THE HAUNTING OF
CALHOUN MANSION

JAMES HUNT

✳ Created with Vellum

PROLOGUE

Prologue – Thirty Years Ago

The late-night snowstorm made it difficult to see on the drive up the mountainside. Devon Farr gripped the steering wheel of his BMW with both hands, the heat blasting through the vents struggling to warm the vehicle against the cold. He had been woken in the night by a call from a Detective Salvor who was at the Calhoun estate.

Devon was the financial consultant for Richard Calhoun and his business ventures. The pair had worked together for the past twenty years, and Devon's account with Calhoun Enterprises made up the bulk of his yearly revenue. With only two other accounts signed to his firm, Richard Calhoun was Devon's most important client.

The detective hadn't told Devon much other than he was needed at the estate. But Devon's stomach churned from the nervous thoughts that plagued him on the way over. Something bad had happened. Good news never arrived in the middle of the night.

After the next curve in the road, Devon caught the glow of more lights up ahead through the storm. And when his own headlights shone upon the open gates of the Calhoun estate, his mouth hung open in shock. "Oh my God."

The massive three-story structure was painted in the blues and reds of emergency vehicles which clogged the long stone driveway. An officer guarding the entrance walked over and gestured for Devon to roll down his window.

Devon complied, the wind and snow whipping past, causing the officer to shout above the noise of the storm.

"Sir, I'm going to have to ask you to turn around and leave," the officer said, his voice booming with authority.

"I-I was called by Detective Salvor," Devon said, and then fumbled his hands for his ID, the cold stealing his dexterity. "I handle the Calhoun business finances. I'm friends with the family."

The officer checked the identification and then pointed to a patch of open space near another parked squad car just inside the gated entrance. "You can park your vehicle there and walk up. It's too crowded for you to drive."

Devon nodded and rolled up his window. He had been sluggish from the late hour, but the frigid cold had woken him up. He parked in his designated area and shut the car off. He paused for a moment, staring up at the house, a sense of doom rushing over him. He tightened his grip on the steering wheel, his fingers aching from the cold, and shut his eyes. He couldn't stop shaking.

None of this was right. None of this was supposed to be happening.

But Devon told himself that he didn't know the whole story yet, and he blamed the shaking on the cold as he opened his eyes. He struggled with the door, the wind pummeling the car with snow flurries, but he finally escaped and started his long trudge up to the house.

Devon flipped up his collar and pulled the scarf tighter around his neck. The snow refused to let up, the forecast calling for two feet of fresh powder by morning. He blinked, his eyelashes batting the snowflakes from his eyes, but it was still hard to see. The closer he moved toward the house, the more figures emerged from the haze of white, red, and blue. He passed ambulances and squad cars, and people running around in a frenzy. He watched a gurney with a covered body being loaded into the back of one of the ambulances, and he stopped.

The gurney disappeared into the back of the ambulance, and the doors shut. One of the officers smacked his hand on the back doors three times, and the vehicle started the slow crawl down the snow-covered drive.

Devon forced himself to realize what he saw. Someone was dead.

"Mr. Farr!" A man stood at the top of the front steps

to the entrance of the house and waved his hands. "Over here!"

Devon veered toward the house, keeping his coat pulled tight over his chest, and navigated the steps up to the door carefully. He didn't want to slip and fall and find himself taking a ride in the back of one of those ambulances. "Detective Salvor?"

The detective was a young black man, almost too young for his rank. It must have been a recent promotion. "Mr. Farr, I appreciate you coming out here. Follow me inside so we can get out of this cold."

Devon nodded, and the pair escaped into the warm interior of the mansion. Devon trailed snow into the foyer and wiped the snot that had started to run from his nose and onto his upper lip. "Detective, what is going on? You were very vague over the phone and—"

Devon finally looked over to the grand staircase across from the main entryway and saw Margaret Calhoun, the youngest of Richard's daughters, huddled with a blanket over her shoulders and covered in blood.

"My God," Devon said, aghast. "What in the hell happened here?" He turned to the detective for answers, but Salvor only pointed back to Margaret.

"She called 911 and said that she needed help, but she hasn't said a word since," Salvor said. "I found her inside the library next to her dead sister." Salvor took a breath. "The whole family was murdered."

Devon's mouth hung open, his jaw slack. The skin around his eyes twitched as he struggled to find his voice. "I-I-I don't understand... They're all dead?"

"Richard Calhoun, Bethany Calhoun, and Aubrey Calhoun, all found dead in different areas around the house," Detective Salvor said.

Devon looked back to Margaret. She was a beautiful woman nearing thirty, and she still lived at home like the other sister. Devon had always found that strange, wondering why the girls had never married. It wasn't like they didn't have prospects. "How?"

"I'm sorry?" Detective Salvor asked.

Devon turned toward Salvor, suddenly flushed with rage. "How did this happen!"

"I'm afraid I can't discuss the investigation with you at this time," Salvor said, keeping his voice calm in hopes of easing Devon's hysteria. "I called you because you were listed as an emergency contact for the family. Margaret isn't talking; the medic told me she's in shock. But I was hoping a friendly face would help coax some answers out of her about what she saw."

Devon looked to young Margaret. He knew the girls well, but he had always struggled with interactions that went beyond the boardroom. But he knew that if he didn't cooperate, the police would look closer at him. And he didn't want that. Not now. He nodded, swallowing to try and gather some spit in his mouth. "Okay. I'll try it."

Detective Salvor led Devon over to the staircase where Margaret sat on the third step. A paramedic was checking her vitals, shining a light in her eyes, but through it all, Margaret remained stoic and motionless.

Devon bent over, placing his hands on his right leg

as he tried to get into Margaret's line of vision. "Margaret? It's Devon— Mr. Farr."

When she didn't respond, Devon glanced back to Detective Salvor and shrugged.

"Keep trying," Detective Salvor said.

Devon sighed and faced Margaret again. He had never been close with Richard's daughters, and he was at a loss of what to say. "Can you tell me what happened tonight?"

Nothing but silence; Margaret staring into an empty void, her eyes wide as a full moon. Her face was pale, all the color gone save for two red spots that sat high on her cheeks, a thin line of red around her lips, which contrasted against the vibrant splashes of blood that covered her face and body. The woman looked like she had done the killing herself.

After another minute of silence, Devon leaned back and flapped his arms at his sides. "I'm sorry, Detective. I wish I could have—"

"They won't leave," Margaret said, repeating the words through chattering teeth. "They won't leave."

Devon remained frozen, but Detective Salvor stepped in, taking over the line of questioning. "Who won't leave? Are the killers still in the house?"

The skin around Margaret's mouth twitched, almost as if she were trying to smile, but the micro-expression passed quickly, and she repeated herself.

"They won't leave," Margaret said.

Salvor turned to the other officers nearby. "I want another sweep of the house. Check every room. Let's move!"

The officers broke away to their assignments and Salvor tried pressing Margaret once more, but she had gone mute again, and Detective Salvor gave up. He led Devon away from Margaret and the staircase so the pair could speak in private.

"She's lost her mind," Devon said.

Detective Salvor pursed his lips in the way that people did when they wanted to say something but knew they shouldn't. "Look, it's going to come out anyway, but I need you to keep quiet about it until then, okay?"

Devon nodded.

Salvor grimaced and then bit on his lower lip before he continued. "I was the first on the scene, and I have never walked into a bloodier crime scene than the one I found tonight. Everyone, save for Margaret over there, was carved up like a Thanksgiving turkey."

Devon staggered a step backward but caught himself before he fell.

"Do you know if the Calhoun family had any problems with anyone lately?" Detective Salvor asked. "Anyone trying to ruffle some feathers?"

Devon cleared his throat. "No. Not that I know of."

"I know that Mr. Calhoun was a wealthy man," Salvor said. "The entire West Coast knows who he is. But I didn't just call you here to ask you to speak with Margaret."

Devon swallowed, and he broke out in sweat beneath his coat, but he tried to remain calm. "What else can I help you with?"

"Mr. Calhoun had a vast private collection of

jewels," Salvor said. "My officers and I have swept the entire house, but we can't find anything. I was hoping you knew where they might be located?"

"You think this is about money?" Devon asked. "You think that someone butchered an entire family because they wanted money?"

Salvor held up his hands. "We haven't been able to find anything that was stolen. All of Bethany Calhoun's jewelry was still in her room, and none of the silverware was taken, so my only guess is that whoever did this was after the jewels that Mr. Calhoun kept in his private collection."

Devon shook his head. "No. I'm afraid Mr. Calhoun was very private about his personal collection. I heard that he'd built a special vault for the jewels and placed it somewhere in the house, but I don't know where he put it." He looked to Salvor, studying him closely. "Do you have any suspects?"

"No," Salvor said. "With the amount of snow that's falling outside, we couldn't find any tracks around the house. We found some bloody footprints, but it will take forensics some time before they're able to tell who it could have been."

"Do you think Margaret did this?" Devon asked.

"I don't know what I think at this point," Salvor answered, his tone defeated. "The chief is going to want an update from me soon, and right now I don't have shit." He looked to Devon. "That's why I was hoping you could tell me if you knew about the jewels. If I can prove that they're gone, then I'd have a motive for the murders."

Devon nodded gravely and turned back to Margaret Calhoun, who remained stoic and quiet on the staircase. He had worked for Richard Calhoun for the past twenty years. He had thought they had been close. He had thought they were friends. But after tonight, he was beginning to think he didn't know his friend at all.

*T*he man was almost dead. It wouldn't be much longer now. A few more minutes and Mr. Haggerty's life would end. The old man had been a fighter, but he couldn't outlast Father Time.

Dressed in her scrubs, Nicole Harper waited in the living room, checking the time on the large grandfather clock across the room that ticked off the seconds with a steady cadence. She tried to focus on the clock's rhythm instead of the quiet sobs coming from the bedroom down the hall.

The family had known he was going to die. They had known for a long time. It was as inevitable as the fact that the grandfather clock would ring when the hands fell onto the hour. But for as long as Nicole had been involved in the hospice industry, she knew that no amount of preparation could prepare someone for the death of a loved one.

Since the family had arrived yesterday afternoon, Nicole had been nothing more than a ghost in the house, moving about to make sure that Mr. Haggerty's pain levels were manageable. He was already far past the point of consciousness, his body weakened by the cancer that he'd been fighting for the past eighteen months.

But still, his family stood around his bed, taking turns holding his hands, desperate for him to know that they were still by his side. And while it may have been the family's first up-close brush with death, Nicole was a familiar acquaintance with the Grim Reaper.

While most people feared death, Nicole didn't, and neither did most of her patients. To the sick that Nicole cared for, death was an escape from their pain.

The old clock chimed and Nicole stood. She moved quietly down the narrow hallway, passing pictures of Mr. Haggerty's family on the wall. The captured memories revealed a life filled with love and happiness. Moments he must have cherished to have them framed. And now they would be all that remained of his existence in this world.

Nicole paused at the door to Mr. Haggerty's room, his family crowded together inside. "Excuse me." She never raised her voice above a whisper as she stepped into the room, weaving between the grandchildren, children, cousins, and siblings that had come to pay their respects to a man that they loved. She walked to the bedside and gently pressed her fingers against Mr. Haggerty's wrist.

Cancer had ravaged the old man, his body withering away to nothing more than a skeleton. His skin was sallow and thin, his muscles atrophied, and his hair nothing but thin white wisps on the top of his head. He was no more than a shadow of the man that filled the pictures in the house.

Every eye in the room was focused on her. She felt their stares, their hopes, their wishes that the man they cared for so deeply was able to hold on for a few more minutes. Nicole took her time. She wanted to be sure before she called the time of death.

But after a solid minute of no pulse from Mr. Haggerty, Nicole knew that it was over. She carefully placed the old man's wrist back on the bed, her touch lingering on his hand for just a moment longer than was necessary before she raised her head.

A room of rheumy eyes stared at her, waiting for the inevitable news that she was charged with delivering to a family that didn't want to hear it.

"He's passed," Nicole said.

The declaration triggered tears, and Mr. Haggerty's daughter buried her face into her husband's shirt, muffling the sobs.

"I'll let you say your final goodbyes," Nicole said, addressing the rest of the room, the faces glazed with a mixture of expressions ranging from shocked to sad to blank. "Take your time." She weaved around the bodies toward the door, again keeping her head down, and it wasn't until she returned to the living room that she was able to breathe again.

Nicole waited in the living room and watched as one by one the family members left the room and either walked outside or sat on the couch, glaring blankly at their phones. She wondered how many of them would post this as some kind of social media status update.

In the seven years Nicole had been a hospice nurse, she had watched death transform from a dignified, natural process to something leveraged on social media to earn likes and comments. Something that was meant to be personal and sacred had become digitized and presented to a world that held little respect for anything that couldn't bring them joy.

And while Nicole understood that people grieved in different ways, she was still saddened to see how most people never took the time to process their grief. Nicole was one of them.

Unlike the Haggerty family who would slowly have time to work through their pain, Nicole would be given another assignment upon her return to the office, where she would be thrust into a similar situation and the process would start all over again.

Most of the patients that Nicole took care of lived in nice homes. It was a vast improvement over nearly every hospital that she had worked in, where break rooms were falling apart, and there was never a time during your twelve-hour shift that provided a moment of peace and quiet to take a breath.

There was always a patient, a doctor, a colleague, someone who needed something, and after five years of running herself ragged, she had decided to make the switch. But her hospice experiences weren't always pleasant.

Some families were cruel and bitter, treating Nicole

as nothing more than another servant to be ordered around. And the patients weren't always as kind as Mr. Haggerty had been, because everyone faced their own deaths differently. And while most took their final moments as an opportunity to make amends and peace for those that they had troubled relationships with, some clung to their anger as their lifeline.

Thirty minutes passed, and everyone but Mr. Haggerty's daughter had left the room. Nicole debated on whether or not to disturb the daughter, but she knew that it didn't take long for the body to start to decompose.

Once the time passed to an hour, Nicole returned to the bedroom, finding the daughter by her father's bedside, holding a lifeless hand, staring down at a man who was no longer with her.

"Mrs. Thompson," Nicole said, quietly stepping into the room.

"I can't leave him." Mrs. Thompson's voice was thick with phlegm. Of all of Mr. Haggerty's family members, she had taken his illness and his slow decline the hardest. She was the only one who visited her father regularly. And from their interactions with each other, Nicole knew they were very close.

Nicole walked around to the other side of Mr. Haggarty's bed and saw the tears that had dried on Mrs. Thompson's cheek. The expression of loss on her face was one that Nicole had seen on a thousand other family members. There was always someone unwilling to let go.

Mrs. Thompson scrunched her face in preparation

for tears, but she held them back with a few deep breaths and slow exhales, and then she cleared her throat. "When I was a little girl, my father worked a lot. He would be gone on business trips for weeks, but he would always tell me that he would come back on a specific day. And each time, no matter the circumstances around the trip or weather, he always made it home on the day he promised. Every time."

"Your father was a good man," Nicole said. "I didn't know him as well as you, but even in the short time that we had together, I could tell that he cared for his family very much. He loved you."

Mrs. Thompson nodded. "He was a good father." She kissed Mr. Haggerty's hand, her lips lingering on the brittle and frail skin before she gently returned the hand to the mattress. She turned her bloodshot eyes to Nicole, the light from the window framing her face. "Thank you for making him feel comfortable. He told me that you were very kind."

Nicole smiled. "He was a wonderful patient."

Mrs. Thompson took a moment to wipe her eyes. "You must be tired of people like me. People who just can't let go."

Nicole shook her head. "Not at all."

Mrs. Thompson nodded. "What made you want to do this? Take care of the dying?"

It was a question that Nicole received often, but she never tired the explanation. "I was very close with my grandmother when I was younger. In many ways, I thought of her as a mother figure more than my actual mother. But when my father moved us across the country and away from her, I didn't get to see her very often." Nicole bowed her head. "She got sick, and she didn't tell anyone. By the time I found out about it, she was already gone."

"That's terrible," Mrs. Thompson said. "I'm sorry."

"Thank you," Nicole said, and then cleared her throat. "She died alone, and in a lot of pain. So at her funeral, I promised that I would do whatever I could to take care of those that couldn't care for themselves. No one should have to go through this alone."

"That's very noble." Mrs. Thompson turned back to her father and kissed his forehead, then whispered something in his ear that Nicole didn't hear. It was meant to be private. Eyes filling with tears, she walked to the door, but stopped and turned around one last time.

"Thank you," Mrs. Thompson said. "Thank you for giving me time."

"You're welcome," Nicole said.

Once the daughter was gone, Nicole finished her work, collecting the equipment and slowly preparing the body to be transported from the room and into the back of a van. It would then be taken to the mortuary chosen by the family, where the body would be prepped to be buried.

And as Nicole went about her duties, she thought of all of the love that she had seen amongst the family members, particularly between Mrs. Thompson and her husband. Because for as many times as Mrs. Thompson had come to visit, her husband was always there with her, offering support, a kind word, a shoulder to lean on or a hand to hold. From her perspective, they seemed to be a very happy, very supportive couple.

But Nicole knew better than most how looks could be deceiving. She had thought her own marriage was solid as a rock until three months ago when her life was turned upside down. Only time would tell if she and Jake would survive, or if they would fall to the wayside as another footnote of failure in the book of love.

2

*A*fter Nicole had packed up the gear and the men from the funeral home retrieved Mr. Haggerty's body, she said her final goodbyes to the family, who again thanked her for caring for their father. She appreciated their kind words, but like the Haggerty family, it was time for Nicole to move on.

Traffic was terrible on her drive back to the office, but Nicole reveled in the snail-like pace on the highway. It provided the needed time to decompress.

Caring for the dying in their final moments was taxing and emotionally draining. And while Nicole had never regretted her move from hospital work to hospice care, there were times when she wondered how many more hands she could hold before she was numbed to the idea of death.

That's why, in the moments after, Nicole enjoyed being alone. It gave her a chance to recharge, reboot, get back into the right frame of mind. It was her time to hit the reset button.

When Nicole worked at the hospitals, she always had patients that she liked, and patients that she didn't like, but because of the fast pace and hectic nature that the hospital's environment provided, there was rarely time for her to really connect with the people that she was caring for. But working in a home, seeing the same patient every day for hours, weeks at a time, it was hard not to become attached to the individuals under her care. And every time she drove away after one of her patients had died, a little piece of her was chipped away.

Nicole was warned by several co-workers and her boss not to become emotionally vested in the patients, and she had done her best to adhere to those standards, but with every new patient, she found it harder and harder to keep herself from becoming involved. Because like Mr. Haggerty's daughter, Nicole felt like she had lost someone too. Not in the same category as losing a father, but a friend.

By the time Nicole reached her company's headquarters on the outskirts of San Francisco, she felt a little better, but she was drained. She found a parking spot near the front, shortening the distance she had to carry the gear she packed up from the Haggerty household. She popped the trunk and managed the two boxes in one trip, aided by a gust of wind that brushed up against her backside. The automatic doors opened, and she was greeted by the reception desk's permanent smiling face, Lisa.

"Hey, Nic," Lisa said, then stepped from behind the

desk and plucked the top box off of the pile in Nicole's arms.

"Thanks, Lisa," Nicole said, catching her breath. "You'd think the hills around here would keep me in better shape, but I get winded just from stepping out of the car."

"I hear that," Lisa said.

The pair of women walked through the narrow halls of the office. Unlike the Haggerty home, the workplace didn't hold the same warmth, though the people inside were friendly enough. However, Nicole spent so much time out in the field that the only time she actually made it back to the office was when she was at the end or beginning of an assignment.

Nicole dropped the box off at the locker room where the equipment was stored. It was rare that a patient in need of hospice care owned the necessary equipment, so most of it was rented out along with the nursing services.

"I scheduled the bed to be delivered for tomorrow," Nicole said, pushing the box toward Dan, who ran the locker, keeping track of the hundreds of thousands of little items that came in and out of the building.

"No worries." Dan set the box of unused catheters and syringes aside as he rested his forearms on the counter and leaned closer toward Nicole. "Some of us are heading out in a few minutes to grab some drinks at The Pour House. You want to come?"

Dan's smile was inviting. He was a good-looking man, trim and fit for someone who spent his days cataloging medical supplies. He was a few years younger than Nicole, and he seemed unfazed by the wedding ring that occupied space on her left hand.

"Can't tonight," Nicole said, being friendly but firm. "But you guys have a good time."

"I'll take a shot for you," Dan said, straightening up. "I hope you like tequila."

Nicole laughed. "Not on my worst day."

Nicole walked away, Lisa following. Once they were a safe distance away from the locker room and Dan's ears, Lisa leaned closer to Nicole. "Someone hasn't given up."

Nicole rolled her eyes. "I don't know why he keeps trying." She pointed to her ring. "Maybe I should just wave it in front of his face the next time I see him."

"Oh," Lisa said, suddenly surprised. "I thought— never mind."

Nicole slowed and grabbed Lisa's arm, pulling her closer. "What?"

Lisa worked her mouth from side to side, struggling to keep quiet until the words spilled out like a stream of water from a faucet. "People still think you're getting a divorce." She covered her mouth with her hand once she was finished, her green eyes wide as saucers.

Nicole lowered her head, shutting her eyes. "I should have known better than to think that would stay quiet."

Lisa removed her hand from her mouth, hands raised as if she thought that Nicole was going to hit her. "So, are you *not* getting a divorce?"

"No," Nicole answered, then winced and shook her head. "I don't know. We're going to therapy. We're trying to fix it." She exhaled, a headache starting to form at a pressure point right between her eyes. She closed her eyes and gently massaged the point of contention.

"It's good that you guys are trying to work it out," Lisa said, trying to sound encouraging. "It just takes time to get back to a good place after you guys stopped talking to one another. You know?"

"Yeah," Nicole dropped her hand, opening her eyes to a field of black spots that peppered her vision for a few seconds before she saw clearly again. "I just wish people would mind their own business."

Lisa shrugged. "People like to gossip."

"Yeah." But deep down Nicole knew that she only had herself to blame. The rumors had started after she had exploded on Jake during a phone call while she was at the office. She couldn't even remember what he wanted to ask her, but her response had nothing to do with his question. Something inside of her had just snapped, and she tore into him, screaming over the phone at the top of her lungs.

"Hey," Lisa hugged Nicole. "It's going to be alright."

Nicole patted Lisa's back and then nodded. "Thanks." The pair broke apart. "You know Dan might be interested in me, but you should go have drinks with them tonight."

Lisa blushed, and she looked down at her shoes, picking at her fingernails. "I wasn't invited."

"It sounded like an open invitation to me," Nicole said.

"Nicole!" Susan Horner stepped out of her office, making eye contact with Nicole. "I need to speak to you before you leave."

"Sure thing," Nicole called back.

After Susan disappeared into her office, Nicole slouched.

"I didn't like the sound of that," Nicole said.

"Well, maybe it's a good thing," Lisa said, smiling.

Nicole smoothed out the front of her scrubs and took a deep breath. "When was the last time that you spoke with Horns, and it was about something good?"

Lisa hesitated and then smiled wider. "I can't remember?"

Nicole snickered and then headed down the hall to Susan's office, using the same strategy of talking to her boss as she did with removing a band-aid. Get it over with quickly.

Nicole knocked on the door before she entered and saw Susan sitting behind her desk, head down, scribbling her signature over pages of documents.

"Sit down," Susan said.

Nicole quietly occupied one of the two empty chairs in front of Susan's desk and waited to see what her boss and overlord wanted.

"I have a new assignment for you," Susan said, finishing the last of her signature with an aggressive flick of her wrist. "It's out of state."

Travel had been one of the reasons that led to the

start of the troubles in her marriage. At least that's what the therapist said.

"I'm only sticking to assignments around San Francisco," Nicole said, keeping her tone pleasant. "I already cleared it with HR."

Susan scooped up all of the paperwork that she had been working on and stacked them in a neat pile on the corner of her desk. "I'm aware of that. But I'm in a pinch right now, and everyone else I would normally ask is already working rotation."

"Susan, look, I'm—"

"It pays four times the normal rate," Susan said, hoping that cutting to the chase would help her cause. "And the employer requested you by name."

Nicole frowned. "They did?"

"Yes," Susan said, sounding as surprised as Nicole. "They're looking for a nurse who has experience in taking care of patients with dementia and Alzheimer's, and you're one of the top nurses in the state for that kind of work. Taking on a wealthy client like this is a great resume booster. You might be able to get more work with a higher-end clientele after this case."

Nicole hesitated. Four times the normal rate wasn't chump change. With that kind of money, it could change a lot of things for her, open up some options that hadn't been available before. She and Jake had wanted to buy a house and had been saving up for one until she found out about the affair.

After that, talk of a house and their future together had been put on hold, and while therapy was helping their situation, she wasn't sure if it was doing enough.

It seemed like Nicole was forced to make a decision for the both of them, and while a part of her had wanted to leave, it was hard to move on. Because she had the memories of seven good years with Jake, and those memories weren't just pictures she could take off the wall of her mind and put away.

"So?" Susan asked. "What do you say?"

3

*N*icole sat in her car in the parking lot outside of her apartment building. The car's engine had long since gone cold, and she could see the light in the living room window on the second floor to their apartment. She knew that Jake was home, and she dreaded going inside.

Before the affair, Nicole couldn't wait to rush through the door. Her home with Jake had been her safe haven, her personal escape from the rest of the world. But now all of that love had been replaced with dread, and doubt, and hate, and it made her sick inside, filling her heart and mind with poison.

Nicole took a breath and stepped out of the car. She walked slowly to the stairs and fidgeted with her hands, a side effect of the anxiousness that started in the pit of her stomach and then spread to her extremities. She hated the feeling, but she'd gotten used to it over the past few months.

The door was unlocked, and Nicole paused with

her hand on the doorknob as she replayed the event from three months ago in her mind. If she shut her eyes now, she could see it as if it happened yesterday.

Nicole had come home for lunch to surprise Jake, who had started working from home more. But when she entered the apartment, she found her own surprise: moans coming from their bedroom down the hall.

It took a few seconds before Nicole could make herself walk. The floor became uneven, and she lost her balance twice, catching herself on the walls as she neared the bedroom door. It was cracked open, and the moans grew louder. Her heart caught in her throat, and she broke out in a sweat. She was convinced that she was in a dream and that she would wake up and everything would be fine.

But when Nicole opened the door and saw Jake in bed with another woman, she felt her heart break in two as both of them gasped at her presence.

Nicole opened her eyes, a tear falling from the corner and down her cheek. She stared at the closed door to her apartment and quickly wiped the tear away before she opened the door and stepped inside.

It was quiet, and all of the lights were on. She paused at the foyer, her feet planted on the rug by the entrance, waiting for the sounds of betrayal to be heard once again. But there was nothing.

"Babe? Is that you?" Jake called from down the hall.

"Yeah." Nicole's voice cracked, and she cleared her throat. "Just got home." She hung up her purse and walked down the hall to the second bedroom, which Jake had converted to his office.

Jake turned around in his chair, closing his laptop, and smiled. "Hey."

Nicole didn't return the smile. "Hey."

While the pair had made some progress at therapy over the past few months to try and heal what had been broken, there was still a hint of awkwardness in their interactions with one another. Neither was quite sure what to say.

"How was work?" Jake asked.

"Good," Nicole answered, then picked at one of her fingernails as she stared at her hands. "I got a new assignment."

"Oh," Jake said, his voice softening. "Mr. Haggerty passed today?"

Nicole nodded.

"Nic, I'm sorry," Jake said. "I know you said he was a good guy."

There was genuine sorrow and regret in Jake's voice, and Nicole appreciated the words. "His entire family had been waiting for the past two days. His daughter never left his side. You don't see things like that in most families. It was heartbreaking and refreshing all at the same time."

"It's really incredible what you do. Honestly. I know I wouldn't be able to do it." Jake stood and walked to her, but when he reached to hold her, she stepped back, and he stopped. "Sorry, I just thought—"

"It's fine." Nicole smiled and then hurried down the hall to the kitchen, calling back to Jake when she opened the fridge. "What did you want to do for dinner?"

Nicole bent down and rummaged through some of the leftovers they had from the weekend. "Looks like we have some Chinese food left, and pizza—" She straightened up, finding Jake leaning against the kitchen counter with his arms crossed.

"Are you all right?" Jake asked.

"Yeah, I'm fine." Nicole shrugged and grabbed the Chinese food and shut the fridge. She moved to the microwave and set the timer for three minutes to heat up the chicken fried rice.

"It's just that Dr. Matthews said we should talk to one another whenever we feel like something is off," Jake said. "You know, to make sure that we're communicating with one another?"

The microwave hummed as the Chinese food spun slowly around. Nicole nodded, and just like that, Nicole was thrust back into the dark corner of her thoughts where she was plagued with doubt. Doubt in herself, doubt in her marriage, doubt in the man standing next to her.

"You're right," Nicole said, trying to be productive. "I'm sorry."

The microwave beeped, and the kitchen fell quiet. The pair stood close to one another, Nicole staring down at the oven top while Jake stared at Nicole.

"The new assignment is out of state," Nicole said, turning to face Jake. "Up in Washington."

Jake arched his eyebrows. "Oh. I thought we agreed that you wouldn't take any more assignments out of state while we were... figuring things out."

Nicole spun around and leaned her backside

against the stove. She crossed her arms. "I know. But the client is willing to pay me four times the normal rate. I guess they're looking for a hospice nurse who has some specialization in caring for patients with dementia." She shrugged. "I thought it could help with the house."

Jake smiled. "The house? You haven't talked about the house in a long time."

Nicole tilted her head from side to side in a mild gesture. "I know, but… I don't know. I guess I was thinking about the future."

Jake nodded, still smiling. "I think it's great that you're thinking about the future. In fact…" He held up a hand and then sprinted out of the kitchen, returning quickly with a piece of paper in his hand. "Take a look at that."

Nicole grabbed the paper from his hands. It was a house listing. "Where did you find this?"

"I was looking online today during my lunch break," Jake answered. "It's a little pricey, but look—" He pointed to the address. "Right on the coast. It overlooks a bluff so you can see the beach and the ocean. It's a dream house."

Nicole stared at the picture, trying to remember what that dream house looked like before Jake's infidelity. She handed him the picture back, grabbed the Chinese food out of the microwave, and sat down at the kitchen table.

Steam rose from the container as Nicole used her fork to push around the rice. She took a few bites. It was almost too hot to eat.

Jake stepped from the kitchen, but he didn't join her at the table. "Are you going to tell me what's bothering you?"

Nicole huffed. "It was a long day."

"Okay," Jake said, trying to be calm. "I understand. We can just talk about the assignment another time—"

"I've already decided to take the assignment," Nicole said.

Jake's calm exterior started to crack. "Don't you think we should talk about this first?"

Nicole slammed her fork down on the table. "Did you talk to me before you slept with another woman in our bed?"

Jake's cheeks had flushed red, and he looked away. She knew how embarrassed and ashamed he was of his actions. She had struck the only nerve that could hurt him.

Nicole watched him, immediately regretting the outburst. She shook her head. "Jake, I'm sorry. I don't know why I said that."

Jake nodded, trying to shrug it off, but having a difficult time. "It's fine."

"No," Nicole said. "It's not fine. I shouldn't have…" She shut her eyes, tired of wrestling with conflicting thoughts in her mind. "I'm still learning how to remember to be with you again." She opened her eyes and saw that Jake was looking at her again. "I'm trying to remember how it was before."

"Me too," Jake said. "But we don't have to ignore what happened." Jake walked to her side of the table, taking a knee and her hand. "I know that what I did to you was the worst kind of betrayal. And if I could go back in time and stop myself, or erase it, I would. I'll never forget what I did. I'll never forgive myself for hurting you." He squeezed her hand tighter. "But acknowledging the past doesn't mean we have to forget the future. It doesn't mean that we have to give up everything that we still want."

Nicole nodded. "I know. And I'm trying. It's just taking longer than I thought." She shut her eyes and shook her head. "I don't know why I can't let it go."

"I'm not asking you to let it go," Jake said. "I'm just asking for a small bit of trust that I won't repeat my mistakes."

Nicole cracked a smile, this one not as forced as the one that she felt before. "I can do that." She took a breath and exhaled, feeling better, but she knew that she needed to find a healthier way to decompress. She couldn't keep ambushing him and expect him to keep taking the abuse.

"So what's the job?" Jake asked.

"Nothing," Nicole answered. "I'm going to turn it down. I shouldn't leave when we're still trying to work things out."

Jake nodded, but then glanced around the apartment. They had been living in it since before they were married, nearly seven years. And every day the space got smaller and smaller. Both of them had wanted a house, and it was earlier in the year that they had finally started planning to buy one, but their financial planning was derailed after the affair, as they had used the cash that they were saving to pay for the therapy sessions.

"I mean, I could go with you," Jake said. "If that's okay with the employer."

Nicole was surprised. "Really? Work would let you do that?"

"Sure," Jake shrugged. "Most of my programming is project-based now anyway, and I don't think they'll mind where I work so long as the work gets done. And besides, I used to travel with you all the time before we got married."

"That's true." Nicole rubbed her thumb across the top of Jake's hand, his skin warm.

Their earlier days of travel together had been fun. They went all over the country, living weeks at a time in different cities, seeing new places and trying new things. It was a whirlwind, but it didn't last forever after Jake was hired to his current position in San Francisco, and it was here they chose to settle down. But it appeared that settling had been one of the problems that had led to the infidelity in the first place.

"What do you think?" Jake asked.

"I can ask if it's okay," Nicole answered. "You're sure you want to come with me to another job?"

"I meant what I said about doing what it took to fix our marriage," Jake answered. "And part of fixing the present is preparing for the future. I still want a house. I still want to start a family. I still want all of the things that we talked about before I screwed up. I told you that I wanted to make things right, and if this will help us get on a path to success for the future, then that's what I'll do."

It was good to hear him say that, but Nicole was suddenly nervous. Nervous about slipping back into the old days, nervous about letting herself trust him again, nervous about grabbing hold of the future that they wanted together that she had been so adamant about wanting to let go. But she knew that if she was going to give their marriage another try, then she'd have to eventually take a chance on trusting Jake again. She just hoped that she was strong enough to handle it.

4

---

*N*icole stared out the window of her rear passenger seat and watched the waves of the Pacific crash against the rocky coast. The water sprayed up and over the rocks, the white foam clinging to the rough surfaces before a gust of wind or another wave caused them to vanish. The process was repeated with every wave, over and over. It was an infinite loop.

Nicole leaned back into her seat, Jake sitting next to her, looking up at the mountains to where they would travel. When she had spoken to the lawyer handling the patient's care, Nicole had requested that Jake come along, and they were so desperate to find the help that they didn't protest.

Nicole only hoped that she wasn't falling back into old habits, and she hoped that she was putting her trust into the version of the man that she had fallen in love with, and not the version that had broken her heart.

"Quite a view," Jake said.

Nicole nodded. "You'd think after living in San

Francisco for as long as we have that I'd be used to the water by now, but it still has the power to mesmerize me."

Jake glanced on the other side of the road, away from the coast, where there was nothing but wooded trees. "How much farther do we have to go? I know you said it was up in the mountains, but I haven't seen any signs of civilization for miles."

"I'm not sure," Nicole said. "I didn't get a lot of details about the location other than the address and that we would have our own living quarters."

"I just hope that it's not one of those hostel situations," Jake said. "I'm too old to be thrust back into some kind of open living space. I need my peace and quiet."

"I guess we'll find out soon enough." Nicole twisted her fingers together in her lap. She was unusually nervous about this new assignment.

Jake reached for her hands, and the ball of nerves in her stomach transformed into a furnace, causing her cheeks and neck to flush red. It had been a long time since he made her feel like that by the touch of his hand. "Everything is going to be fine."

The road veered away from the coast and eventually winded up through the mountains. The incline grew a little bit steeper, and the road became slightly narrower, and the forest that crowded on either side of the asphalt became thicker until the driver finally noted their arrival.

"And we're here," the driver said.

Both Nicole and Jake glanced ahead to the iron

gates, their jaws dropping from the massive home behind the walls.

"I think I understand how they could afford to pay four times the normal rate," Jake said.

The house was three stories, with spiral towers on all four corners of the rectangular structure. It was a mixture of brick and stone, and the sun warmed the earthy colors, which helped blend the massive home into the surrounding forest and mountain landscape.

And as Nicole looked up at the house, she saw a woman standing in one of the windows. She was young and beautiful, dressed in an evening gown, which Nicole thought strange. "I wonder who that is?"

"Who?" Jake asked.

Nicole looked to her husband and then pointed back to the house. "There in the wind—" Nicole lowered her finger. The woman in the window was gone.

The driveway from the gate to the front entrance cut through an immaculately well-kept yard dotted with small patches of gardens and sculptures, ending at a circular drive with a fountain stuck in the middle of it. The drive stopped between the fountain and the front doors, where an elderly gentleman held the door open for a tall, strikingly beautiful woman in a business suit that pulled at the natural curves of her body.

The driver opened the door for Nicole, and she stepped out just as the woman stuck out her hand to greet Nicole.

"Mrs. Harper, I'm Melissa Farr, Ms. Calhoun's attorney."

Nicole smiled back, trying to avoid the over-whelming greeting. "It's nice to meet you, Mrs.—"

"It's miss," Melissa said. "How was the trip?"

"It was great," Jake answered. "I've never flown first class before."

"We enjoy taking care of the people who work for Ms. Calhoun's estate," Melissa said, always keeping a smile across her face, which was accentuated by the red lipstick that contrasted against her creamy white skin. "Don't worry about the bags. Donald will take care of them for you."

The butler who opened the door for Melissa relieved Jake of their luggage without a word and quickly scurried back up into the house.

"He'll put your things in the guest house around back," Melissa said, then gestured up toward the front door, which was still open. "Let's head inside and discuss a few things."

Nicole and Jake followed Melissa up the steps and inside, where Nicole realized that she was standing in the most expensive home that she had ever seen.

Between the marble floor, the crystal chandelier, and the paintings of people that Nicole didn't recog-nize hanging on the walls, she had never seen such opulence in her life, and it only became more and more impressive the farther she walked into the house.

The floors were polished wood, the door handles finely-polished silver, and the crown molding near the ceiling had swirly painted gold running over it. They passed multiple living rooms, and Nicole caught a brief glance at the towering stacks of books in the library that were beckoning her to read them.

A few more rooms down from the library, Melissa entered a small office, which was surprisingly modest considering the décor they passed through the hallway.

Melissa sat down behind the desk, and Nicole and Jake occupied the chairs that were on the opposite side. A stack of paperwork was at the center of the desk, and once everyone was settled, Melissa's smile vanished as she switched from greeter to lawyer.

"Before we get started, I wanted to cover a few things with you," Melissa said. "During your time here at the Calhoun estate, you'll have all three square meals delivered to you and unlimited snacks. Our chef at the estate is well-versed in nearly any dish you could imagine so if you create a list of favorite meals, she will be able to prepare them for you. Are there any food allergies I should pass along?"

"No shellfish," Jake said. "I'm deathly allergic."

"Noted," Melissa said, smiling. "And you, Mrs. Harper?"

"No allergies for me," Nicole answered.

"Very well," Melissa cleared her throat. "As employee and guest to the Calhoun estate, I must inform you of some general rules." She looked at Jake. "Mr. Harper, you'll not be allowed into the main house during your wife's contract with the estate. You will have access to the guest house and the outside of the surrounding grounds, but under no circumstance are you allowed in this house."

Jake raised his eyebrows. "Is there a reason for that—"

"Ms. Calhoun is very particular about the individuals that she wants in her home," Melissa said. "Seeing as how your wife is taking care of her, I was considerate enough to allow you to come along. But if these rules are unsatisfactory, then I will be happy to have Donald gather your things, and we'll put you on the next first class flight home."

Nicole and Jake exchanged a glance, and despite the rough patch that the pair had gone through, they could still practically read one another's minds. She knew that he wasn't completely sold on the idea of being confined to the guest house, but if the size of the main house was any indication of what they would be living in, she figured it was more than enough space for him to live for the next few weeks. And with the pay, it seemed to be a deal that he was okay making.

"That's fine," Jake said, looking back to Melissa.

"Good," Melissa said, then gathered up the paperwork that was on her desk and placed it in front of Nicole and Jake. "In addition to the main house being off-limits, neither of you are to enter the woods that surround the house. Understood?"

Nicole and Jake nodded.

"Excellent," Melissa said. "Before I discuss any medical information about my client, I need both of you to sign these Non-Disclosure Agreements. Take your time to read them over."

Jake picked up his NDA first and frowned, skimming the first page and then flipping it over to the next. When he looked up from the papers, he laughed. "A gag order preventing us from going to press? What in the world would we have to talk to the press about?"

"The items disclosed in the contracts are non-negotiable," Melissa answered, unfazed by Jake's incredulous tone. "Again, if you find these conditions—"

"Do you mind if I speak to my husband in private?" Nicole leaned forward, cutting Melissa off before Jake exploded.

Melissa flashed a pleasant smile. "Of course." She leisurely walked out of the room and closed the door behind her.

"This is ridiculous." Jake made zero effort to keep quiet. "I mean I can't come into the house? I can't speak to the press? It's like Nazi Germany took over this place."

"Will you calm down?" Nicole asked, keeping her voice hushed, knowing that the walls in a house this old were probably paper-thin.

"This doesn't bother you?" Jake asked.

"Why would it bother me?"

Jake picked up the NDA. "Have you ever had to sign something like this for any of the patients that you've taken care of before?"

"No," Nicole answered. "But I've worked with some people who have done it before with some of the wealthier clients. It's not that out of the ordinary."

Jake calmed a little bit. "I just don't like being told things I can't do, when there's no rational reason for me not to do them."

Nicole smirked. That had been one of Jake's more

endearing qualities when they first started to date all those years ago, but the longer that they were together, the more frustrating it became. But since they started therapy, he hadn't been so judgmental. She figured he was trying to keep her happy for as long as possible, but seeing it now was almost a welcome surprise. It was normal.

"If you don't want to do this, we can go back," Nicole said.

Jake took a minute to calm down, and she saw the wheels turning in his head. "No. We're going to make it through this, and we're going to do it together. I promised you that I would be here." He reached for her hand. "I'm here to stay."

Nicole smiled. "Thank you."

After another minute, Melissa knocked on the door and then poked her head inside. "Everything all right?"

"Yes," Jake said. "I'm sorry if I came off as a jerk."

"Not at all." Melissa handed both of them pens, and they signed on the dotted line. Once Melissa ensured everything was in order, she planted both elbows on the table and looked at both of them. "Now, let's discuss my client."

5

*M*arried people talked. Melissa knew that, and Nicole assumed that was the reasoning behind having Jake sign the NDA. It was inevitable that Nicole would talk to her husband about what was happening at work. So instead of trying to play the game where Nicole was forced to keep quiet, she chose to bring Jake into the fold and make him legally culpable for anything he might do or say should Nicole relay sensitive information to them. It was smart.

"Ms. Calhoun has had a very horrific life," Melissa said. "A few years ago, she began the early stages of dementia. For a time it was enough for the estate staff to handle and manage, but as it has worsened over the past year, we've sought out more professional help to handle her deteriorating condition."

Dementia and Alzheimer's were horrific diseases and affected the body as much as the mind. Nicole had seen their effects firsthand. "How bad is she?"

"It depends on the day," Melissa answered, sighing and showing the first sign of human emotion that Nicole had seen from her since they started the conversation. "Some days she's normal, or at least as normal as she has ever been, and then on other days, she won't stop throwing tantrums. It's very up and down."

"What do you mean, 'normal as she has ever been'?" Jake asked. "Has she suffered from other illnesses in the past?"

Melissa clasped her hands together and leaned forward. "The NDA agreements weren't just because of Ms. Calhoun's current medical situation. Her family has been the point of contention in this area for a very long time."

"What do you mean?" Nicole asked.

"Her father, Richard Calhoun, was one of the state's wealthiest individuals, and the wealth he accumulated over his lifetime also came with enemies." Melissa looked away and took a moment before she spoke again. "Thirty years ago, Ms. Calhoun's family was murdered, in this house."

"Oh my God," Nicole answered.

"She was the only survivor?" Jake asked.

Melissa nodded. "Her father, mother, and sister were all killed."

"How did she survive?" Jake asked.

"No one knows," Melissa answered. "The police came to the house and found Ms. Calhoun sitting next to her sister, covered in her blood, completely catatonic. She hasn't spoken a word since that night thirty years ago."

Nicole shivered. "That's awful. Was that her only family?"

"Yes," Melissa answered. "Richard Calhoun was an only child, and so was his wife. Ms. Calhoun's sister, Aubrey, never bore any children, and she never married. Margaret Calhoun is the last of her family."

Nicole leaned back into the chair, the plush velvet lining unable to soften the blow. She understood what it was like to be alone. She had felt like she was living on an island for the past three months. But even knowing the betrayal that she felt at the hands of her own husband, she couldn't comprehend what Ms. Calhoun would have gone through after losing her entire family in one night. A trauma like that changed a person. It created a timestamp of before and after.

"It's the combination of Ms. Calhoun's current medical condition, along with her family's past, that we have the contracts," Melissa said. "I can't tell you the number of reporters and media who have tried to get the scoop on what happened all of those years ago, but it's my job to protect her from the vultures who are looking for a quick and easy meal." She hardened her gaze as she looked between both Jake and Nicole. "I trust that I won't have a problem with you two."

"No," Nicole answered quickly. "Of course not." She looked to Jake, who nodded.

"No," Jake said. "No problem here."

"Good," Melissa said. "And while I'm sure you read the contract thoroughly, I want to remind you of a few stipulations. Anything that is said, seen, or heard on this estate is to be kept on this estate. Once your contract has expired with us, your silence about your experience here will continue for the rest of your days. If it doesn't, then I promise that I will bring a lawsuit against you that is so big it will put you behind bars."

There was no love lost in Melissa's tone, and Nicole had no intentions of testing her limits.

"We will honor the agreement," Nicole said.

"Yes," Jake replied, keeping his answers short.

"All right then," Melissa said. "Mr. Harper, you are free to head toward the guest house to get settled. I need to keep your wife here to discuss the duties of the house."

The door swung open the moment she was done speaking, and the butler from earlier was already standing guard.

"Donald will show you the way," Melissa said.

"Right." Jake slapped his hands on the armrests and then stood. He looked at Nicole. "I guess I'll see you at dinner."

Melissa remained quiet until Jake was gone and the door was shut behind him. "Now then." She opened one of her drawers and removed a red folder, which she handed to Nicole. "Inside you'll find the daily and weekly schedule for Ms. Calhoun. She's very particular about her routine, so you must keep to the strict schedule."

"Okay." Nicole opened the folder, finding the contents incredibly detailed. The schedule was timed down to the last minute.

"The chef already knows the meals she likes, so you'll only have to bring them to her," Melissa said. "If you discover that she's not eating, then let the chef know, and she'll prepare her back-up meals until we find something that Ms. Calhoun will eat."

Aside from the rigidness of the schedule, everything was pretty routine in regards to duties. Daily checks for cognitive abilities, blood pressure, heart rate. A monthly blood sample was drawn and sent to a lab for testing. Medications and exercises for physical therapy were also included.

"Does she have a gym at the house, or will I be taking her to another location?" Nicole asked.

Melissa's face deadpanned. "Ms. Calhoun is to never leave the estate. Under any condition. Whatever Ms. Calhoun needs will be brought to her. It's why you're here."

Sensing that Nicole had said something wrong, she quickly nodded. "Of course, I'm sorry."

Melissa stood and pointed to the folder. "Do not lose that. Follow me."

Nicole quickly followed Melissa out the door, struggling to keep up with the tall woman's long strides.

"Unlike your husband, you'll have access to the main house to perform your duties," Melissa answered.

"Is there a reason why he's not allowed in the house?" Nicole asked.

"Yes," Melissa answered, but she didn't expand on her response. "The first floor of the house is all of the gathering areas. Formal dining room, library, study, living room, and other leisure areas, along with the kitchen and a few bathrooms. The second floor is mostly bedrooms and offices, along with Ms. Calhoun's master bedroom."

Nicole nodded as they passed the second floor and headed toward the third, staying close behind Melissa on the journey to the top.

"I mentioned that you'll have full access to the house, but there is one room that you will never, under any circumstances, enter." Melissa threw a sharpened glance at Nicole, stopping to turn around as she stepped onto the third floor.

A few steps down from Melissa, Nicole kept her hand on the smooth wood of the rail as she looked up at the lawyer, who was made taller by the two steps above.

"Do I make myself clear?" Melissa asked.

Nicole nodded. "Of course."

Melissa turned around and restarted their tour onto the third story. Nicole followed and saw Melissa stop outside of a blue door. It was out of character with the style of the rest of the house.

The blue had faded, and the paint was peeling. It hadn't been maintained like the rest of the house, and Nicole found that odd as she stepped closer to get a better look.

"Why is it blue?" Nicole asked.

"I don't know," Melissa answered. "All I know is that when I took over handling the estate and other assets for the Calhoun family from my father, I was instructed to ensure that no one entered that room. It remains locked, and I've been told that only Ms. Calhoun has the key, though I have no idea where she put it."

Nicole studied the door, the old relic standing out of place in the hallway. She took a step closer, her hand involuntarily reaching for the worn brass knob, and it wasn't until Melissa snatched Nicole's wrist that she stopped.

"What are you doing?" Melissa asked.

Nicole stuttered. "N-n-nothing." She swallowed and then reclaimed her wrist. "I'm sorry." She shook her head. "I don't know why I did that." She rubbed the flesh that Melissa had grabbed and stepped back from the door.

Melissa eyed Nicole with a curious gaze. "I was told by your employer that you're one of the more polished nurses in the company."

Nicole cleared her throat. "I do my best to put the right foot forward from the beginning."

"And is that what you're doing now?" Melissa arched her eyebrows. "Putting the right foot forward?"

Nicole lowered her gaze, inadvertently staring at the tips of her shoes. The laces on her right sneaker were loose, a few steps away from coming undone. After gathering her strength and stringing together the jumble of thoughts in her head, Nicole lifted her eyes to meet Melissa and then cleared her throat. "I under-stand that you're trying to do your job thoroughly. I can see that you've dotted all your T's and crossed all of the I's. But I am good at my job, Ms. Farr, and in the seven years that I have been working in hospice care, I have never had a complaint filed against me or any wrongful accusations. Ms. Calhoun is in the best of hands."

Nicole had made sure to keep her voice even-keeled. She needed to make sure that the lawyer was confident in Nicole's abilities to take care of her client. There was nothing worse than dealing with the family members or friends that didn't trust the people taking care of the sick. Her relationship with the individuals surrounding the elderly was just as important as the relationship with the patient themselves.

"I hope you're right," Melissa said, then turned and walked back toward the staircase. "Now, you might notice that all of the lights in the house remain on at night, but that is perfectly normal. And at no point are you to turn off any of the lights in the common areas around the house."

"Yes, I understand," Nicole said.

"Good," Melissa said. "Time to meet the lady of the house."

6

*N*icole followed Melissa to the second floor to the master bedroom, where Ms. Calhoun spent most of her time. Melissa entered first, and when Nicole stepped through the door, she was surprised by the vast space inside.

The ceilings were vaulted, at least fifteen feet high. Gold and white striped wallpaper covered the walls, along with several paintings. One of the paintings was an empty chair with a spotlight on it surrounded by darkness.

The painting hung above the wall at the head of the king-sized bed, which sat upon a four-post bed frame. Thin white cloth draped over the sides, and the ceiling fan billowed the sheets to life, and it was through these billowing sheets that Nicole saw Ms. Calhoun on the other side of the room.

"Ms. Calhoun?" Melissa asked, her tone much sweeter now that she was speaking to her employer. "I have someone that I'd like you to meet. Someone who will be helping take care of you."

Nicole stepped past Melissa and walked toward Ms. Calhoun. The old woman had her back turned to Nicole, the sunlight from the window draping a silhouette around her, and she stopped a few feet behind her new patient. "Ms. Calhoun, my name is Nicole."

Ms. Calhoun slowly turned around, her expression stoic.

Nicole smiled and extended her hand. "It's wonderful to meet you, ma'am."

Ms. Calhoun didn't look down at Nicole's offered hand, but her fading blue eyes locked onto Nicole's green ones. The woman was old, but a life of leisure and staying indoors had kept her skin mostly smooth.

But it wasn't a healthy smooth. The rounded cheeks, shoulders, and arms were plump, but had the kind of muscles that were soft and mushy underneath. Her skin was pallid, almost grey. Ms. Calhoun wore no makeup and no jewelry, save for a thin gold necklace around her sagging neck. She had her hair done in a perm; the white hairs curled into thin wisps that resembled summer clouds against an afternoon sky.

Melissa finally rescued Nicole from the awkward silence, pulling her back toward the door and away from Ms. Calhoun.

"It was good seeing you again, Ms. Calhoun," Melissa said, her tone still sweet, but raising the volume of her voice even though she had moved closer to her client. "Nicole will be back in a little bit to check on you. Bye-bye."

Melissa draped her long left arm around Nicole's shoulders and then steered her out of the room and back into the hallway, returning to her normal business tone once she was certain she was out of her client's hearing range.

"Well," Melissa said. "There she was."

Nicole glanced back to the open door. "Does she leave her room much?"

"No," Melissa answered. "The house is kept in an immaculate condition for her, and she does nothing to enjoy it. Same thing with the surrounding grounds. She doesn't go outside. All of her meals are brought to her room."

"Was she like that even before her diagnosis of dementia?" Nicole asked.

"Yes," Melissa answered. "However, I was told she still wandered about the house, even made a few visits to the blue door to poke around inside, but that was decades ago."

Nicole frowned, glancing back to the room. "If she experienced such a trauma like watching the death of her family all those years ago, did she try counseling? Therapy? Was anything done after—"

"Mrs. Harper, you were brought on board to help with Ms. Calhoun's current condition," Melissa said. "Not to dig up her past. She doesn't like it when people talk about it around her, so do not bring it up. You'll only cause the poor woman more pain than she's prepared to handle. Understood?"

Nicole didn't agree with the policy, fully aware that

past traumas could rear their ugly head in an aging patient, especially one with early-onset dementia. But now wasn't the time to rock the boat so early on in the trip.

"I understand," Nicole answered.

"Good."

Melissa led Nicole down to the first floor where she was introduced to the rest of the staff. All of them had gathered in the kitchen, which looked like it belonged behind the scenes of a major restaurant instead of the empty home it currently occupied.

"This is the rest of the estate staff," Melissa said. "I had them all come in this morning so they could meet you."

Nicole studied the faces staring back at her and saw that none of them were happy about the gathering. Nicole suspected that she was cutting into their workday, and she understood how precious the time in a day could be.

The first man she greeted was Donald, the butler that had helped them with their bags. He was an older gentleman, Nicole pegged him in his mid-sixties, but from the way that he easily carried the luggage from the car, she could tell that he was still in good shape. The only signs of his aging were the bald head and wrinkles that had creased the mounds of fat that collected under the jowls.

"Donald Weiss, ma'am." The butler clicked his heels together and then offered a slight bow. "Your things are waiting for you to unpack in the guest house."

Nicole stepped forward, offering her hand to the butler, who stared at it with a measure of surprise. But unlike Ms. Calhoun, he finally shook her hand.

"If you need anything, Mrs. Harper, please don't hesitate to ask," Donald said, and then before Nicole could reply, he was already out the door.

The next of the three was the chef, Kate Mills. Dressed in her culinary whites, complete with hat, she fit right in with her surroundings. She was around Nicole's age and very pretty. It was the ice-blue eyes that Nicole noticed first. She was blonde, tan, and even with the chef's coat on, Nicole could tell that she had a nice figure underneath it, and the moment she touched the chef's hand, she felt a pang of jealousy run through her. Jake had cheated on her with a blonde.

"It's great to meet you," Kate said. "It'll be nice to have another woman on the staff. The boys are not much for conversation."

"I'm sure we'll find something to talk about," Nicole said, and then she wiped her palm on her side, not even realizing that she did so.

The last of the three, and by far the biggest and most menacing, was the groundskeeper and maintenance man, Rick Dunst. With fists the size of Nicole's skull, she didn't offer to shake his hand.

"Rick will be the person to contact if you need anything fixed around the guest house," Melissa said.

"Well let's hope that we don't add more work for you," Nicole said.

Rick grunted, crossing his big arms over a chiseled chest. "We'll see." The shirt that clung to his body was already drenched in sweat. The hard stare combined with the hard body made for a combination that Nicole didn't want to get mixed up in.

With the introductions complete, Nicole followed Melissa back to the front of the house, reviewing the schedule that had been put together, when Melissa spun around as Donald opened the front door for her.

"I'll check in with you tomorrow and see how things have been going," Melissa said. "If you have any questions about the schedule or about the house, please don't hesitate to call me. I'd rather you ask before you do something that you might regret."

Nicole shrugged off Melissa's comment. She was used to family members treating her as if she were incompetent. It was a defense mechanism to protect themselves over the fact that they couldn't take care of their family by themselves. But Nicole was surprised for a lawyer to give such a comment. "I'll be sure to do that."

"And remember that Ms. Calhoun's schedule must be followed down to the strictest detail," Melissa said. "You won't have a lot of downtime during your stay here during working hours, so make sure you don't fall behind."

"I won't," Nicole said.

"Good." Melissa tugged at the bottom of her jacket, straightening it out, and then forced another smile that parted her red lips and exposed her picture-perfect teeth. "I hope we have an enjoyable work relationship." She extended her hand, and Nicole shook it. "Goodbye."

"Bye." Nicole couldn't help but smile as she watched Melissa leave, her easy strides long and assertive on her path to her car. She glanced back down at the schedule in her hand, realizing that she was already behind on her work for the day. "No rest for the wicked."

7

*I*t took some time to locate all of the supply closets that Nicole would use for most of her work around the house, but once she managed to find those areas, she was off to the races. The schedule called for Nicole to check on Ms. Calhoun every twenty minutes to ensure she was comfortable.

A few notes had been made of what to look for when Ms. Calhoun was distressed. Because the woman didn't talk, the staff was forced to learn the non-verbal cues to figure out what their employer wanted.

When Ms. Calhoun placed her hand on her throat for extended periods, it meant that she was thirsty. An open mouth signaled that she was hungry. If she laid on her stomach, that meant she wasn't feeling well, and if she hugged her arms across her body, it meant that she was mad.

Most of the gestures made sense in Nicole's mind, but as she checked on Ms. Calhoun throughout the first few hours, she saw no such signs of distress.

The old woman simply kept sitting by the window, staring out through the glass. Her eyes didn't seem to be focused on anything particular. Nicole made a few attempts to speak to Ms. Calhoun, remembering to keep her tone as conversational as possible. Her years caring for the sick and elderly had taught her that while those people needed care and support, they didn't need to be talked down to.

They were still people, and they still wanted their dignity. Nicole tried to honor that by always speaking to her patients as if they were still healthy. They didn't need to be reminded of their limitations or the bleak nature of their future. Their illnesses did enough of that every day.

Nicole walked over to Ms. Calhoun's side, staring out the window with her. "I imagine it was a wonderful place to grow up." She smiled. "All of that wide-open space." She glanced down at Ms. Calhoun, who didn't respond. "Is there anything I can do for you before I bring up your lunch?"

Ms. Calhoun remained motionless, staring out the window. She kept her hands folded in her lap, and Nicole wondered if that was one of the non-verbal cues. The cold shoulder was evident, and Nicole suspected that her new patient didn't enjoy her company.

But Nicole had worked with patients who didn't like her before, and in the end, she had managed to win them over. It was part of why Nicole enjoyed her work, it was the challenge of taking an impossibly bleak situation and turning it into memories for people to enjoy.

Because in the end, that's what mattered most to people, just enjoying the little time that they had left, and she hoped that she could do the same for Ms. Calhoun.

Nicole descended the stairs and headed to the kitchen, hearing the clank of dishes before she entered and saw Kate at the stove.

"Is Ms. Calhoun's lunch ready?" Nicole asked.

Kate turned around. "Almost. Be just a minute."

Nicole nodded and hung back by the kitchen door. She watched Kate work, the skilled hands moving quickly between pots and pans, adding ingredients and measuring spices. Nicole had never been a good cook. Her mother had tried to teach her growing up, but her mother's golden touch never rubbed off on her.

Unable to stand the silence while she waited, Nicole cleared her throat, hoping to make at least one friend while she was here. "So how do you like working for Ms. Calhoun?"

"It's not bad." Kate shrugged, keeping her back to Nicole. "It pays well, and it's easy. Since the old bat doesn't talk, she never complains about my cooking." She glanced over her shoulder. "Not that there is anything to complain about."

Nicole nodded. "Good to know."

"So who was that I saw heading around to the back?" Kate asked. "The man that was with you."

Nicole cleared her throat. "My husband. Jake."

"Husband?" Kate spun around, wiping away the sweat that had collected on her brow. "Must be nice to bring your man on work trips." She scrunched up her face. "Or is it all work and no play?"

Nicole blushed, turning her eyes away from Kate as she tried not to stumble over her words. "It's the first time we've taken a trip like this in a long time."

"Trying to spice things up?" Kate asked. "Probably not too hard. Your husband is a good-looking man."

That familiar pang of jealousy thrummed through Nicole, but she tried not to dwell on it. This woman had no idea what Nicole had just gone through, no idea that the pair hadn't touched one another since the affair.

But despite her efforts to drown her doubt, Nicole wondered if Jake would find Kate attractive. Kate was the kind of woman that men dreamed about when they were stuck in a long-term relationship. The fantasy girl.

"So how do you like it so far?" Kate asked, setting a tray with dishes while the food in the pan behind her billowed steam.

"Everything is fine," Nicole answered, keeping her tone cordial. "First time I've worked in a place this big."

"And I bet it's the first time you've ever had a client like Ms. Calhoun," Kate said, shaking her head as she glanced around the kitchen. "The old bat is off her rocker."

Nicole frowned. "She has dementia."

Kate looked from the dishes and arched her eyebrows. "I wouldn't be so sure about that. I mean, you know what happened here, right? The murders?"

"Melissa told me about them, yes."

THE HAUNTING OF CALHOUN MANSION

Kate scoffed. "Yeah, I'm sure she gave you the glossed-over version. But did she tell you that they never caught the person who did it? Tell me how a person who killed a family of three, victims who also happen to be some of the wealthiest people in the country, gets away? And how in the hell was Ms. Calhoun the only survivor? That just doesn't add up to me."

Nicole gestured to the stove behind Kate. "Food is burning."

"What? Oh, shit!" Kate spun around, quickly removing the skillet from the stove, and turned on the vent to help clear out some of the smoke that had gathered. She plucked the burnt contents from the skillet with a pair of steel tongs. "Well, I don't think that's edible anymore." She dropped it in the trash and then opened up the refrigerator and removed something from a piece of Tupperware. "I don't think she'll mind some leftovers." Kate dumped the contents onto a plate and then placed it in the microwave, setting the timer for three minutes before she turned her attention back to Nicole. "I mean, don't you think that it's strange how she just so happened to have gone silent after her family was killed?" She leaned over the counter, planting her elbows on the steel. "She was found covered in blood. How do you think that happened if she wasn't the one slicing away?" She faked a few stabbing motions with her hand.

"I don't speculate on the past of any of my patients," Nicole said.

Kate pushed herself off the table and held up her

hands. "Hey, I get it. Don't want to ruffle any feathers, especially on the first day. But just so you know, this place doesn't have any cameras or anything. Which I also found strange. I mean what kind of a rich person doesn't have some type of security for their stuff? Especially with that vault hidden somewhere around here."

"Vault?" Nicole asked. "What vault?"

"The one that Ms. Calhoun's father built to store all of their precious jewels. Diamonds, sapphires, rubies, it was said old Mr. Calhoun had the biggest jewel collection in the state. Millions tucked away in a vault, and no one knows where it is, except for that crazy old bat, and she hasn't said a peep since the murders. Not that she needs the jewels. Her father also had a nice investment portfolio, which has provided all of the modern comforts that you see before you."

The timer on the microwave beeped, and Kate grabbed the plate from inside and quickly transferred it over to the tray, blowing on her fingers because it was so hot.

Nicole walked over and picked up the tray, but before she turned away, Kate stopped her.

"And, hey, if there's anything that I can do for you and your husband to keep it interesting," Kate said, bouncing her eyebrows up and down. "I can prepare some chocolate-covered strawberries or give you a can of whipped cream to fool around with." She giggled in a way that Nicole suspected garnered her more attention than other women. She was flirtatious and oozed sexuality without trying.

"I'll let you know," Nicole said, then quickly cleared her throat and left the kitchen before she was forced to suffer any more of the adolescent innuendos.

Nicole tried not to let her interaction with Kate mess with her head, but she found it difficult as she replayed the conversation in her head on her way to the second floor.

"A can of whipped cream," Nicole said, muttering under her breath.

She imagined how it would feel to be with Jake again in that way. Even before the affair, their love life had been scant, and her sex life was currently on a five-month drought.

The thoughts in her mind swirling, Nicole didn't notice that Ms. Calhoun had moved and stood up from her chair by the window and was currently facing her, staring at Nicole with the same blank expression that she had worn all morning.

"Lunch for you, Ms. Calhoun," Nicole said, forcing herself to focus on her work and leave the questions for the next time that she and Jake attended therapy. "Leftovers from last night. Would you like to eat by the window? Or in bed? I could help you down to another room if you'd like a change of scenery?"

Ms. Calhoun didn't react. Unsure of where she would like to eat, Nicole placed the food tray on the end of the bed, making sure that it wouldn't spill, and then walked toward Ms. Calhoun.

Nicole touched her throat, trying to mimic the signs that she had read in the documents about Ms.

Calhoun's non-verbal cues. "Are you thirsty? Or hungry?"

Nothing caught the old woman's attention as Nicole drew closer, but with only a few feet between the pair of them, it was too late for Nicole to protect herself when Ms. Calhoun brandished an empty water glass that she had been holding behind her back.

Ms. Calhoun screamed as she raised the glass high above her head, and then flung it down at Nicole's feet as the old woman lumbered forward.

Nicole raised her arms to block the glass, but when it crashed at the ground near her feet, she had little time to react before Ms. Calhoun picked up the vase from a nearby table and smashed that on the ground as well, still screaming at the top of her lungs.

Nicole retreated toward the door, her eyes locked onto the open black hole that was Ms. Calhoun's mouth. She couldn't see anything but that empty void, and the closer it moved toward her, the more Nicole was convinced that she would be swallowed whole.

"Ms. Calhoun!" A black and white blur crossed Nicole's field of vision and restrained the hysterical woman. It was Donald. He managed to calm Ms. Calhoun's outburst. The screaming had stopped, but Ms. Calhoun continued to breathe heavily.

Nicole backed up against the wall, catching her own breath and trying to figure out what had triggered the old woman. Had she said something? Done something to set her off? She didn't think she had, and Melissa hadn't written down anything that might trigger a reaction like the one she had just experienced.

It wasn't the first time that Nicole had been forced to deal with violent patients, but that had been the first one where she had been attacked with such rage.

"Are you all right?" Donald walked over to Nicole and checked her for any injuries.

Nicole nodded, but when she spoke, her voice was in a high-pitched tone. "I'm fine. I think." She slowly pushed herself off the wall and examined her arms and legs. None of the glass that shattered had managed to hit her legs, but there was a nasty gash on her left arm, and a drop of blood had already fallen to the carpet.

"Oh my, that is a nasty cut," Donald said.

Nicole looked from the wound to Ms. Calhoun, who had returned to the other side of the room, staring out the window. The old woman was perfectly calm, as if nothing happened.

"Let's get that fixed up." Donald gently guided Nicole by the crook of her elbow out of the room and into the hallway.

Nicole glanced back one last time before she left, getting a glimpse at the back of Ms. Calhoun, wondering if there was any truth to the chef's claims that the old woman had been the one to murder her entire family.

8

*N*icole winced when Donald applied the rubbing alcohol to sterilize the wound and apologized for the twentieth time.

"Sorry," Donald said, his voice sheepish.

"It's fine," Nicole replied.

Once the wound was cleaned up, Donald placed a fresh bandage over the cut and then nodded, satisfied with his work.

"Almost good as new." Donald put away the supplies and then turned back to Nicole. "Are you sure you're all right beside the scratch?"

"Yes," Nicole answered, forcing herself to sound more cheerful than she felt. She knew that she would get over it, but it would just take some time. That was all.

But while Nicole might have been able to fake her emotions, Donald slumped forward on the stool. "She has been getting worse over the past few months. I didn't want to believe it, but after today, it's hard not to see the signs."

"You've known Ms. Calhoun for a long time?" Nicole asked.

"Yes," Donald answered, and then a smile broke through the worry. "I've been in the service of the Calhoun family for forty-three years." He straightened up a little, trying to return to a more professional posture. "Ms. Calhoun was already a grown woman when I came to work here. She was so lovely. The apple of Mr. Calhoun's eye." He chuckled. "Everyone loved her."

Nicole smiled. The picture that Donald painted was a far cry from the one that the chef had given her, and she rather liked this one more. "What was she like? Before?"

Donald slid back into the memories as easy as slipping a foot into a well-worn fleece-lined slipper. It was warm and cozy and familiar. Nicole had noted how easy it was for older people to do that. She figured it was maybe because their memories were of a more highlight reel at this point in their lives. Only the really good, or the really bad, caught their attention like the flicker of gemstones at the bottom of a still pond. And Donald reached into the still waters and plucked one from the depths and smiled as he recounted the tale.

"She has a wonderful smile," Donald said. "And the most infectious laugh. Once she got going with the giggles, it didn't take long before everyone around her was in the same condition. And she was devoted to her family."

"It must have been hard on her," Nicole said. "Losing everyone the way she did."

Donald nodded, and the smile faded from his face along with the memories. "It was the loss of her sister that hurt her the worst. Of course, she loved all of her family, but the bond with Aubrey... It went beyond blood. They were friends. Best of friends." He glanced around the room, which was small and empty, save for the small table and chairs where they sat. "I should have been here."

Nicole reached for Donald's hand, lending comfort. "What could you have done?"

"I don't know, but I know that I could have done something." Donald's voice quivered the longer he dwelled on the failures of his past, and he kept his face turned away so that Nicole couldn't see his expression. "I could have stopped the person responsible."

Nicole squeezed Donald's hand, and the pressure caused him to look at her. The old man was hurting. "I've been around people who are in pain my entire life, and the one thing I've learned is not to fight it. Because the harder you fight against the pain, the more it fights back, and I don't think that's something you want to do, is it?"

"It's hard not to fight back," Donald answered. "It's hard to just take it."

"It always passes," Nicole said.

Donald nodded and then took a deep breath. "I suppose you're right."

Nicole thought about what Donald had said about Ms. Calhoun's family, and then realized why she thought the house looked different. "There aren't any pictures of her family hanging up." She looked to Donald for an explanation. "Why?"

"After the murders, Ms. Calhoun was silent as a church mouse," Donald answered. "Wouldn't speak about anything to anyone. Not even me. Lord knows that I tried to get her to open up." He frowned, slouching forward, and the raw emotions made him show his age. "She walked through this house like a ghost. Saying nothing. Looking at nothing. She wouldn't eat. Couldn't sleep. I thought that she was going to die from starvation." He paused, fiddling with his hands, twisting his liver-spotted fingers. "One night, it must have been close to three am, I heard this blood-curdling scream. It was so loud, so piercing, I thought all the glass in the house would shatter. I sprang from my bed and rushed down to the master suite where I'd heard the screaming, and when I entered the room, I saw Ms. Calhoun standing over the shattered remains of the picture frames in the room. She had torn them off all the walls, breaking them. She had stepped on a lot of the glass, which had dug into the soles of her feet. Bloody footprints were all over the room, and she just wouldn't stop screaming."

"What did you do?" Nicole asked.

"She wouldn't tell me what was wrong," Donald answered, lost in the memory. "She just kept scream-ing, kept stomping the broken glass with her bare feet. She wouldn't stop, so I had to finally pick her up and carry her out of the room to get her fixed up. She cried, but she never spoke a word."

"What happened next?" Nicole asked.

"Exhaustion finally caught up with her," Donald said. "She slept for almost three days, and when she finally woke up again, she seemed... better."

"Did she speak?" Nicole asked. "Did she say anything?"

"No, she was still quiet, but there was something different about her," Donald answered. "She was more like herself than she had been before, but also..." He trailed off.

Nicole leaned forward. "What?"

Donald looked at her. "Only she wasn't herself. I know that sounds odd, but when she finally woke up and got out of bed, it was like she was a different person. I mean, she had been different since the murders, but... Her eyes had changed. The color had dimmed. I didn't think something like that could happen, but it did. And then, after she woke up, she started taking down all of the pictures in the house. She did it calmly, and when I noticed what she was doing, I walked over and started to help." He shrugged. "And ever since then, she's just been a ghost drifting through these halls. She started eating again, and sleeping, though I don't think that she sleeps through the entire night." He frowned, struggling to find the words. "It's like she's waiting for something. Something that I can't help her with. Maybe she doesn't even know what it is, but..." He finally leaned back and shook his head. "I don't know. I think I'm just tired."

Nicole understood the pressures that came with taking care of someone that you loved. And with the communication barrier between himself and Ms. Calhoun, Nicole imagined that only made the situation more difficult.

"It sounds like you've done everything you can to help take care of her," Nicole said. "I don't think that there is anything else that you could have done. And I'm here to help with all of that now, so you don't have to go through it alone."

Donald smiled. "You're a good person, Mrs. Harper. I knew it the moment I saw you. Your husband is a lucky man."

Nicole matched the smile that Donald gave her, but inside she felt that pang in the center of her stomach that hollowed out her extremities. It was a side effect from anyone who brought up the mention of Jake without her expecting it. She didn't know when the feeling would stop, only that she knew that until it went away completely, she would never truly be ready to be happy again.

Donald stood. "If you need to change out the bandages on that cut, you can come in here to find the medical supplies." He moved toward the door and then stopped before he left, turning around to face Nicole once more. "And I wouldn't worry about Ms. Calhoun having another outburst at you again."

"Why do you say that?" Nicole asked.

"She tends to have one whenever she meets someone new, but it always dies down," Donald said. "Sometimes I think that that's the only way she knows how to say hello anymore."

Nicole nodded her thanks, and Donald left her in

the room to contemplate how to handle her next inter-action with Ms. Calhoun, because while Donald might have had some fond memories of the woman, her own interactions combined with what Kate had said about the old woman's past had already planted the seeds of doubt in Ms. Calhoun's innocence.

9

*N*icole went about her chores and duties, careful to mentally record her interactions with Ms. Calhoun to determine if there was anything particular that she had done to trigger the previous outburst.

But every time that Nicole walked into Ms. Calhoun's room to either give her medicine, food, water, or just for the general twenty-minute check-ups, the old woman wouldn't even look her in the face. She just kept staring out the window, focused on nothing in particular. As far as Nicole could tell, the old woman didn't even notice that she was there.

Once Nicole collected Ms. Calhoun's dinner, she made sure to follow the instructions of shutting all the curtains in the master bedroom and the rest of the rooms on the second floor. Even though the sun was still shining and it would be setting soon, Ms. Calhoun usually spent the rest of the night in bed, in the dark.

Nicole wasn't sure how that was going to help her

dementia, and she was concerned about the lack of activity for Ms. Calhoun in the daily schedule. While the woman took a steady dose of medicine and her nutrition seemed fine, there was no real form of exercise other than the allotted walking-around time, which was to be done at Ms. Calhoun's leisure. Nicole knew that a good physical routine could combat the effects that dementia had on the mind.

But seeing as how it was her first day and she was still getting acclimated to Ms. Calhoun's routine, she didn't want to upset the woman any more than she already did. What was most important now was gaining her new patient's trust, building a relationship that would help Ms. Calhoun buy into the exercises that would help make her feel better.

It was a wonder that the woman had remained in the shape she had without any type of exercise. If she hadn't been outside in decades, then her body and bones must be incredibly frail.

All of this filled Nicole's head on the walk from the main house to the guest house on the back-left corner of the lot. The orange light of the sunset reflected off the windows and prevented Nicole from being able to see inside, making what she found a surprise.

"Hey, I'm—" Nicole stopped, and she was still close enough to be bumped by the door as it knocked her backside after it swung shut.

"Hey." Jake stood with flowers in his hand, more candles than she had ever seen in one location, and dinner on the table. "I figured since it was the end of your first day that I could surprise you. New place. New us. You know?"

Nicole remained by the door, surprised by the gesture. "Wow. I—" She covered her mouth and then shook her head. "I wasn't expecting this."

Jake, flowers still in hand, walked over to her, never breaking eye contact. "I want us to get back to the place we were before I royally screwed up. I told you that I meant what I said about doing whatever I needed to do to fix us, to rebuild the trust." He was standing right in front of her now, close enough for her to smell the cologne that he had applied. He smelled nice. "I love you, Nic."

He handed Nicole the flowers, and she took them from his hands. She hoped that he wouldn't say anything else because she wasn't sure what more she could say in return other than "Thanks."

But her wishes were granted, and he walked her to the table, taking the binder from her hands, which she had been studying on her walk back from the mansion, and sat down at the dinner table.

"Where did you get all of these candles?" Nicole asked.

"A plus of having your own personal chef is that you have more time to decorate and set a nice ambiance for the meal." Jake smiled from the other side of the table.

It was a small, square dinette set, and Nicole placed the flowers in the vase in the center, which blocked Jake from her line of sight. Both of them laughed, and Jake moved the flowers to the left.

Nicole glanced down at her plate, which was

covered, the steam collecting on the inside of the dome, blocking her view of the food. "What is it?"

Jake smiled. "Take a look."

Nicole lifted the cover off the plate, her face blasted with steam. She winced, turning her head away, and then smiled when she saw the steak on the plate.

"Filet mignon," Jake said. "With brussels sprouts and a baked potato."

It was her favorite meal. And because they had been saving for a house and then paying for the therapy sessions, it had been a long time since she had been able to enjoy it.

"We could have this every night," Jake said. "Can you believe that? Kate can make this every single night!" He laughed and then removed his dome, triggering another column of steam.

But as happy as Nicole had been about the food, she only latched onto the one word that mattered to her, and that was the name of the gorgeous chef.

"You spoke with Kate?" Nicole asked, her voice rising an octave.

"Yeah, I wanted to make sure she could do this before I set out all of the candles," Jake answered, the smile slowly fading as he looked down at her steak. "Is something wrong?"

Niccle shook her head and then cleared her throat, picking up one of the knives. "No. Everything looks great." She grabbed her fork and started to cut into the steak.

"How was your day?" Jake asked, digging into his steak.

Nicole watched the blood ooze from the slice down the middle. She liked her steaks rare. "It was… stranger than a normal first day."

"How so?" Jake asked, shoving a piece of steak into his mouth as he reached for the bottle of wine that had been airing out.

Nicole speared a hunk of meat with her fork and frowned. "She attacked me."

Jake stopped pouring, arching his eyebrows in surprise. "She what?"

Nicole held up her arm, revealing the bandage that Donald had applied, and then popped the steak into her mouth. "He said that she goes off on strangers sometimes, but—"

"He?" Jake asked.

"Donald," Nicole answered, still chewing. "The butler—Wow, this is really good."

"Are you going to file a complaint?" Jake asked.

"A complaint with who?"

"The lawyer, Melissa, your own company," Jake replied. "She could have hurt you."

"That's the thing," Nicole said, and she leaned forward. "I don't think she was trying to hurt me. I mean the stuff she was throwing kept landing near my feet. The only reason that I got hurt was because the pieces bounced up and scratched me."

"Nic," Jake said, setting his fork and knife down. "She could have seriously hurt you."

"She was fine for the rest of the day." Nicole shrugged it off, digging into her steak. "I actually tried to see if I could recreate what happened before, but she was completely normal. Well, I suppose docile is a better word."

"I just don't like the idea of you being in a dangerous situation," Jake said.

Nicole started to chuckle, the first few blasts coming out involuntarily before she was able to get it under control.

Jake paused. "What's so funny?"

"You have just been laying it on so thick lately," Nicole answered, starting to feel a little light-headed from the wine. "Makes me think that you might have done something wrong." She popped another piece of steak into her mouth and then slathered some butter on her baked potato.

Jake quieted down, and it was his silence that finally forced Nicole to realize that she had made him upset. And for a brief moment, she felt bad about what she had said. The words had come out of her involuntarily. But then she remembered how *he* had made *her* feel. She remembered the embarrassment and shock. She remembered the rage that had coursed through her veins, and how it made her doubt everything about herself, and him.

The doubt hung over her life like a storm cloud in those peanut comic strips, following her around wherever she went. At work. At home. At the grocery store. At the movies. Out to dinner, even driving on the highway. It was always there, gnawing away at her ability to move past the pain of the affair.

Because as far as Jake had come, and as sincere as all

of his apologies had been, there was always the doubt that he would slip back into his old habits.

"What?" Nicole asked, her tone suggesting she was ready to pick a fight.

She wasn't sure why she had done it, other than the fact that it made her feel good. But it was that fleeting good feeling. The kind where you would eat an entire tub of ice cream late into the night and then have the worst sleep of your life, waking up the next morning feeling gross and tired. And just like the ice cream, she knew that she would feel bad after this.

"Nothing." Jake kept his head down, staring at the food on his plate. He always went quiet whenever he was upset. But Nicole couldn't stop talking.

"How did the conversation with Kate go?" Nicole asked, reaching for the wine. "The pair of you get along all right?"

Jake finally looked up. "Don't do this, Nic."

"What?" Nicole smiled, keeping the overly cheery tone up as she shrugged, the rim of her wine glass only inches from her lips. "I'm just making conversation. I talked to her today too, you know." She winked at him and took a sip. "She thinks that you're cute."

Jake stared at her with that dead-eye glare she was so familiar with. "Nicole, I really don't want to make this into something, okay? So why don't we do what our therapist said whenever we're getting into an argument about nothing and just hit the reset button? Okay? Can we do that?"

Nicole could hear the pleading in his voice. He really wanted it to stop. He really wanted this to be a nice dinner. But that little voice in the back of Nicole's head just wouldn't let her stop, that cloud of doubt egging her on. "Arguing about nothing? I wouldn't say fucking another woman is nothing, Jake, but maybe that's just how you saw it."

Jake removed the napkin from his lap and slapped it on the table. "I am tired of you lording it over me, Nicole. Yes, I made a mistake. Yes, I wish I could undo it, but I can't. It's done. And, yes, maybe I have been bending over backward for you to try and make amends, but I do it because I want to save our marriage! Something that you don't seem to care about anymore."

"Oh, I don't care?" Nicole stood up from her chair, planting her palms into the table and leaning forward. "I cared by not sleeping with someone else, Jake! I showed that I cared by being faithful to you!"

"By not sleeping with anyone, including your husband?" Jake asked, now standing himself. "How in the hell is that keeping a marriage alive? The only thing you were doing was slowly suffocating both of us. I mean, Jesus Christ, Nic, we had done nothing for each other."

"So you sleep with someone else?" Nicole shot the words back at him and hoped that they stung. Judging by the look on his face, she knew they did.

Jake helplessly flapped his arms at his sides. "I don't know what else to do, Nic. I really don't. If you want to work this out, I still do. If you want me to leave, I'll leave. If you want a divorce—"

"Is that what you want?" Nicole asked, the bite in

her tone dissolving into the quiver that was reserved for when she was about to break down. And she didn't want to break down here, not now. "Do you want a divorce, Jake?"

"No," Jake answered. "I want to fix this, Nicole, but if you won't forgive me for what happened..." He signed and then rubbed his eyes before pinching the bridge of his nose the way he did when he had a headache. "I don't know."

Jake was quiet for a minute, staring at the floor, and then he returned to his seat, picking up his fork and knife, and started eating his food.

Nicole watched him for a minute, and when he felt her gaze on him, he finally looked up, shrugging his shoulders.

"It's filet mignon," Jake said. "I'm not going to let it go to waste."

But Nicole had lost her appetite. She said nothing as she walked toward the bedroom where Donald had placed her luggage and then closed the door, pressing her back up against the sturdy wood, wondering how she was going to fix the mess that she kept making in her own bed. She knew that Jake was sincere in wanting to fix their problems. She knew the regret he expressed was genuine.

And every time Nicole thought she was able to let the past stay where it should remain buried, something triggered her. But now she was starting to think she was making excuses, and she knew the reason why she had asked Jake if he wanted a divorce. Because it was all she had been able to think about since she found out about the affair.

But Nicole couldn't bring it up. Not even in therapy. Every time she thought she was getting close, the words gathering near the back of her throat, she froze. She couldn't go through with it, no matter how many times she had tried. It was becoming infuriating. And frightening.

She knew that she was running out of time if she wanted to save her marriage. Jake wouldn't stick around forever, even though he said he wanted to fix his mistake. It was up to her now, and she had no idea what she would do.

10

*A*lone in bed, Nicole couldn't sleep. She tossed and turned beneath the covers, unable to quiet her mind. She kept reliving the conversation at dinner. She knew that she shouldn't have snapped at Jake, especially without any actual proof he had done something wrong. But she was still learning to deal with her emotions after the affair.

It wasn't the first time that Nicole had tossed and turned at night, alone in bed. The pair had slept separately ever since the affair, and Nicole had been surprised at what the therapist had told her when she brought it up in one of their sessions.

"Stop it." Valerie Wickets was a sprightly woman, inquisitive yet direct. She had the uncanny ability to make you feel better and worse at the same time. "For the pair of you to heal, to really heal, you'll need to start by getting back into the marriage bed together. I'm not telling you to start having sex again, but you need to refamiliarize yourself with each other's touch.

Start slow, and then build from there, but step one, by far, is making sure that both of you sleep in the same bed."

Nicole knew that it was the rational decision to make, but she couldn't bring herself to clear that step. She couldn't bring herself to sleep in the same bed that had been the source of all their problems. Even when Jake threw the bed out and bought a new one, she still couldn't do it. She didn't even like being in that room, in the apartment... all of it was too much.

Deep down, Nicole knew that she needed to start trusting Jake again. After all, it had been three months since the affair, and they had ten weeks of couples' therapy under their belt. He was doing everything that the therapist had suggested, and he was consistent.

And what had she done? Nothing but shoot him down at every turn, rubbing his nose in it like he was a dog that piddled on the carpet. If he had done that to her and the roles were reversed? Nicole didn't have any doubt that she would have left weeks ago.

But Jake had stayed, despite the abuse that she had given him at every turn. Every nice gesture, every small token of apology, she had turned it against him. It was her turn to make the decision if she wanted to fix their marriage.

Nicole took a breath and then looked at her closed door, highlighted by the moonlight streaming through the window. She flung the covers from her body and then placed her feet on the carpet. She moved quietly toward the door, pausing when her palm touched the brass handle.

It was cold, and she couldn't stop shivering. But she knew that if she couldn't take this step, if she couldn't walk to her husband and lay with him, just sleep next to him in a place that was as beautiful as this, then she wasn't sure she would ever be able to move on. It was now or never.

Nicole opened the door, stepping into the hallway. She saw that Jake's door was cracked open. He had taken the room at the end of the hall.

Butterflies fluttered through her stomach. She hadn't been this nervous since their wedding. She tried not to get in her own head and psych herself out. She had done enough of that over the past few months.

Nicole relived Jake's betrayal every day. She had tortured herself, wondering if he would do it again, unable to part the clouds of doubt and be happy again. But maybe she didn't want to be happy anymore.

Nicole had listened to her therapist talk about how some people self-sabotaged, running away from the good things in their life.

But halfway down the hall, Nicole had no desire to turn around. Because she knew that this could be their last chance. She knew that Jake could only take so much abuse after trying to make things right before he left her for good. She didn't want to lose him. She needed to make an effort before it was too late.

Nicole quietly opened the bedroom door, even though she knew that Jake slept like a rock. Last summer there had been a major earthquake that rocked the house, waking Nicole up in a screaming fit of surprise, only to find Jake snoring logs. It wasn't until the event was over and she punched him in the arm that he woke up.

Jake lay in bed with his back to the door, hidden under the covers. She closed the door behind her and tiptoed to the empty side of the bed. She carefully lifted the covers and slid onto the cold sheets next to her husband.

The bed was larger than one in her own room, and Nicole wiggled over the mattress. Even under the covers, she couldn't stop shivering, and as she neared Jake, she smelled something rotten.

Nicole grimaced but continued to move closer to Jake. But something felt wrong. She was nervous, yes, but there was something else beneath those nerves, something sinister. Her mouth went dry, and the ball of nerves in her stomach went haywire like a row of busted circuits. She grabbed hold of Jake's shoulder and gave him a little shake. He was ice cold to the touch.

"Jake?" Nicole's voice was nothing but a whisper, a puff of cold air escaping from her lips.

The flesh on her arms broke out in gooseflesh, and Nicole shook Jake harder, pulling him from his side and onto his back. "Jake, are you—"

Jake landed on his back, and when his head hit the pillow and rolled to the side, the face staring back at Nicole wasn't the face of her husband. It was the butler, Donald.

The pair of dead, lifeless eyes triggered a scream that started in the pit of her stomach and rose until it escaped from her lips, propelled by a jet stream of frigid air.

Nicole rocketed backward out of bed and hit the floor hard on her backside. The pain traveled from her tailbone all the way up to the base of her skull. She couldn't take her eyes off the bed, or the butler that had somehow taken the place of her husband.

"No." Nicole hyperventilated. Her heart rate skyrocketed. Was she having an episode? Some kind of nervous breakdown?

Nicole retreated until she hit the wall and kept her eyes focused on the bed. Was Donald dead? Had he wandered into the guest house by mistake? Some kind of sleepwalking ritual? Nicole wasn't sure.

"Donald?" Nicole finally mustered up the courage to find her voice. "Are you all right?"

Donald rose straight up from bed, like a zombie in a horror film. He said nothing and was silhouetted by the moonlight coming through the window from across the room.

After a period of stillness, Nicole finally managed to sit up on her knees. But she kept her distance from the bed, remaining close to the wall, one eye trained on the door in case she needed to run.

"Donald, what are you doing here?" Nicole asked.

The butler said nothing, looking straight ahead.

Nicole's courage grew stronger in the silence, fueled by her curiosity, and she hardened her tone. "Why are you here?"

Donald finally turned his head toward Nicole, his expression hidden by the silhouette, and Nicole froze. Her heart leaped into her throat, and she struggled to catch her breath as Donald finally removed the covers from his legs and stepped out of bed.

He walked in slow motion, almost as if he were struggling to move, but it was when he rounded the end of the bed and started his slow shamble toward Nicole that she noticed something running down his hands, tiny droplets of liquid dangling from Donald's fingertips and falling to the carpet.

Nicole retreated back toward the wall, cringing. "Donald, what—"

Quick as a snake bite, Donald snatched Nicole's wrist, and her skin burned. But it was cold like ice instead of hot, and now that Donald held onto her, Nicole saw the wounds that sliced down his forearm all the way to the base of his hand. The gash was deep, blood running over the splayed sides of the flesh.

Unlike the cold grip of Donald's hand, the blood was warm and sticky as it transferred from Donald's open wound and onto her skin.

The blood was all that Nicole could look at until Donald tightened his grip, giving her a shake that jolted her vision upward so that the pair stared into each other's eyes.

Nicole wanted to look away, but she was paralyzed. She watched as Donald worked his lips, trying to open his mouth, his cheeks reddening from the effort.

Unable to escape, Nicole watched Donald's eyes widen with terror until he finally opened his mouth and a swarm of flies flew from the dark cavern of his mouth.

11

*N*icole woke up screaming in her own bed, swatting at her face. She was drenched in sweat, her throat raw from the blood-curdling cries, but when she touched her cheeks, there were no flies.

Jake burst into her bedroom, a large candlestick gripped in one hand, which he held high above his head, prepared to strike.

"Are you all right?" Jake glanced around the room, expecting to find some kind of monster lurking in the darkness, but there was nothing. He finally lowered the candlestick, catching his breath from the quick sprint down the hall.

"He killed himself," Nicole said. "He was in your bed, and he had cut his wrists."

Jake set the candlestick on the nearby nightstand and then sat on the other side of the bed, taking his wife's hand, which was as cold as the corpse that had just grabbed her. "Honey, it was a dream. There's no one here." He squeezed her hand. "Everything is fine."

Nicole glanced down at their interlaced fingers. It had been a long time since they had held hands. Their physical contact over the past few months had been limited to the occasional shoulder bump or arm graze.

But something stirred in Nicole and she quickly withdrew her hand, still hesitant from that cloud of doubt that fogged the future.

"Well," Jake said, breaking the silence. "I don't think I'll be able to fall asleep after all of that." He looked at her and then gestured to the kitchen. "Need a drink?"

Normally Nicole would have told him no, but she still couldn't shake the goosebumps. "Yeah. I think that might help take the edge off a little bit."

Some wine was still left over in the bottle from dinner, and Jake uncorked it and poured them each a glass. Nicole drank half of hers on the first gulp.

Jake raised his eyebrows as he sipped from his own glass. "Thirsty?"

Nicole shut her eyes, cupping the wine glass with both of her palms like it was a sacred artifact. "I could smell the blood. That metallic scent. And I could feel how cold the air was. It was freezing." She opened her eyes and then glanced down at her exposed forearms.

The hairs still stood upright, and she could still see the flashes of blood from Donald's wounds.

Nicole took another drink and then leaned back in her chair. "I don't know why I would have a nightmare like that one I had."

Jake kept the lip of his own wine glass hovering close to his lips. "We're in a new place, a place that just so happens to have a history with murder and death."

Nicole set her wine aside. She was already feeling the buzz.

"Do you want to talk about it?" Jake asked.

Nicole flinched. Between the adrenaline rush from the nightmare and the buzz from the wine, she wasn't sure how much she remembered.

"You know, I had a dream too," Jake said.

Nicole frowned. "You did?"

"I was here." Jake pressed his hands on the kitchen counter. "I think I was working, and it was already dark. I thought that it was weird that you hadn't come back from the main house yet, so I walked outside. All of the lights in the windows were out except for one. It was the far right window, top floor, and I saw the silhouette of someone in the window. I was too far away to see who it was, and I didn't even know if they were looking at me, but I waved, and they just stood there." He touched the back of his neck. "And then I felt this little pinprick on the base of my neck, and it paralyzed me. I couldn't move; not even my eyes. I was just locked in place, staring up at the window, and that silhouette staring right back at me. The longer I stared at it, the more frightened I became."

Nicole hugged herself, remembering the figure in the window that she had seen when they first arrived at the house, and then leaned into the counter. "What happened?"

"That's the thing," Jake answered, laughing to himself. "Nothing happened. And then I heard you screaming from your room, and it snapped me out of the dream." He raised his glass and tipped it toward

Nicole. "So I guess you could say we saved each other from bad dreams tonight."

Nicole smiled. "I guess so."

The pair stood at the kitchen counter in silence, sipping the wine. But for the first time since the affair, the silence wasn't forced or awkward. They had fallen into that comfortable silence that any couple could do that had been together for a long time. And it was the first time since the affair that Nicole found herself enjoying Jake's company.

A knock at the door startled both of them, ending the moment.

Jake walked to the door, looking back to Nicole. "Do you think they heard you screaming all the way from the main house?"

"I don't think so," Nicole answered.

Nicole opened the door, and three men with badges stood outside, along with Melissa.

"Are you Mr. and Mrs. Harper?" The man who spoke was older and possessed a flat, no-nonsense tone.

"Yes," Jake answered.

"Do you mind if we step inside?" the officer asked, already casing the place before he made it through the door.

Jake had always had an issue with authority. His default position with any and all of his interactions with the police was defensive, and Nicole slid off the stool to stop him before he said something that he would regret.

"Is everything all right?" Nicole asked.

Melissa sighed and then exchanged a quick glance with the detective before she spoke. "I'm afraid there was an incident at the main house." She lowered her gaze, and when she looked Nicole in the eye and spoke again, Nicole's knees buckled from the news, and it was Jake who caught her before she hit the tiled floor.

The butler was dead.

*J*ake helped Nicole back over to the kitchen counter, where he stayed with her while the detective questioned them about their nightly routine. Melissa remained by their side, but Nicole sensed that she was more concerned about the image of Ms. Calhoun and the estate than making sure they were innocent of any wrongdoing.

"When was the last time that you spoke with Donald today?" Detective Jon Salvor was a short black man with broad shoulders. His hairline had retreated halfway to the top of his head, but he had tried to make up for it with a thick, unruly gray beard that covered his cheeks and had begun to crawl down his neck.

Nicole remained closed off, still shaken by what she saw in her dream and the news that Donald was really dead. "It was around lunchtime. I brought Ms. Calhoun her lunch, and I ended up getting a cut on my arm."

"How did you get the cut?" Salvor asked.

Nicole glanced toward Melissa before turning back

to the detective. She didn't want to lie to the detective, but she felt an overwhelming pressure to make sure she didn't divulge any information about Ms. Calhoun's condition. "I dropped one of the plates." She cleared her throat, unsure if the lie was convincing. "Donald showed me where the medical supplies were kept, and he bandaged me up."

"Did he seem strange to you?" Salvor asked. "Anything out of the ordinary?"

Nicole shrugged. "He seemed fine. Maybe a little sad, but I don't know if that was out of the ordinary for him. I'd only known him since this morning."

"Is this going to take much longer?" Jake asked, tapping his foot impatiently. "It's late, and we do have work in the morning."

Salvor didn't pay Jake any mind and continued jotting notes down on the pad in his hands. "What time did the pair of you go to sleep?"

"I went to bed at around ten-thirty," Jake said, squinting as he tried to think.

"I went to bed at ten," Nicole answered.

Pen and paper in hand, Detective Salvor looked up from his notes, taking a pause, and raised an eyebrow. "What room did you two sleep in?"

"The end of the hall," Jake answered.

"Well, he sleeps at the end of the hall," Nicole said. "I was in a different bedroom."

Salvor focused on Nicole. "You didn't sleep together?"

Nicole looked to Jake, and then to Melissa, floundering for someone to help her. "No. Is that a problem?"

"It's a problem that neither of you can confirm where you have been all night," Salvor said.

"Detective, this isn't necessary," Melissa said, finally cutting in. "They're both cooperating and answering your questions honestly. I'd ask you to wait before jumping to any conclusions."

Salvor didn't press the issue any further, but he didn't look happy about it, and Nicole grew worried that she had said something wrong. "Did you hear anything suspicious during the night?" Detective Salvor asked.

"We both had bad nightmares," Nicole answered. "I woke up screaming."

Salvor kept a close eye on Nicole. He had a studious gaze, the kind of glance that was able to penetrate through people and leave them exposed. He was a man who saw through the lies.

"How long have the two of you been married?" Salvor asked.

"Seven years," Jake answered. "But I don't see what that has to do with anything."

Salvor turned that inquisitive gaze to Jake. "Have you had any trouble in the marriage recently?"

"Detective," Melissa said, thankfully butting in before Jake hung himself with the rope that Salvor was doling out. "Their personal lives are not relevant at this time."

Salvor turned his attention back to Nicole since she

had been the more willing participant. "Is there anything else you can tell me about this evening?"

Nicole didn't know if she should tell the detective exactly what the dream had been about. She didn't want to lie, but she also didn't want to paint a target on her back, which she already felt one forming.

"Mrs. Harper?" Salvor asked. "Did you hear me?"

"Sorry," Nicole answered. "No. I didn't hear anything out of the ordinary."

Salvor tucked his pen and paper back into the inside of his rain jacket, which had finally dried from the light dew that had sprinkled outside. "I'd like to take a look around the guest house and have my forensic unit perform a sweep."

"No," Melissa said. "Not without a warrant, you're not."

"If these people don't have anything to hide, then I think that you should let me look around," Salvor said, his patience wearing thin. "How about a little professional courtesy?"

"How about a little thing called the Fourth Amendment?" Jake asked.

Detective Salvor took one aggressive step toward Jake before he stopped himself, but to her husband's credit, he didn't flinch. "You wave around that crap like it's some kind of get out of jail free card, but I promise you, buddy." He pointed a long, meaty finger at Jake and narrowed his eyes. "I will find out the truth."

"I think they have answered enough questions for one night, Detective," Melissa said.

"Until this investigation is complete, I'll need the

two of you to stick around," Salvor said. "So don't plan any spontaneous vacations. Because I will track you down. And it goes without saying that the butler's room is off-limits until this investigation is over." He bumped into Jake's shoulder on his way past, and Nicole felt the machismo coming off of both of them. "I'll be back with that warrant."

Jake turned to add a little verbal backstab on the detective's way out, but Nicole saw the look in his eyes, and she grabbed his arm and pulled him back off the ledge.

Salvor slammed the door shut, leaving Melissa alone with Jake and Nicole.

"God, I hate cops," Jake said. "Nothing but a bunch of mindless drones."

"He's just doing his job, Jake," Nicole said, then looked to Melissa. "Is there anything we should be worried about?"

"No," Melissa said, shaking her head. "Unfortunately Donald was dealing with some issues of depression. They haven't given his death an official ruling, but all the evidence points to a suicide."

"That's awful," Jake said.

Nicole nodded, but all she could think about was her dream and the blood dripping from Donald's slit wrists.

"The detective is just performing his due diligence," Melissa said. "I can assure you that you have nothing to be worried about and that all of this will blow over. However." She held up her hand as she spoke. "I want to make clear that you are not to speak to the police without my presence and you are not to go to press about any of this. It's bound to catch wind once the official report is filed, but I'll be performing damage control before it gets blown out of proportion."

Nicole frowned. "I didn't think suicide was a problem to be brushed over."

"No, of course not," Melissa said. "But we all have to move on, and the best way for us to do that is to make sure that we press forward, business as usual." She collected her briefcase and then headed for the door, stopping to turn back and look at Nicole. "Work starts same time tomorrow morning."

"Of course." Nicole smiled, but the moment that Melissa was gone, the smile vanished and she slouched forward on the counter. "God, I can't believe that."

Jake was quiet for a moment and then drummed his fingers on the counter. "Why did you tell the detective that we weren't sleeping together?"

Nicole shook her head. "Because it's the truth."

"Nic," Jake said, rubbing his temples. "The fact that you said that paints us as suspects."

Nicole grew defensive. "But we didn't do anything."

"The guy was looking for excuses to make something out of nothing," Jake said. "The less we tell the police, the better. All they'll do is twist what we have to say into something that doesn't ring true."

Nicole wasn't sure about that, but she had withheld her own information about the dream and the death of the butler. "Should I have told them about the dream?"

Jake walked over to her and pressed his palms against her cheeks. "It was a bad dream. I know that it's probably freaking you out right now, but you don't have anything to worry about." He dropped his hands and then yawned. "Let's go back to bed before the goon squad comes back to waterboard us."

Nicole reached for Jake's hand before he walked away. "Could we sleep together tonight? I think I'm still freaked out, and I don't want to be alone."

Jake kissed Nicole's hand and nodded. "I'd like that."

Nicole walked with Jake to the back bedroom and curled up next to him. And while she wished that the circumstances on this milestone of sleeping together again were different, she couldn't deny how good it felt to lie next to his warmth in bed.

Sleep came quickly, and Nicole rested in a dreamless state. No more bloody premonitions, no more screams, nothing that woke her in the middle of the night. But the next morning, when she cracked her eyes open, her head pounded and her joints ached. She was plagued with the kind of stiffness that accompanied a night of deep, short sleep.

Nicole was on her side when she woke up, and the first thing she saw was wooded trees and the mountain ridge backdrop from the open window. The curtains had been opened, and she lay there in the bed, warm under the covers.

Nicole had never been the kind to linger in bed. When the alarm was off, she was up and ready to start the day. But the combination of the night before, the view, and the warmth under the blankets made her want to go back to sleep.

Nicole rolled onto her back, expecting to bump into Jake, who had always been a late sleeper, guilty of hitting the snooze button for at least an hour before he finally got out of bed. But she was alone.

Nicole touched the space where Jake's body had been, and the moment her fingertip grazed the wrinkled white sheet, she was bombarded with the images of blood, and she quickly withdrew her hand.

Her heart skipped a beat, then hammered quickly. She shut her eyes, trying to erase the image from her mind, but the blood on the sheets was stained on the back of her eyelids, and she saw the large blotches of crimson contrasted against the crisp white of the sheets.

Nicole flung the covers off of her and jumped out of bed, hurrying toward the door, afraid that she had another premonition and that Jake was in some kind of trouble. But when she placed one foot out of the bedroom and into the hallway, just before she called out her husband's name, she heard the light, carefree laughter of another woman in the house, and she froze.

Nicole grabbed hold of the door frame to keep herself upright, and she slunk back into the bedroom as though she were afraid to be caught eavesdropping. But no one was in the hallway. The voices were coming from the kitchen. A woman's voice and her husband.

Their words were muffled by the walls, and while she might not have been able to hear the exact words that were exchanged, she recognized the tone of the conversation clearly.

The light cadence of the back and forth, combined with random giggles. Nicole could shut her eyes and see the flirting as clearly as she had seen the blood on the sheets.

At first, the sound of her husband talking to another woman like that was paralyzing, and she felt foolish for worrying about Jake's well-being. Of course he was fine. He was always fine.

The voices grew louder as Nicole walked down the narrow hallway toward the kitchen. She lifted her chin and turned the corner from the hallway, and she saw Jake and Kate standing there, and while the kitchen island was wedged between them, separating them about three feet, both had leaned forward during the conversation with one another.

And it was Jake who noticed Nicole first, leaning back and clearing his throat as if he had been caught in the act again. Maybe that was only partially true.

"Hey, Nic," Jake said.

"Hey." Nicole shifted her gaze toward Kate. "I didn't realize you made house calls."

Kate smiled and then gestured to the kitchen table behind her, which was already set with plates and silverware and a covered tray. "I brought breakfast over and saw that Jake was already up."

"How did you get in?" Nicole asked.

"Oh, I have a key," Kate answered, then patted the side of a pants pocket. "That's okay, right? I mean, Melissa gave me keys to practically every room in the house. And I didn't go through your stuff or anything like that." She frowned, shutting her eyes. "God, why would I say that?" She laughed.

"It's fine," Jake answered.

But Nicole thought it was anything but fine. She didn't think that it was fine that her husband was alone in the kitchen with a beautiful woman. She didn't think it was fine the way that he blushed red after Nicole walked in and caught him flirting with Kate. Because that's what it was. There was no lying about that.

"How did you guys sleep after last night?" Kate asked, immediately changing the subject. "I mean it was crazy about Donald, right?"

"Yeah," Jake answered, nodding along. "The police came and questioned us after it happened."

"Me too," Kate said. "You know that it was Ms. Calhoun that found him?"

"Really?" Jake asked.

Nicole joined them at the kitchen island. "Did she say anything?"

"No," Kate answered. "Apparently she remembered how to use a phone though. She dialed Melissa until she picked up and Melissa came rushing over when she didn't hear anyone on the other end. I guess she figured there was some kind of trouble."

Nicole frowned, the lines on her brow folding into one another. It was odd that Ms. Calhoun would go into the butler's room. She barely left her room all day yesterday, and according to everyone else, that was normal behavior.

"I know what you're thinking," Kate said, pulling Nicole from her thoughts. "It's hard not to think about it after something like this."

"Think about what?" Nicole asked.

Kate laughed. "You're kidding, right? I mean, thirty

years ago this woman's family is brutally murdered and she is the only survivor? And they never catch the person who did it? And she suddenly goes quiet, never speaking about what happened or what she saw? And now the only person that she's known after all of these years, the person who has taken care of her, someone who was 'practically family' dies, and once again she's the person who finds the body?" Kate shook her head. "She's guilty."

Nicole hadn't gone there in her own head, but now that Kate had brought it up again, it was difficult not to make the connection. Ms. Calhoun was the logical suspect, and Nicole had seen firsthand the violent outbursts that the old woman was capable of. But to overpower a full-grown man, despite Donald's age, in her condition?

"Do you know how he died?" Nicole asked, looking to Kate. "I mean, I know that he killed himself, but do you know how?"

Kate nodded. "I heard the cops talking about it down the hall. I wasn't allowed to go into the room myself, but I was able to catch a few things. He cut his wrists. Both of them slit right down the middle." She mimicked the motion by using her fingers to draw the lines down her forearms. "Bled to death."

Jake grimaced. "Jesus."

And while Nicole was just as shocked and nervous about the news, she was more concerned about the connection between Donald's death and her dream.

"Nicole, are you all right?" Jake asked.

Nicole nodded, turning her mind away from the

images of her dream, or her premonition, or the visit, or whatever the hell it was. "Yeah. I'm fine."

It was quiet for a moment, and then it was Kate who finally broke the silence. "Well, I better get back to the kitchen. The lady of the manor will want her breakfast." She knocked her knuckles against the marble countertop twice and then pointed to Nicole. "I'll see you in a few minutes."

Kate left, both Nicole and Jake watching her leave, but Nicole tossed her eyes back to Jake. She wanted to see if there was any of that shine in his eyes, the kind that she always saw in men when a pretty woman walked past.

But Jake had lowered his eyes, and she wasn't sure if the flush of heat on his cheeks was from her staring at him or the fact that he had been thinking something he shouldn't. If past experience had taught her anything, then she thought that it was probably the latter.

"I need to get ready for work," Nicole said, heading back toward her bedroom, but Jake followed.

"What about breakfast?" Jake asked, leaning into the hallway.

Nicole paused when she was in the doorway. She was usually hungry in the morning. Jake had joked that she was a part wolf the way that she would devour a meal, but as she turned back to the man whom she finally had trusted enough to sleep with the night before, she was only numb. "I lost my appetite."

*N*icole's mind wandered through the endless distractions that had complicated her morning, and a job that was supposed to have been a turning point for her both professionally and personally. Ms. Calhoun was supposed to be the rich client that would catapult her into caring for more high-end clientele, and this was supposed to be a time for Nicole and Jake to return to the way that things had been before the affair. But things had only gotten worse.

Jake had the hots for the chef, Nicole's employer had a past that was as vast and mysterious as the house in which she lived, and the icing on the cake was a murder that Nicole saw in her nightmares.

Nicole stopped in the hallway, carrying Ms. Calhoun's lunch, and took a moment to pause and hit the reset button.

She needed to think clearly, remember why she was here in the first place, and make sure that she didn't do anything to jeopardize the strides that she had made to get here. She still had her job. Jake hadn't slept with anyone (as far as she could tell), and there was still a sick old woman who needed care.

Nicole exhaled the breath, ridding herself of all of the negative thoughts, save for one. Ms. Calhoun.

But as she circled back to thoughts of the old woman, Nicole couldn't help but wonder how she was connected to everything.

Behind the fog of confusion that normally settled in Ms. Calhoun's eyes, Nicole detected glimpses of lucidity. And it was in those moments of lucidity that she believed Ms. Calhoun was hiding a secret, something that she didn't want people to know.

Nicole pushed the thoughts from her head and then walked toward Ms. Calhoun's room, lunch tray in hand, not wanting the old woman's food to go cold. And while Nicole had done her best to not freak herself out about seeing Ms. Calhoun again, she stiffened just before she turned the corner to enter the room, unsure what she would find.

Nicole stepped into the master bedroom and saw Ms. Calhoun in bed, propped up at the headboard with a mountain of pillows at her back, and she relaxed.

"How are you, Ms. Calhoun?" Nicole asked.

Nicole didn't expect a response, but she wanted to create a sense of normalcy in the environment, which was important when dealing with patients that were having trouble with their own reality.

Nicole set the tray down over Ms. Calhoun's lap, and the old woman kept her eyes trained on Nicole. Nicole smiled, but Ms. Calhoun didn't reciprocate the gesture. The old woman maintained her stoic expression, her faded blue eyes studying Nicole the way that a person would study a lamp, waiting for it to turn on.

Once Ms. Calhoun was all set for her lunch, Nicole stepped back and waited to make sure that she ate. Dementia affected motor skills, and they would eventually deteriorate, and she would have to feed Ms. Calhoun by hand.

"I'd eat that before it gets cold." Nicole pointed to the food, but the old woman only stared at her, paying zero attention to the lunch in her lap. "Do you need help?"

Ms. Calhoun, a woman who looked no more dangerous than a caterpillar struggling to cross a sidewalk and into the safety of grass, someone who had done nothing but stare at her with expressions of apathy, suddenly smiled.

The old woman's skin crumpled on either side of her mouth, her lips parting to reveal a set of clean white teeth, her wrinkles folding into one another like an accordion. And while the expression might have meant to be friendly, it was unsettling.

Nicole stepped back, the motion involuntary, and Ms. Calhoun's smile grew wider. But the happiness looked forced, and as Nicole studied Ms. Calhoun, she saw why.

The smile never reached the eyes. The pupils remained expressionless even though the grin stretched from ear to ear. The eyes reminded Nicole of Donald, and his visit last night in her dreams. It was that same dead-eyed glaze that followed her throughout the room as Donald, blood dripping from his fingertips and onto the carpet, leaving pieces of himself behind, tried to talk to her.

Nicole shuddered, blinking away the memories, and when she looked back to Ms. Calhoun, she saw her patient digging into the applesauce with a spoon.

Glad for the moment to be over, Nicole turned toward the door. But just before she stepped into the hallway, someone spoke.

"He didn't kill himself."

Nicole spun around quickly, seeing Ms. Calhoun still focused on her meal, acting as if she had said nothing.

"What did you say?" Nicole asked, frozen at the door, still only half-turned around. "Ms. Calhoun?"

Nicole crossed the room and stopped at the bedside.

"Ms. Calhoun, do you know something about what happened to Donald?" Nicole asked.

Ms. Calhoun speared a single noodle from her macaroni salad and then looked up at Nicole.

The words were there on the tip of her tongue, just like they had been on Donald's tongue the night before in Nicole's dream.

But Ms. Calhoun said nothing, and eventually placed the macaroni into her mouth and continued with her lunch, quiet as a mouse save for her chewing.

*N*icole stayed in Ms. Calhoun's room when she called Melissa. She wanted to see if she would get a reaction from the old woman by calling her out in the open, but Ms. Calhoun said nothing as she ate her lunch, which she was already halfway through when Melissa finally answered after the third try.

"Is this important?" Melissa's greeting was rushed and quiet. "I'm in the middle of something right now."

Nicole ignored the flustered answer. "She spoke."

"What?"

"Ms. Calhoun spoke." Nicole waited, the silence on the other end of the line signaling that Melissa was at least considering the possibility that Nicole was telling the truth.

"She hasn't spoken a word in thirty years," Melissa said.

"I know, but it happened a few minutes ago," Nicole said, glancing back to Ms. Calhoun to see if the old woman would say anything, but she was currently masticating the last bits of chicken pot pie, some of which lingered on the corners of her mouth.

Melissa sighed exasperated. "Mrs. Harper, I don't see how this warrants an emergency—"

"She said he didn't kill himself," Nicole said. "She said that Donald didn't commit suicide."

Another stretch of silence lingered, but this time when Melissa spoke, there was no sigh, no exasperated tone, only the succinct and firm words of a woman who knew her way around the law. "Have you told anyone besides me?"

"No," Nicole answered, thankful that Melissa was taking this seriously. "You were the first person I called."

"Good," Melissa said. "Now, I want you to listen to me very carefully, Mrs. Harper. I don't want you speaking to anyone about this. No one. Do you understand? Whatever you thought you heard must have been a mistake, because I can assure you that the police have—"

"The police are wrong," Nicole said, blurting the words out and working herself into a frenzy. "Do you understand me? The police are wrong about what they thought they found. He didn't kill himself."

"And how do you know that?" Melissa asked. "Because Ms. Calhoun told you? A sixty-year-old woman with dementia who hasn't spoken a word in over thirty years? And suddenly she decides to talk to you, a woman who has worked for her for a single day?"

Nicole shut her eyes, realizing that her outburst had been misplaced. She took a breath, calming herself. "I understand the sensitive history around Ms. Calhoun and her family, but I am not making this up. She spoke. She said that Donald didn't kill himself. We need to do something about this."

"*We* don't need to do anything," Melissa said. "I will handle the communication with the authorities. And if you reach out to them without my permission, then you will be in breach of contract, and I will not only have you fired, but I will take you to court and make sure that you don't have a penny left to your name."

The call ended, and Nicole slouched, lowering the phone from her ear. She pinched the bridge of her nose. A headache was forming.

Nicole pocketed the phone, and when she looked at Ms. Calhoun, the old woman was finished with her lunch, the bits of food still clinging to the edges of her mouth, that dead-eyed smile still plastered on her face.

"Why did you tell me that?" Nicole asked.

But Ms. Calhoun provided no response, and for the first time in her career as a hospice nurse, hate coursed through her veins. Hate for the old woman. Hate for her condition. Hate for being placed into this godforsaken home in the first place.

Nicole stormed over to the bed, plucked the empty tray of food from Ms. Calhoun's lap, and walked out, fighting the urge not to mutter 'stupid bitch' under her breath. She returned to the kitchen, still fuming by the time she arrived, and found it empty.

She set the food down on the tray and then headed

back out into the hallways, not sure where she was going, but knowing that she needed to blow off some steam. But on her way out, she heard something coming from upstairs.

At first, she thought it was Ms. Calhoun talking again, and she raced up the stairs. But when she reached the second floor, she realized that the noises were coming from the third floor. It was soft at first, but familiar.

Slowly, quietly, Nicole reached the top of the stairs to the third floor and then paused. The hairs on the back of her neck stood up, and her stomach lurched.

The noises were heavy breathing, moaning, and the rhythmic cadence of bedsprings. It was of people having sex.

Nicole's mind was thrust back to three months ago, when she had heard those same noises coming from her bedroom. She knew that she couldn't trust Jake anymore, she knew that she was right about him flirting with the chef. Jake had wanted to sleep with her, and he was just waiting for his chance.

Nicole imagined all of the things that she would say to him when she flung open that door and caught them both in the act. She was going to make sure that she got everything off of her chest. This was the moment of her liberation, and when she grabbed the doorknob, quickly turning it, she entered the room with the brash authority of a parent who knew they were catching their child in the act of wrongdoing.

"You son of a bitch, I knew—" Nicole was three

steps into the room and then she froze when she saw the pair of flushed faces turn back toward her.

Kate was on top, her blonde hair cascading down a tanned, toned back, sweat covering her upper lip from the exertion, but beneath her wasn't Jake. It was Rick Dunst. The groundskeeper.

Nicole opened her mouth, stuttering, unable to speak. "I'm…" She stared at them, the pair reflecting the same bewilderment. She finally looked away and then backed out of the room. "I'm sorry. I'm so sorry."

Nicole slammed the door shut, breaking out in a cold sweat in the hallway. She couldn't believe what she had just done. She couldn't believe that she had done something so stupid. She had let her imagination run wild.

Lost in her own embarrassment, Nicole jumped with surprise when the bedroom door opened behind her and Kate walked out, buttoning the top of her blouse.

"I'm so sorry," Nicole said, her cheeks still blushing.

Kate waved it off, her cheeks still flushed, though it wasn't from embarrassment. "It's fine." She gestured to the door. "I got to finish, but he's still upright if you'd like to have a go." She winked, slapping Nicole on the shoulder as she walked past, and then giggled as she bounded barefoot down the hall, shoes in hand, her wavy blonde hair bouncing behind her as she disappeared down the staircase.

The bedroom door opened again behind Nicole, and she turned to find Rick standing in the doorway with his shirt off, sweat still clinging to his body. The man had a ripped physique and a few tattoos that adorned the wall of muscles that was his chest and shoulder. Some were too small for Nicole to see, and the words scrolled along his collarbone were in cursive too sloppy for her to decipher, but she saw the skull centered on his six pack very clearly.

"What the hell are you doing up here?" Rick asked.

Nicole shook her head, still stammering. "I-I-I'm so sorry. I heard the sounds coming from your bedroom, and I thought—" She shut her eyes, pressing her lips together so that her mouth formed a flat line, and took a moment to gather her thoughts. "I shouldn't have barged into your room like that."

The glower on Rick's face told Nicole that he didn't care for the apology, and the hardened, fixed gaze of his eyes pushed her back a step.

"The best thing for you to do in this place is to stick to your job and mind your own fucking business." Rick gave her a look up and down and then curled his lip when he was finished. "Just stay the hell out of my way."

A rush of wind blasted Nicole in the face as Rick slammed the door shut, and she turned to leave, thankful that the altercation had ended.

But when Nicole reached the staircase, she stopped and turned back to Rick's closed bedroom door. She thought of what Ms. Calhoun had said about Donald not killing himself. She knew that it was a jump to think that Rick had something to do with it, but the way that he looked at her was frightening.

He didn't kill himself.

Nicole stopped at the top of the stairs, and then glanced back to Rick's closed bedroom door, Ms. Calhoun's words still ringing clearly in her head. Everyone thought that the old woman was crazy, losing her mind, but that didn't make her wrong.

Between the interactions with Ms. Calhoun, the call to Melissa, and her unintentional interruption of Rick and Kate, Nicole stayed on her toes. She heeded Rick's advice and made sure to stay out of his way, though it wasn't hard considering most of his time was spent outside the mansion, while Nicole's job kept her indoors.

The only time Nicole ventured outside was the walk from the mansion to the guest house to have her lunch, finding Jake already at the kitchen table, still hunched over his laptop.

"Not taking a lunch break today?" Nicole asked, hoping that sliding into a normal conversation would negate the fact that she had been so weird this morning. She wasn't in the mood for any further communication missteps or awkward encounters. She had met her daily quota.

Jake kept his attention on the screen, and Nicole

walked over to him, stepping behind him so she could read the screen.

Instead of his coding work, there were a series of internet browser windows open with different articles with some disturbing headlines.

Three Dead in Calhoun Manor.

Killer Still at Large.

No Suspects Named.

Margaret Calhoun Lone Survivor.

Did Margaret Kill Family Over Money?

Nicole frowned. "What are you looking at?"

"The murders from thirty years ago," Jake answered, still reading one of the articles that he had open, the one titled No Suspects Named. "Have seen any of this stuff?"

Nicole stepped away, heading to the lunch waiting for her on the counter. "No." And she had no desire to learn the gruesome details. But she wasn't surprised that Jake had looked the family up. He had always had a fascination with serial killers. Ted Bundy. Charles Manson. Ed Kemper. They had watched more documentaries on those psychos than she cared to count.

Jake pointed to the monitor, his fingertip smudging the screen. He did that all the time to Nicole's laptop. It drove her nuts. "Every member of the family was killed with a, and I quote, psychotic passion."

Nicole focused on her turkey sandwich on marble rye.

Jake looked up from his monitor, a little too giddy. "Can you believe that?"

"Yeah," Nicole said. "That's pretty crazy."

"And!" Jake held up his finger like an exclamation point, his excitement growing. "The police found a set of bloody footprints in the house that didn't match any of the family members."

Nicole relaxed at this information. It had been the first sign of proof of a suspect other than Ms. Calhoun since Nicole had come here. "So it was someone else?"

"That's what the authorities believed thirty years ago, and you know who was the lead investigator on that case?" Jake smirked. "Detective Jon Salvor." He shook his head, looking back to his computer. "No wonder the guy was so hot to try and figure out what happened here. He never caught the first killer."

This piqued Nicole's interest, and she walked over to Jake, sandwich in hand, and peered over his shoulder. Most of the articles pegged Ms. Calhoun as the murderer, but he moved through them too quickly for her to even read what had been written.

"The press blew up over this case," Jake said. "People followed it for years. Hundreds of reporters and investigators tried to get in contact with Ms. Calhoun to request an interview, but all of them were denied. She didn't speak with anyone. Not even the police."

"Right," Nicole said. "Because she hasn't said anything in over thirty years. The events shocked her to the bone."

"But she did talk to one source," Jake said, smiling, as he opened up another window. "I found this small newspaper operating in Oregon. One of their reporters traveled to the mansion in hopes of getting an interview. This was about a year after the murders had taken place, and most of the press had died down, at least from all of the major media outlets, but a lot of smaller newspapers were still trying to get an exclusive, knowing that if they did find something, it would help boost their readership. Anyway, the reporter from this newspaper, the Portland Journal, camped outside the estate gates. Right there on the road. The cops were called to try and remove them, but since he wasn't actually squatting on the property, the authorities couldn't do anything. But the guy was out here for six days. And on the last day, just as they were about to pack up and go home, Ms. Calhoun comes out of the house. Alone. She strolls right up to the gates, staring at the reporters, and grabs hold of the iron bars. The reporter went up to her, hoping to get an exclusive. He started asking questions about the murders and what really happened the night her family was killed, and she says this." He stopped and pointed toward the screen, and Nicole leaned closer for a better look.

I was so scared. I had never seen so much blood before in my life. But there was nothing I could do. My father had done something horrible, something that I never could have imagined him doing. We were all shocked. I just couldn't believe he would have done something like that to us. They're all gone now. All of them except for my sister.

Nicole leaned back, her hands gripping the back of Jake's chair, while he looked up at her, unable to wipe the smile from his face.

"It was the dad," Jake said. "He must have snapped and killed everyone."

Nicole frowned, re-reading the excerpt. "But what

about the set of footprints that were found. You said they didn't match anyone else in the family."

"No," Jake said. "They didn't. They were large footprints, which led authorities to believe that they were a man's foot, which was why they never really considered Ms. Calhoun a suspect. But two years ago, a group of forensic experts reexamined some old murder cases, and the Calhoun Estate Massacre was one of them. They said that the bloody footprints could have been enlarged due to smears, and the size of the shoe could have been misinterpreted because of the style of shoe that the killer wore."

"What kind of shoe did they think could have made the prints?" Nicole asked.

"They think that it could have been a snowshoe, which made sense because of the snowstorm the night of the murders," Jake answered. "One of the worst blizzards on record."

Nicole raised her eyebrows, finding herself sucked into the gossip, the intrigue, and mystery. "What kind of shoes was Mr. Calhoun wearing?"

Jake smiled. "That's a good question, and it's something the reporter tried to answer, but he couldn't because the police didn't mention the types of shoes worn by any members of the Calhoun family, nor was the shoe size of the family members ever made public."

"Are you saying the police could have lied?" Nicole asked.

Jake shrugged. "They were a powerful and wealthy family. I mean, look at what we had to go through for you to take care of a dying woman. A lot of people thought that it wasn't Ms. Calhoun herself that covered everything up, but the business partners of Mr. Calhoun. Even with most of the family dead, there was still a lot of money to be made with Mr. Calhoun's vaults, and I don't think the people involved in those business interests wanted their profits to go down the tube. Who would want to buy a vault designed by a man who murdered his family?"

Nicole nodded. "I can understand that." She then pointed to the excerpt from the article. "How come this didn't make bigger news? I mean, Melissa told us that Ms. Calhoun hasn't spoken since the night of the murders. If she did finally break her silence, how come it didn't show up in any of the major news outlets? Why wasn't it a bigger story?"

"Because the tape recorder that the reporter used to record his conversation with Ms. Calhoun was taken from him," Jake said, and before Nicole could roll her eyes, he held up his hands. "I know how it sounds, but just think about it for a second, all right? It's not impossible to think that someone close to Ms. Calhoun and his father's business stopped the tape from going public."

It made sense. People did crazy things for money, and if someone thought that the wrong publication was going to affect their bottom line, it would be easy to get rid of the evidence. "So who did the reporter say snatched his recorder?"

Jake smiled. "Donald Weiss."

Nicole arched both of her eyebrows. "The butler?"

Jake nodded, unable to wipe the grin from his face.

"It's quite the tangled web. And what's even more insane is that regardless of what actually happened the night of the murders and who killed who, the truth is that since the authorities never arrested the killer—"

"The killer is still at large," Nicole said.

"Hard to imagine someone getting away with something so terrible," Jake said, looking back at the screen, and then he straightened very quickly. "Oh, and guess whose father was very close to the Calhoun family?"

"Who?" Nicole asked.

"Melissa the lawyer," Jake answered and then pulled up a picture. "I found this photo of all of them in one of the articles that I read. Look."

The image filled the screen, and Nicole took a closer look as Jake pointed everyone out. "That's Robert Calhoun, the titan of the industry, and that's Devon Farr, his wife Maggie, and little Melissa in her arms. Crazy how that's all connected."

But Nicole wasn't looking at baby Melissa. Her eyes were locked on the picture of a young woman next to Mr. Calhoun. "Who is that?"

"That?" Jake asked. "Oh, that's Richard Calhoun's oldest daughter, Aubrey. Ms. Calhoun is here, too, look. And that's Bethany Calhoun, Richard's wife, and Ms. Calhoun's mother."

Nicole had seen Aubrey Calhoun before. She had been the woman she saw in the window when they first arrived at the house. "When was this picture taken?"

"Um, it looks like about a month before the murders," Jake answered. "Why?"

Nicole focused on her turkey sandwich. "No reason." But she wanted to know how she might have seen a woman who had been dead for thirty years.

The sandwich, despite her recent assumptions of Kate, was quite good. The woman might have been a little too promiscuous for Nicole's own taste, but there was no denying her talents in the kitchen.

Or the bedroom. At least from what she heard.

Nicole almost told Jake about the encounter, but she held back, not wanting to explain why she was snooping around, tracking down sex noises in the mansion. After their many attempts at unsuccessfully reconnecting, she didn't think her false accusations of more infidelity would help.

"I have to get back to work." Nicole brushed the sandwich crumbs from her scrubs and then paused when she reached the door, making eye contact with Jake. "And unless I remember correctly, you still have work to do?"

Jake spread his arms in a helpless gesture. "But I'm in the middle of solving a thirty-year-old murder!"

"Whatever you say, Columbo." Nicole laughed as she shut the door behind her. The smile lingered on her face as the sun warmed her cheeks, glad to leave her interaction with Jake on a good note.

There had been small stretches where she had briefly fallen back into the ease of their relationship before the affair, but it was eventually spoiled by those horrible memories.

Halfway back to the house, the good mood still radiating off of Nicole like the sunshine above her, movement in her peripheral vision pulled her attention away from the mansion and toward the wooded area at the end of the open field.

Rick had stepped out of a shed, shovel in hand, and disappeared into the woods. Woods that were supposedly off-limits. Nicole stopped and watched until she couldn't see him anymore.

Sparked by the curiosity that Jake had given her with his investigation into what was happening with the Calhoun murders from all those years ago, Nicole found herself drawn to discover what the groundskeeper might be hiding out in the woods. And what secrets he might be burying with that shovel he was carrying.

Once Nicole entered the woods, she tried to move as quietly as possible, but the dense foliage on the ground made it difficult to move stealthily between the trees.

Nicole pressed her hands against the smooth trunks of the maples that she stepped around, losing herself in the wilderness. She turned around, unable to see the mansion anymore, and nervous about not finding her way back.

But she refused to give up. She wanted answers, and the truth was pulling her deeper into the woods.

Staying aware of her surroundings, Nicole walked for another five minutes before she came across a small clearing, where she saw a small mound of dirt piled next to a hole in the ground.

It was a grave.

But whose body was it for? Was it for Donald? No, the police had taken his body to the morgue to be examined by the medical staff to ensure that his injuries aligned with the current theory that involved him committing suicide.

"Hey!" A strong hand gripped Nicole's shoulder and spun her around. The strength from the hand paralyzed Nicole, and she stared up into the hardened gaze of the groundskeeper. "What the hell are you doing out here? Did you follow me?" Rick glanced around, making sure that she had come out here alone, then tightened his grip. "I asked what the hell you are doing here?" He rattled her shoulder, and Nicole tried to wiggle away, but he was too strong. She was at his mercy.

Dirt was smudged on Rick's face, mixed in with the sweat and oils from his skin where he tried to wipe both off on his cheek. Sunlight cast through the trees, illuminating the left side of his face, casting the other half in dark shadow, which only accentuated the hardened lines of his face from his menacing expression. "I told you to mind your own business."

Nicole knew that she should have been scared, and she should have apologized, but something stirred within her, a defiance that she hadn't harnessed in a very long time. She had been walking on eggshells ever since the affair, afraid to speak her mind.

Nicole grabbed Rick's wrist, her palms and fingers sliding from the sweat. With one hard twist, she removed his hand. "And what the hell are you doing out here? The woods are off-limits. What are you hiding?"

Nicole braced for the aggressive storm that she

knew was coming, but was thankful to find that she was wrong, and Rick backed down.

"It's for the butler," Rick said.

Nicole frowned, skeptical that this man who had been so intimidating during their time together would suddenly be okay telling her the truth. "The butler isn't here."

"Yeah, no shit," Rick said. "But they're bringing the body back to be buried with the rest of the family."

"What are you talking about?" Nicole asked.

Rick said nothing as he pointed behind Nicole, deeper into the woods. She turned around, half expecting to be ambushed by him, knocked out and then shoved into the hole that he had been digging and buried alive before she could regain consciousness, smothered beneath all of that dirt and debris.

But when she turned around, she saw what she had missed because of the dense cluster of trees that surrounded the small clearing, and the overgrowth of grass and bushes. It was a small graveyard.

The Calhoun family graveyard.

"It was stated in the estate's rules that anyone in the service of the Calhoun family for greater than thirty years, having served the family faithfully, would have the full rights and be buried with the Calhoun family as if he were a part of the family himself," Rick said. "I don't make the rules, I just dig the graves."

When Nicole turned around and faced Rick again, he was smiling at her. "And you like doing that kind of work?"

Rick stepped close enough for Nicole to feel the

heat and stench radiating off of his body. "I enjoy getting what I want. And you know what I want?"

Nicole shrank backward, realizing that she had pushed the boundaries too far. She couldn't take him all alone. And she had walked so far out into the woods that she didn't think that anyone would be able to hear her scream. "I don't care what you want."

"Are you sure about that?" Rick said, matching Nicole step for step on her retreat. He held a predator's gaze, and when he licked his lips, Nicole knew she needed to leave quickly.

Knowing that she was only going to get one chance at this, she took one step toward Rick, who grabbed her throat, and while he thought that he had managed to ensnare his prey, she thrust her knee up into his groin as hard as she could.

Rick groaned from the contact and immediately released Nicole as she darted away from the brute and sprinted blindly into the woods.

Tree branches smacked her face, the hands of the forest grabbing at Nicole's side, trying to prevent her from leaving. The longer she ran and saw nothing but trees, the more she began to worry that she had run in the wrong direction and that she was currently sprinting deeper into the forest. She didn't know the area well enough to find her way back home if she had gotten lost. She could always scream for help, but that would only make it easier for Rick to find her.

But just before she was about to scream bloody murder from frustration, Nicole broke through the tree line and stumbled into the open field behind the mansion.

Fatigued and out of breath from the sprint, Nicole only managed to walk a few more yards before she hunched forward, hands on her knees, and caught her breath. She glanced behind her, afraid that Rick might have recovered and chased after her, but the longer that she stared at the edge of the forest line and saw no movement, she thought that Rick probably shrugged off his losses.

Nicole straightened up, her body soaked with sweat, small dark patches staining the scrubs that she wore. It took five minutes before she finally caught her breath, and she realized just how out of shape she was, but all that mattered was she had escaped.

But she was far from safe.

Nicole needed to figure out what to do next. Obviously, Rick needed to be reported. She reached for her throat to see if it was tender. It hurt, but she thought that might be from her sucking wind. She needed to check a mirror to see if she had any bruises. If she didn't, then it would be a he-said-she-said situation, and that wouldn't lead to a desirable outcome for either herself or for Rick.

Could she tell Jake? She thought that he would believe her, but what would he do about it? He had never been a violent man. She didn't think he had ever been in a fight in his life. Rick was a behemoth, and she was convinced that the man could knock her husband down with a single blow.

Nicole turned toward the manor and thought that a

call to Melissa was in order, but first, she needed to speak to Jake. That was important.

But when Nicole turned away from the mansion and toward the guest house, a figure in one of the top floor windows caught her attention. She paused mid-step, a cold prick running from the base of her skull and down her spine.

Nicole looked up to the top floor window and saw Aubrey Calhoun staring down at her. She was motionless, but she was up there, Nicole was certain of it. She also happened to be standing in the window of the butler's room. And Nicole wanted to know how Aubrey could be standing up there when her grave was in the woods behind Nicole.

Once inside the mansion, Nicole sprinted toward the stairs, bounding up the steps two and three at a time, and never broke stride once she reached the third floor. It wasn't until she was five yards away from the closed door of Donald's bedroom that she slowed.

Yellow police tape still covered the door from when the forensics team had entered the day before. But what was more concerning was the fact that the seal of the tape hadn't been broken. No one had opened that door since the police had closed it last night, which made seeing Aubrey Calhoun in the window impossible.

Nicole looked behind her, making sure that she was alone, and then faced the door. The crime scene tape was stretched taut over the entrance, and Nicole knew that she couldn't open it without giving away that someone had gone inside.

Nicole reached for the doorknob, but then stopped

herself. If the police came back to examine the crime scene, she didn't want to leave her fingerprints on the room of the man who had been murdered, so she retrieved a pair of cleaning gloves from the supply closet.

Nicole opened the door, and the police tape broke, falling to either side of her as she stepped into the room.

The space was small, orderly, and without much decoration or flair. If Nicole hadn't known that Donald lived inside, she would have thought that it was unoccupied.

But her few interactions with Donald painted the picture of a man who was dutiful and simple, much like the room where he lived. He was a shadow, going about his daily business with a quiet and efficient manner of a man who felt rewarded by nothing more than a job well done. And he had tried to reach out to her for help.

"I'm trying, Donald," Nicole said, whispering to herself.

But while she found the room undisturbed, she didn't find Aubrey Calhoun. Had Nicole not experienced everything she had upon her arrival at the house, she would have thought that was crazy. But a part of her believed that there was a presence in this house, something that she couldn't exactly see all the time, but was always there.

Like the way that Ms. Calhoun always looked just to the left of her, never really making direct eye contact, almost like she was looking at someone else that was in the room with them.

Nicole saw the yellow evidence markers that the police had left behind. She saw that one of them was on the bed, which was neatly made. Another was on the nightstand adjacent to the bed where an alarm clock sat, along with an empty pillbox.

A few other items were tagged, but when Nicole looked at the bathroom, the open door allowing her to see inside, she saw the edge of a crimson lake.

"They found you in the bathroom," Nicole said.

Nicole stepped toward the bathroom, her breathing shortening to little gasps by the time that she saw the lake of blood that had crusted onto the bathroom floor.

The blood was so bright against the white tile and tub that it didn't seem real. It looked too much like someone had spilled a bucket of paint. And unlike the night that Ms. Calhoun's family was butchered, there were no bloody footprints to suggest that what happened here was anything but the suicide that the authorities believed occurred.

Inside the tub, there was even more blood, but it had been smeared, probably from when they removed Donald's body.

But why the puddle of blood outside of the tub? Did he leave his wrists hanging over the side? Why? If he made it all the way to the tub to slit his wrists, then Nicole would have thought that he would have kept his arms in the tub. Why stretch his arm out like that?

It could have been a last-minute spasm, something that Donald had no control over as the last bits of life slowly drained from his body, but she was just guessing at this point. Either way, none of this still explained how she had seen Aubrey Calhoun in the window.

Nicole wasn't sure what she expected to discover, but it wasn't what she found. She stood by the sink, staring at the congealed pile of blood that had collected on the floor, then turned to leave before the door slammed shut.

A heavy whoosh of cold air blasted her in the face, and the door cracked loudly against the frame upon contact.

Startled from the sudden slam of the door, Nicole reached for the brass knob. It was locked.

"Hey!" Nicole pounded her fist against the door, rattling the wood and the frame. "Hey, let me out of here!" She repeated the gesture, hoping that whoever was on the other side would quit playing games and let her go, but she received no answer.

The light flickered above her, and Nicole stepped back from the door. She again felt the prick of cold on her body, and she hugged herself to keep warm. The light continued to flicker and then finally shut off, casting Nicole into darkness.

It was teeth-chattering cold, and the longer the darkness lingered, the lower the temperature dropped. But what was worse than the cold was the presence that she felt in the bathroom with her. She wasn't alone.

"Aubrey? Aubrey Calhoun?" Nicole whispered into the darkness. "Are you in here?"

Nicole waited for a reply, but she received nothing. She reached for the doorknob again and tried to open it, but it was still locked. She shut her eyes, and just when she thought that she might go into hypothermic shock, the incandescent light bulb glowed to a soft dim.

Even though it was a small amount of yellow light, Nicole still squinted when it turned on. The dull yellow glow was like the first rays of dawn that broke through the dark of night.

"H-h-hello?" Nicole watched her breath puff from her lips in a small cloud of mist. Frozen, she remained hunched, arms crossed over her chest, grabbing onto her arms as she tried to keep warm, and then she saw movement on the floor.

Nicole retreated until she bumped into the wall, and it was there she remained as she watched Donald's spilled blood bubble on the tile.

She flattened her back against the wall, her eyes locked onto the simmering blood, which had lost its crimson flare, transforming into a black tar-like substance.

A breath tickled Nicole's ear, and she quickly turned away, swiping at the nape of her neck as though someone was trying to whisper in her ear. And while she couldn't hear the exact words, she heard the rattling sounds of a raspy voice, struggling to speak, as though talking out loud was painful.

Nicole kept her eyes shut. She didn't want to look. She didn't want to see anything else that might give her nightmares. And just when the cold and the dark and the absurdity of everything that was happening to her reached a crescendo, a voice broke through the noise.

Help.

Nicole stopped shivering and slowly opened her eyes. She recognized the tone of the voice, and she knew that whoever was speaking really was in trouble. It was the desperate plea of someone that had exhausted all of their options, and when her vision adjusted and she stared down at the puddle of blood, a phrase was written in the blood.

Save her.

The light brightened, and Nicole reached for the door handle in the same instant, finding that it was unlocked. She bolted out of the bathroom, through the room, and into the hallway. She didn't stop running when she reached the stairs, nor did she stop running when she reached the first floor.

Nicole kept going, her path taking her out the front door and into the sunshine, which blinded her, and she slammed into a body, a pair of hands catching her before she fell backward.

19

———————

"Mrs. Harper?" Concern was laced in Detective Salvor's tone as he kept hold of Nicole. "Are you all right?" He looked past her, probably searching for whatever thing that she had been running from, but there was only the open front door of the Calhoun estate. He looked back at her. "What happened?"

Nicole didn't know how to explain what she saw. She certainly didn't know how to tell the detective, who she believed thought that she knew more than she was letting on, how she broke into a crime scene room that she was specifically told not to enter and tell him that she received a message written in a dead man's dried blood by... what? The ghost of Aubrey Calhoun? Was that what she had seen in the window?

"Mrs. Harper." Detective Salvor's voice hardened. "What happened?"

Nicole wasn't even sure why the detective was here. Had he come to speak with herself and Jake again?

What more questions could they answer? Or maybe he had found something about them?

"I found something," Nicole said. "About Donald's murder."

Detective Salvor frowned. "Murder? What makes you think he was murdered?"

Nicole retreated toward the estate and the still-open front door. "Follow me."

Nicole walked back inside, and Detective Salvor remained close.

"I know that I wasn't supposed to go in there, but I saw someone," Nicole said when they reached the top floor. "I was standing outside in the back, and I saw them in the window."

"You saw someone in the window of the butler's room?" Detective Salvor asked. "Who was it?"

"I don't know." Nicole lied. She wasn't sure she was ready to divulge the fact that she was seeing dead people.

"You don't know?" Salvor was skeptical.

"I was too far away to make out the features of their face, but I know that it was a woman," Nicole said, and the more she spoke about it out loud, the more confident she became of what she saw. "And when I came up here, I—"

Nicole stopped, and Detective Salvor walked up behind her, looking at the closed door to the butler's room.

"That can't be right," Nicole said.

The police tape was back up over the door, the seal

unbroken. It was like Nicole had never even walked into the room at all.

"What are we looking at here, Mrs. Harper?" Detective Salvor shifted his focus between the door and Nicole.

Nicole frowned. "It's still sealed."

"And is it not supposed to be that way?" Detective Salvor narrowed his eyes, all of his attention focused on Nicole. "I'm not in the mood for games, Mrs. Harper, so I need you to tell me what happened."

Nicole floundered, trying to find a way to explain all of this.

"I walked into the room, and it was empty," Nicole said. "I couldn't find the woman, but I went into the bathroom, and saw the blood and the tub where Donald was killed. And then the lights flickered and the bathroom door shut, and it got cold, really cold." She inadvertently hugged herself as she remembered the way that her skin transformed into nothing but goosebumps, multiplying over her body like braille. "Then, the blood on the tile started to bubble. Like it was boiling or something, but it was still cold. I screamed for help, but no one came." She shut her eyes, shaking her head, knowing that the detective was going to brush all of this off. But she needed to keep going because there was the smallest possibility that he could find something in her story that would help his investigation. "And then it was dark, and I heard a whisper, and then..." She swallowed, realizing how dry her mouth was. "I opened my eyes, and I saw that something had been written in Donald's blood. It said 'Save her.'" She took a breath and then locked eyes with the detective. "And then the lights came back on all the way, the door was unlocked, and I ran until I collided into you outside."

Detective Salvor was quiet for a while, and to his credit, he didn't immediately dismiss what Nicole had said. There was no sigh, no eye roll, no grimace that betrayed what the detective might have been thinking. He simply asked, "Then why was the seal unbroken if you entered the room?"

"I don't know," Nicole answered.

Again Detective Salvor remained quiet. There wasn't a lot that he could do other than try and make sense of something that made zero sense in his mind, and then he finally gestured to the butler's room. "Let's have a look."

The door hinges groaned when Detective Salvor pushed the door inward, breaking the seal, and the pair lingered in the hallway, staring inside. Nicole held out the smallest sliver of hope that whoever she had seen in the window would suddenly be inside, vindicating her, but the room was exactly how it was when she had entered only moments ago: empty.

Detective Salvor entered, stopping in the middle of the room, and saw the open bathroom door. Nicole waited with bated breath as the detective lingered in the bathroom, and she hoped that he saw what she had seen. But after a few minutes in the bathroom, he stepped out and shook his head.

"There's no writing in the blood, Mrs. Harper," the

detective said. "The scene doesn't look like it's been disturbed at all."

Nicole shook her head and then finally walked to the bathroom. "No, that's impossible—" But when she passed Salvor and looked into the bathroom herself, she saw that he was right. There was nothing.

Nicole stepped out of the bathroom, trying to convince both herself and the detective of what she had seen. "It was there. I swear to you. Why would I lie? Why would I lie about breaking into a room where you clearly told me that I wasn't allowed to be inside? It doesn't make any sense."

Salvor pointed toward the door. "Then explain to me how the seal on the door remained unbroken. I know that you couldn't have climbed through the window. There's no possible entrance. It's too far from the roof. I checked out that angle last night when I was examining the crime scene."

Nicole didn't have a good answer. And now that she was staring into the face of her own delusions, she was afraid that she was losing her mind along with Ms. Calhoun. "I know what I saw!"

"Saw what?" Melissa hovered in the doorway. She was dressed in a trim black suit with a sky blue blouse, her hair flowing down her shoulders with a shine that made it look like she had just come back from the salon.

"I think you need to start including psychological checks on the people that you hire, Ms. Farr." Salvor walked past Melissa and out of the room, disappearing down the hallway.

But Melissa stayed, looking back to Nicole, who was on the verge of tears. "Mrs. Harper, can you explain to me what you're doing up here?"

Nicole wanted to quit, right then and there, but she knew that it wouldn't solve anything. And she couldn't forget the message that had been written in the blood.

"I'm sorry, Ms. Farr." Nicole forced a smile, and then quickly wiped her eyes. "I thought I remembered something that would have helped the police, but I was wrong."

Melissa narrowed her eyes. "I gave you specific instructions not to speak to the authorities without me present to represent you and the estate."

"I know," Nicole said, bowing her head. "I overstepped my bounds." She kept her head bowed until Melissa spoke.

"Just get back to work," Melissa said. "It's almost time for Ms. Calhoun's supper."

"Of course." Nicole quickly excused herself from the room and then headed down the hall. It seemed that Aubrey's message had been for Nicole's eyes only. Now she needed to figure out who needed to be saved, and who they needed to be saved from.

*N*icole contemplated telling Melissa and the detective about her encounter with Rick, but she decided against it. She had no proof that he had attacked her, and what was more, she had no proof that he had done something wrong. She wasn't sure if he was related to anything that was happening with the woman that she saw in the window, or the handful of other strange occurrences that she had experienced since her arrival at the mansion, but she needed to collect more evidence, something tangible, if she was going to get any allies in her quest for the truth.

Nearing the kitchen, Nicole slowed when she heard the familiar hushed tones of a lover's quarrel, and she stealthily crept toward the kitchen's entrance.

"The jewels weren't in the coffins like we thought, and now that nurse is looking around," Rick said. "If she goes to that fucking lawyer, then we're in trouble."

"If she says something, you'll just deny it," Kate said.

Nicole frowned. So Kate wasn't so innocent after all.

"But if she says something, then that fucking lawyer might dig a little deeper into my records," Rick said. "They can't know who I am."

And who was he? Nicole imagined everyone had gone through a background check. Had Melissa missed something?

"I'm not going back to prison," Rick said. "Not for anyone or any amount of money."

Before Kate could respond, a door slammed and the kitchen fell quiet. Nicole waited to see if she heard Kate crying, but Nicole was surprised to hear her whistling a tune.

Nicole waited a little bit longer before she finally turned the corner to make sure that Kate didn't think that she was spying on her.

"Hey," Kate said, the smile on her face a little too chipper. "Dinner's on the table there."

Nicole said nothing as she picked up the tray. She studied Kate's body language, and she saw nothing that gave her the impression that Kate was rattled. Confused, she carried Ms. Calhoun's dinner to the second floor.

But before Nicole reached Ms. Calhoun's room to bring the woman her food, another whisper tickled her left ear. She froze, looking behind her, but she saw no one.

The whisper was different than the one she heard in Donald's bathroom. That had been one voice. But what she heard now was a collection of voices, a room full of whispers blending together in a single monotonous tone.

Nicole stepped closer toward Ms. Calhoun's room, and the whispers faded. She stopped. She stepped back down the hall toward the stairs, and the whispers grew louder. Knowing that this was something she needed to investigate so she could finally discover who or what was trying to reach out and contact her, Nicole walked down the hallway, following the whispers all the way to the room with the blue door.

Tray still in hand, Nicole stopped, remembering what Melissa had said about the one rule of the house and the only place that she wasn't allowed to enter. But there was something in this house that wanted to tell her something, and she had grown curious enough to want to know the truth.

Pulled closer by the whispers, Nicole walked all the way up to the blue door. Balancing the tray in one hand, she slowly reached for the blue door's handle, the whispers growing louder and louder in her mind, and the moment that her hand touched the handle, the whispers stopped.

Nicole froze. It was like a loud stereo had suddenly shut off, and the silence that took its place was just as deafening as the noise itself.

Just to try, Nicole wiggled the handle, but it was locked. She wasn't surprised. Melissa didn't strike Nicole as someone who trusted people with the honor system.

Still waiting for the whispers to return, Nicole slowly leaned her ear closer to the door and pressed it against the side. She heard nothing, but she knew that she hadn't imagined the whispers. They were on the other side. They were real, just like everything else.

Nicole closed her eyes, concentrating. Maybe she could reach out to whatever was trying to contact her like they were talking to her.

"Can you hear me?" Nicole asked, her own whisper reverberating off the door, giving it a slight echo. "If you can, it'd be great to know what exactly it is that you're trying to tell me."

Nicole waited, concentrating harder, trying to reach out with her own mind, and she repeated the questions in her head. "Hello?"

A heavy thud smacked from the inside of the blue door, the force hard enough to send Nicole back a few steps, and she dropped the tray of food in surprise.

The china and glass shattered on the tray when it hit the floor, pieces of porcelain intermixed with the lasagna and garlic bread that had been prepared, the glass of juice staining the blue carpet a darker shade.

"Shit." Nicole dropped to her knees, quickly picking up the food and the bits of glass and pieces of porcelain, taking care not to cut herself in the process. But while she collected the food and broken pieces of the tray, she glanced at the blue door.

The faded hunk of wood that protected whatever was on the inside of that room was now quiet and still. It didn't rattle or shake. No more whispers either. But one thing was perfectly clear: there were answers on the other side of that door.

*K*ate wasn't very happy about having to cook up another meal for Ms. Calhoun, but the woman didn't protest too much. At least not verbally.

And while Nicole waited for the food to finish, she thought that she might take the time to pry into Kate's relationship with Rick a little more.

"So how long have you and Rick been a thing?" Nicole asked, trying to rely on the power of girl talk to spark some gossip. She had never been good at it, but she thought that she could fake it for a few minutes.

"I wouldn't really call us a thing," Kate answered, the majority of her attention focused on the steaming skillets on the stove, but she turned around and gave a little wink. "More like a fling."

Nicole tried not to grimace. The thought of anyone having a fling with a monster like Rick made her sick. "Has it been going on for long?"

"Not too long." Kate was busy working about the

stove, adding ingredients. That was something that Nicole noticed about Kate, she was always moving. She didn't like to sit still.

"Did you meet Rick here, or did you know him before the job?" Nicole asked.

Kate froze, only for a moment, just long enough for Nicole to notice.

"We met here," Kate said, ending the conversational note in her voice.

Nicole was certain Kate was hiding something, and she slowly reached into her pocket for her phone, and then remembered the rule about not having her mobile device when she was working in the mansion, so recording her was out of the question.

"The last time we spoke, you kept talking about how you thought that Ms. Calhoun killed her family," Nicole said, shifting gears. "Do you think she did it for the money?"

Kate spun around, transferring the soup from the pot and into the bowl, some of the yellow broth splashing onto the tray. "I don't know what the hell goes on inside the mind of that woman. She's insane, and that's all there is to it." She turned back around and then transferred the grilled sandwich next to the soup and pointed to the tray. "You're all set. Try not to drop this one, because I'm clocking out." She then quickly left the kitchen before Nicole could get another word in.

It was the first interaction with Kate where Nicole saw her be uncomfortable. She thought to follow her, but she decided against it.

Careful not to spill the tray, Nicole moved cautiously up the stairs to the second floor. She listened for any more whispers but heard nothing.

Nicole found Ms. Calhoun in bed, and the old woman smiled that unnatural smile again when she saw her dinner on the tray.

"I'm sorry it's a little late," Nicole said, gently setting the tray down over the old woman's lap. "I spilled the last one."

Ms. Calhoun didn't acknowledge anything that Nicole said, turning her focus on the soup in the bowl, and then delicately slurped as loud as possible. When she finished, she looked to Nicole and then smiled again, but this one was different.

The smile reached her eyes, and it made her look normal. More human.

"You're trying to be funny," Nicole said.

Ms. Calhoun clapped her hands and then returned to her soup.

Watching Ms. Calhoun now reminded Nicole of her own grandmother, the funny old woman who used to slip her candies at the dinner table when her mother wasn't looking and helped feed the dog her vegetables when she was tired of eating them. She was eight-year-old Nicole's favorite person.

Nicole knew that it was a long shot, but she sat on the edge of Ms. Calhoun's bed and folded her hands in her lap. "Can you talk, Ms. Calhoun, and you just choose not to?"

Ms. Calhoun remained focused on her soup, still slurping loudly, but no longer smiling about it.

"Sometimes trauma can steal a person's voice," Nicole said. "I know what happened to your family. I can't imagine what it was like to see such violence."

The old woman set the spoon down in the soup bowl, the metal handle clanging against the rim, which was trimmed with gold.

Nicole slowly reached for Ms. Calhoun's hand. She wasn't sure how the old woman would react to being touched, but Ms. Calhoun didn't scream or yell. She didn't throw a fit. Ms. Calhoun simply placed her other hand on top of Nicole's, her two plump, pale, and frighteningly fragile hands engulfing Nicole's in a sandwich, and looked Nicole square in the eyes.

In her years as a hospice nurse, Nicole had seen a variety of expressions from people suffering from dementia and trauma. People handled death in all kinds of different ways. Some were scared, others angry, others glad to finally be rid of the pain that had been plaguing them for so long.

But the grief that Nicole saw in the grey eyes of Ms. Calhoun, a woman who had gone through so much tragedy in her life, was beyond anything that she had seen on another living face before. Her eyes watered and reddened, and her mouth trembled.

Nicole leaned closer, knowing that if she could just get the woman to speak, to find out why or what was happening in the house, what she had seen the night of the murders, she knew that all of it could help her find out what the hell was going on in the house. And who she needed to keep safe.

"Ms. Calhoun, please," Nicole said, pleading with

her. "If there is something that you want to tell me, something that you think could help me figure out what happened to Donald, to your family, then you should talk to me."

The old woman struggled, the tremors along her face growing wilder the longer that she held it in, but Nicole didn't receive the answer she wanted. Instead, Ms. Calhoun forced another smile and then returned her attention to the soup. If Nicole wanted answers, then she would have to find them elsewhere.

Disappointed by the outcome, Nicole collected the dishes after Ms. Calhoun finished her dinner and then meandered down the hall, head hung low, trying to figure out her next move.

When she reached the first floor, Nicole perked up when she heard the heightened shouts of people coming from down the hall. Tray still in hand, Nicole walked down the hallway, careful not to make her presence known, and realized that the heated voices were coming from the lawyer's office.

The door to the office was cracked open, allowing what should have been a private conversation to leak out into the hallway. Nicole moved closer to listen but made sure that she didn't cast a shadow.

"I need to speak to her again," Detective Salvor said.

"No," Melissa replied. "That is out of the question. I'm not going to have you berate an old woman so you can continue to grasp at straws, Detective."

"I'm not grasping," Salvor said, though his voice had that exasperated quality that typically aligned with someone who was on the cusp of desperation. "The medical examiner is taking another look at the wounds that Mr. Weiss sustained. He doesn't think the blade that was used to slit Mr. Weiss's wrists is consistent with the blade that was found at the crime scene—"

"Only because *you* requested the second examination." Melissa laughed, matching the same level of desperation in the detective. "How much longer do you want to drag this out, Detective? Donald killed himself."

"No one here knew him well," Detective Salvor. "And the one person who did won't speak because of something that happened thirty years ago. This house has been marked with more death than it should, and you and I both know that whatever is happening here is strange."

Nicole knew that was true, and the detective didn't know the half of it.

Salvor's voice softened. "Your father was close to the Calhoun family. They were good people. Your father would have let me speak to her again—"

"My father is dead," Melissa said, a nasty bite to her tone. "And if you had done your job thirty years ago, then you wouldn't even be questioning what happened to Donald in the first place. You're obsessed with this case, Detective, because you never found the killer, and now you're desperately trying to link Donald's suicide to some bigger conspiracy."

Detective Salvor was quiet, and when he spoke again, he sounded tired. "You're right. I didn't find the killer. And I never found the jewels either. And maybe I am trying to fix what I couldn't do thirty years ago, but all I'm asking for is a chance."

"Unless you come back to me with a subpoena or a warrant, you will have no further contact with any member of the Calhoun estate's staff," Melissa said. "And considering how you showed up today without one, I suspect that you couldn't convince a judge to give you one."

Nicole leaned away from the cracked door, sensing the conversation was done, and hurried back to the kitchen just before Detective Salvor stepped from the office and left the house.

The kitchen was empty, and Nicole placed the dirty trays on the counter and took a moment to catch her breath and to process what she had just overheard in the hallway.

"There you are."

Nicole jumped, quickly turning to the kitchen's entrance, where she saw Melissa standing. "What?"

"I've been looking for you," Melissa entered the kitchen, making great strides not to get too close to anything that might stain her outfit. She wasn't the kind of woman that enjoyed getting her hands dirty. "I need you to start taking on a few of Donald's responsi-bilities until I can find a suitable replacement. You'll be compensated of course for the extra work." She cleared her throat and then removed a small list of duties and handed them to Nicole. "I don't really know exactly what he did, but that was what I was able to pull from his file."

"File?" Nicole asked, looking up from the paper. "What file?"

"I keep files for all of Ms. Calhoun's employees," Melissa answered. "Yes, even you, Mrs. Harper. It's all laid out in the contract that you've already signed." She looked down at the list and then back up to Nicole. "Are we going to have a problem with this?"

Nicole studied the list a little more carefully. Most of it was just taking care of more personal things for Ms. Calhoun, which Nicole didn't mind since it would provide her a little more time of getting to know her. "No, it's fine."

"Good." Melissa exhaled in relief, and in that quick omission of fatigue, Nicole caught the glimpse of a woman who looked very tired. She then dug into her pocket and brought out a ring of keys. "These are keys to most of the rooms of the estate. You'll need access to some of them to fulfill Donald's duties. But I don't want you to get any ideas and start snooping around." Melissa raised her eyebrow in the way that a classroom teacher would to a class who was about to be on their own for a little while. "I trust that you won't stretch yourself beyond your means, Mrs. Harper?"

"No," Nicole answered, taking the keys from Melissa. "I won't.

"I'll be in my office if you need anything."

Nicole watched the lawyer leave and again contemplated telling her about her encounter with Rick. But telling her about the interaction would also force her to reveal what she had been doing out there in the first place. And the way that the detective was still snooping

THE HAUNTING OF CALHOUN MANSION

around, looking to pin Donald's murder on anyone, made her want to keep out of the spotlight.

But Nicole found it interesting that Melissa kept files on the employees. She was willing to bet the files would hold some interesting pieces of information on everyone that worked for Ms. Calhoun, and they might provide some leverage and insight into Rick and Kate.

*N*icole tried her best to balance her normal work with the new duties that Melissa had assigned her, along with the sudden compulsion to figure out what the hell was happening in the house. She hoped that looking into the safe in Melissa's office would grant her more information, but Melissa never left her office.

Between her tasks and responsibilities, Nicole stared down at the set of keys that Melissa had given her. There were dozens of them, and all of them were roughly the same size, though they varied in shine and color. But there was only one room that she wanted to check.

The blue door room.

Nicole returned to the third floor, making sure that she was alone before she made her way over to the forbidden room. She stood outside of it for a moment, almost afraid of what she would find on the other side.

But that was only if she could get inside.

Nicole studied the keys in her hand, unsure of which one, if any, would unlock the mysteries on the other side. She glanced down the hallway one last time to make sure that she was alone and then began testing out which key might unlock the door.

She started with the older-looking keys, thinking that since the door was so old, that it would also make sense that the key was old too. But none of the rusted or fading brass keys did the trick, and as she worked her way up to the newer keys, she felt her hope diminish.

Finally, on the last key, Nicole shut her eyes and whispered a little prayer, hoping that it would work, but she was denied once again.

Nicole checked the time, realizing that she was now behind her already-tight schedule, her job suddenly the last thing on her mind. But Nicole knew that if she didn't catch up now, then she would be overwhelmed tomorrow.

The first item on the task was preparing the master bathroom for Ms. Calhoun for her morning routine. But the only routine that Nicole knew about was the staring contest that the old woman had outside her window with the vast sweeping nature of the entire mountainside.

Then Nicole saw that she would be helping Ms. Calhoun bathe. And while she had performed these duties for other patients in the past, she wasn't looking forward to it.

The cleaning supplies were on the first floor on the east wing of the estate, and when Nicole went to collect the necessary items, she saw that they were out of bleach. But not to fear, the all-powerful list was there to tell her to head into the cellar, where the bulk of the house supplies were kept in storage.

Nicole entered the cellar through the kitchen entry, still finding no trace of Kate, so she figured that the chef was upstairs having her fun with Rick. Nicole gagged at the thought.

The stairway from the kitchen and into the cellar was narrow and dark. She flicked on the light switch at the top of the stairs, and she saw the responsive glow at the bottom. It wasn't much light, but it was better than wandering around in the darkness.

Nicole walked down the steps, surprised and disappointed with herself that she wasn't able to get the image of Kate and Rick out of her head. She didn't want to know what kind of sick relationship that they had together, but somehow, it made her think about her own relationship with Jake.

Did people think she was stupid for sticking with Jake? After cheating on her in their apartment, in their bed, breaking the most private and intimate moments of their lives? She had been angry and upset, but even after all of that, she couldn't bring herself to leave him.

Because she remembered what it was like before Jake had cheated. She remembered the life that they shared together before he broke her heart, shattering her world into a million different pieces. And while some of those memories were now tainted by what he had done, she could still see them, feel them, taste and smell them. She could transport herself into the world of love that she remembered before her heart was broken.

Nicole paused when she reached the bottom of the stairs, knowing that she was judging Kate the same way that everyone who knew about the affair had judged Jake. She only told a few friends and close family members about the ordeal. It was too much for her to keep bottled up inside and hold it alone, but after she had told those people, she regretted it.

Because now, moving forward, even if Nicole and Jake were able to return to the kind of love and trust that they had before, other people wouldn't be able to move on from what Jake had done. He was now forever painted as the man who had cheated, and those labels were very difficult to remove.

Nicole rubbed her eyes, a headache forming from the tireless arguments in her head. She was only making herself exhausted, running herself ragged until she couldn't think straight.

"One problem at a time, Nic," she said, taking a breath to help rid herself of the negative energy.

The cellar was large, at least larger than the narrow staircase suggested. But from what Nicole could see at the base of the stairs and the dim yellow lighting that the overhead bulbs provided, the cellar was the same square footage as the kitchen above them.

A combination of food stores, freezers, and supply shelves lined the walls, and Nicole walked past the pantry items and toward the back where she saw more of the cleaning supplies. She wasn't sure if keeping both items stored in the same place was up to code, but she figured that the Calhoun estate didn't receive many inspections. And even if they did fail, Nicole was sure that Melissa would be there in a flash to make sure that everything was smoothed over.

Oh, leaking gas? Not a problem at all. We'll just throw money at it until it goes away.

Nicole had never had that kind of money, and she doubted that she would, not unless she stumbled upon the Calhoun family jewels that were supposedly hidden still somewhere in the house.

But then she would need to still try and figure out a way to break into the vault, built by a man who had supposedly been the greatest vault designer in the country. She'd have better luck playing the lotto.

Nicole found the spare bleach on one of the shelves and then grabbed the handle, which was covered in dust. From the look of the supplies down below, the estate had ordered everything in bulk. The cellar was almost like some kind of storm shelter for the end of the world. She had never seen anything like it before.

Bleach in hand, Nicole headed for the stairs, but along the way, the hanging incandescent lights dimmed, then flickered on and off exactly like they had done in Donald's bathroom, and Nicole froze in her tracks.

Nicole spun around, her eyes straining in the darkness to make out any shapes, and the oddly-formed shadows that she did see gave off sinister and monstrous appearances. "Who are you?" Nicole spat the question with a hint of fear, and the lights flickered bright enough for her to see her own breath, and that familiar spike of ice pricked the base of her skull.

Still unsure if the ghost that was chasing her was friend or foe, Nicole unscrewed the cap for the bleach and then held it out in front of her, ready to splash anyone or anything that could be waiting for her. It crossed her mind that it could still be Rick seeking her out for some kind of revenge, especially after the conversation that Nicole overheard between Kate and Rick in the kitchen. He didn't seem like the kind of man who was quick to let something go, and she was in no mood to play any kind of game with him to see who would break first.

"Enough!" Nicole raised her voice, frustration and anger now overriding her fear. "I don't know what you want, but if you want my help, then you better give me something more than riddles written in blood!"

The cellar remained quiet and still save for the buzz of the incandescent lightbulbs, jettisoning her air from her mouth and her quick breaths.

Then, when Nicole was deciding if she should make a run for the stairs, the lights cut out, and the temperature plummeted even colder. It was like jumping into a lake during the winter, breaking through the thin sheet of ice that covered the water like a shiny glaze, and all of your senses and muscles and organs seized up at once as a million knives touched your skin.

Nicole dropped the bleach, and it spilled over the floor. She couldn't move, couldn't blink, and she realized that she couldn't even breathe.

Panic took over at that point, but when she tried to scream, there was nothing. It was like she was caught in some kind of limbo, but being stuck here was a strain on her body, a pressure building up in her that she didn't think she could stop.

And then one of the lights overhead provided dim light. And beneath it stood a young woman. The same woman that Nicole had seen in the window when she first arrived at the estate and again standing on the inside of the butler's room.

This was the first time that Nicole got a good look at the woman. All of her other interactions had kept a building between the two of them, with glass and brick and concrete.

It was Aubrey Calhoun.

The first thing that Nicole realized was that the woman was beautiful. She had long, wavy brown hair, porcelain skin, and an hourglass figure. Her face could have landed her on the cover of any number of beauty magazines. It was the kind of beauty that would have drove men wild had she still been alive.

Nicole knew that she should have been frightened since this was the closest that she had ever come to an actual spirit, but she only felt concerned. Because Aubrey Calhoun looked sad and worried. And based off of Aubrey's previous message, she was probably concerned about her sister.

The woman said nothing, and Nicole opened her mouth to speak, but like her very breath, her voice was stolen from her. She couldn't do anything. She couldn't move, couldn't blink. Whatever this woman wanted to do to her, she would have free rein.

Aubrey Calhoun reached into her pocket and grabbed something. She clutched it tight in her fist and then knelt, pressing whatever she held onto the floor. She looked at Nicole and smiled, tears forming in her eyes.

And then as clear as the woman's image appeared, it slowly faded, growing weaker and weaker, and as Aubrey disappeared, Nicole found that she could move again.

Nicole managed to take a step forward, and her heart skipped a beat. It jumped so hard in her chest that she thought that the muscle would burst from her body and land on the floor. She locked eyes with Aubrey, who was barely an outline of a figure anymore, nothing more than a shadow's shadow.

And then she was gone.

The lights turned back on, and Nicole stumbled forward three steps, drawing in a deep breath, and then coughed from the sharp and unexpected inhale. She hunched forward, catching her breath. She spun in circles, but all that remained of her encounter with Aubrey Calhoun was the slightest chill in the air and the fact that she couldn't stop the tremor of her left hand.

Nicole headed for the staircase, but she stopped when she stepped on something on the floor. She lifted her foot and glanced down, stepping out of the way so her shadow didn't block the light.

When Nicole moved her head out of the way, she

saw a key. She stared at it for a moment, certain that the key wasn't there before she walked into the cellar, or before Aubrey had appeared. It had been left for her, and without being told what room it was for, Nicole knew that it was the key to the blue door.

*N*icole collected the key off the floor and clutched it tightly in her fist. She left the bleach behind, the chores that she needed to complete far from her mind, and stopped herself before she reached the blue door.

Everything that she had done so far, she had done alone, and Nicole knew that if she were to make a case for what was really happening in this house, and to the people in it, then she would need proof, but what was more, she needed someone else to believe in that proof.

She needed to tell Jake.

Nicole hurried toward the guest house, and she kept her head on a swivel as she looked for any signs of Rick lurking about in the gardens. But she saw nothing and arrived at the guest house unharmed.

Unable to slow her momentum when she reached the guest house, she burst inside, catching Jake's attention immediately. He looked up from his laptop. He was in the same spot where Nicole had left him after lunch earlier in the day.

"Nic, what's wrong?" Jake stood up and lowered the screen on his laptop. He hurried toward her, giving her a look up and down to make sure that she wasn't hurt. "What happened? Did—"

"I saw her," Nicole said, blurting it out. She didn't know how to keep her cool at a time like this, and she thought it best to just get on with it and see how crazy Jake thought she was. "The woman in the window, the one that I saw when we first arrived. I've seen her twice more now. It's Aubrey Calhoun."

Nicole studied Jake's reaction, looking for any signs that he might decide to call the bus of white coats to come and whisk her away.

"Okay," Jake said, walking on eggshells. "What happened—"

"I think this is a key to the blue door," Nicole said, opening her palm and showing him the old brass key in her palm. At first, she was worried that the key in her hand had been nothing more than a figment of her imagination. She was afraid that she had seen things that weren't there, but when Jake plucked the key from her hand and held it in his own, there was no doubt it was real.

Jake scrunched his face in confusion. "Blue door?"

Nicole realized that Jake hadn't been around when Melissa explained the rules of the main house because Jake wasn't allowed there. "It's the only room in the mansion that I can't enter."

Jake looked at the key, then looked at Nicole. "What makes you think that this is the key to the blue door?"

Nicole went through what happened to her during the day, even telling him about the interaction with Rick, and she would have been lying if she said that seeing him get angry over what the groundskeeper had told her didn't make her feel slightly better about their chances of reconciling.

"We need to call the police," Jake said once Nicole had finished the bulk of her story. "They need to know what Rick did to you, and they need to know what you found."

"I already told you that the detective doesn't believe me," Nicole said. "I tried to show him the words that I found written in blood, but when we returned to the room, it was like I had never even been inside at all." She pointed to the key. "But this is the first piece of tangible evidence that I found that we can use. This helps prove I'm not crazy."

Jake glanced at the key once more. "I don't know, Nic." He shook his head and then handed the key back to her. "I mean, that key might not even work, and if it does, then you would have breached the contract that we signed." He sat on the edge of the kitchen table and crossed his arms. "I took a closer look at that thing, and we signed over a lot of our legal power to the Calhoun estate. If we break any part of the clause in that contract... we could go to jail. Serious jail."

Nicole hadn't thought about the real consequences of her actions. She had been so consumed with trying to prove that she had been right about what she had seen that she had thrown all caution to the wind. But there was something in the way that Ms. Calhoun would look at her now, and the way that the mystery woman looked at her too. Something was wrong here, and she believed that she was the only person that could fix it.

"We need to take that chance," Nicole said, clenching the key in her fist.

Jake cracked a half-smile and arched his left eyebrow up. "We?"

Nicole blushed and stared down at her shoes. "Well, I figured you'd want to help—"

Jake touched Nicole's hand, and she looked up. He was smiling down at her. "I would do anything to help you. I hope that you know that."

Nicole smiled. "Thanks."

Jake nodded and then glanced out the window toward the mansion. "Let's just hope that we don't get told on by any of the other staff members."

Nicole looked toward the mansion as well, and she shook her head. "I don't think we'll have to worry about Rick and Kate going to Melissa." They might kill them, though.

Nicole and Jake crossed the open backfield from the guest house and into the mansion. Most of the lights were still on, as they normally were during the night. It had been one of the rules and stipulations of the staff members who slept in the mansion. They could turn off the lights in their own rooms, but they were to never touch the lights in the hallways or the common areas. They were to stay on at all times.

"I can't imagine what they pay in electric costs," Jake said, glancing up at all of the chandeliers that were burning bright in the rooms they passed. "I mean, it's just so wasteful."

Waste was the farthest thing from Nicole's mind as she spotted the blue door down the hall. She glanced down at the key once more, and she saw her hand shaking. She was afraid.

It wasn't an uncommon reaction, especially after everything that Nicole had seen so far. She suspected that many people would have turned tail to run, but she didn't. She decided to stay, to keep pushing despite the terrible consequences that might follow, and she did this because she believed that this was the right thing to do.

The thought was empowering, and Nicole smiled. After nearly three months of being stuck in a neutral position, she was glad to know that she still could move forward. She was glad to know that she was still able to fight.

Nicole reached the door first and already had the key out and ready. But before she placed the key into the lock, she paused, then turned to look back at Jake.

"I don't know what we're going to find inside," Nicole said. "I don't know if it will... do something to us."

Jake swallowed. He was nervous. "Well, there's only one way to find out."

Nicole nodded and faced the door again. She guided the key into the lock, and once the old brass-ware was fully inserted, she shut her eyes, praying that it would unlock, praying that whatever she found on the other side of the door wouldn't kill her.

Nicole held her breath as she twisted the key to the left, and this time there was no resistance when she turned the lock, and instead heard the distinct thud of the lock disengaging. Nicole opened her eyes, smiling as she looked behind her and saw Jake with a matching grin.

Nicole left the key in the lock, turned the old brass knob, and pushed the door inward as she took her first steps inside.

*N*icole wasn't sure what she expected to find when she stepped into the room. A part of her thought it would be something terrible, like the bodies of all of the victims that the house had claimed over the years, stored away and sealed up in plastic bags, their decomposing bodies staring back at her with whatever horrific expressions that they had worn on the moment of their deaths.

But there were no bodies. Nothing horrific at all, only boxes.

Jake entered behind Nicole, sporting the same perplexed expression that she wore. "What the hell is all of this?" He approached the nearest tower of boxes and then opened the top one.

"Jake, wait!" Nicole lunged for Jake and grabbed his wrist, stopping him. "We don't know what's inside. It could be dangerous."

Jake laughed. "Like they're booby-trapped? Nic, I

don't think that there is anything in here that is going to hurt us."

Nicole released Jake's hand, and she nodded. "All right." She stepped back and let Jake finish opening the box. It was too tall for her to see inside, so when Jake reached into the box, she couldn't see what he was grabbing. And what he pulled out wasn't what she had expected.

Jake held a picture frame in his hands. It was old but in good condition. He studied the picture and then handed it to Nicole, who eyed it curiously.

"What else is inside?" Nicole asked.

Jake pulled out another picture frame with an old photograph inside. "It's nothing but pictures." He set the box aside and then opened the one beneath it. He shuffled through the packing papers and then pulled out a photo album. He flipped through the pages, revealing more old photographs inside, then stopped as he looked around the room. "There must be over one hundred boxes in here." He looked at Nicole. "Do you think all of them are pictures?"

Nicole remained quiet. She still held that first picture in her hands. It was a family picture. A father, mother, and two young girls were all dressed in their Sunday best, but none of them were smiling. "I think this is Mr. Calhoun."

Jake walked around behind her and glanced over her shoulder to the picture below. "Yeah, I think you're right." He nodded and then moved to the family album that he had pulled out. "These are all family photos of the Calhoun family." He flipped through the pages very quickly, and the paused when he neared the middle of the book. "This is the picture that was used in the papers after the murders."

Nicole walked over to get a better look at the picture, and her heart skipped a beat when she saw one of the young women in the photo. "That's Aubrey." Nicole tapped her finger over the woman. "She's the woman I saw in the window."

"You're positive?" Jake asked, his voice thick with skepticism.

Nicole studied the picture more carefully, making sure that she didn't think it could be someone else, but the longer that she stared at the photograph, the more she was convinced that was the same woman.

"Same hair color, same look, same eyes." Nicole took a breath and then exhaled. "That's her."

"Aubrey Calhoun," Jake said. "What are you trying to tell my wife?"

The pair sifted through a few more stacks of boxes, trying to see if there was anything else stored inside the blue room, but all they found were pictures in a variety of picture frames.

"I can't believe that they just packed all of these memories up," Jake said. "I mean, wouldn't it be good for a person with dementia to be able to see pieces of the past?"

Nicole knew that it would, but she also remembered what Donald had told her about the effect the pictures had on Ms. Calhoun after the murders. "Donald told me that he took them all down because

Ms. Calhoun didn't want to look at them anymore. He said they were driving her crazy."

Jake frowned. "Why would they be driving her crazy? Do you think she was feeling guilty?"

"Maybe," Nicole answered. "But it could just be survivor's guilt. I see that in a lot of people after they watched their family members die."

Jake was quiet for a moment, and then he picked up one of the frames from the box and held it in his hand. He studied it for a moment, and then set it back down. "Maybe we should show Ms. Calhoun the pictures."

The thought had already crossed Nicole's mind, and she had decided against it the moment it entered her head. "I don't think that's a good idea. She's not a stable individual. Looking at all of these faces might make her crack."

"And you're saying that she hasn't cracked already?" Jake asked. "Look, I'm not saying that we parade all of these in her face like some sort of interrogation. But we need to do something to get her talking. She is the only one that is still alive that really knows what happened that night. And there might be a correlation to what happened that night, and what's happening now."

Nicole sighed, rubbing her temples. "This is crazy."

"Hey." Jake stepped closer and grabbed hold of Nicole's hand. "You've always told me when you watch someone pass on that you can feel something leave the room. Something more than just the last breath." He squeezed the hand. "If you really are seeing someone, if this truly is some kind of contact from beyond our own reality, then just think of what you can do with that in helping other people. To really know that there is something beyond the life that we live in this world?"

Nicole hadn't considered that this was something more than just discovering what happened to Ms. Calhoun's family on that Christmas night thirty years ago. But she weighed the possibility of what this could mean for people, for her work.

"What pictures should we take up there?" Nicole finally asked the question, her way of agreeing to the plan. "We can't lug all of these boxes up the stairs, and I doubt we could pull Ms. Calhoun out of bed."

Jake handed her the picture in his hand, and Nicole studied it. "Remember how I told you how Ms. Calhoun was hovering over her dead sister's body when the police came?" He pointed to the picture. "I don't think it's a coincidence that you've seen Aubrey Calhoun around the house."

The picture that Nicole held, which was encased in a charcoal frame with a golden-edged rim, was of two young women. Judging by their age in the picture, Nicole surmised that it must have been taken just before the family's death. Ms. Calhoun and her sister were smiling in the picture together, but Nicole wasn't sure how the old woman would react when she finally showed her the picture in real life.

Nicole carried the picture, pressing the face of it against her stomach, as she and Jake walked up to the second floor to Ms. Calhoun's room. Nicole was nervous, but she wasn't sure why. Ms. Calhoun hadn't acted aggressively toward her since their first interaction together. In fact, the old woman seemed to have tried to help Nicole find out more about the truth, in what limited capacity her mind allowed.

When they reached the second floor, Nicole stopped, glancing down at the picture again. She looked at Jake. "Are you sure this is a good idea?"

"It's the only way that we're going to get answers," Jake answered. "Unless you want to try and crack the vault that is Melissa, the lawyer."

Nicole knew that wasn't going to happen. The woman was sealed up like Fort Knox. The only way they would uncover the truth was if they did it themselves.

"All right," Nicole said. "Let's go."

Nicole walked to Ms. Calhoun's room. The door was closed, and the light was off. She glanced back to Jake before she opened the door.

"I'll do the talking," Nicole said. "You're just here as a witness, and to make sure that she doesn't try and kill me."

"What if she kills me first?" Jake asked.

Nicole held Jake's gaze. "Then it was nice knowing you." She caught Jake's smirk before she turned away, and then she took a breath as she opened the door.

Light flooded into the room through the crack in the door, stretching toward Ms. Calhoun's bed where the old woman was asleep under the covers.

Nicole entered quietly and didn't turn on the lights, instead letting the light from the hallway flood the room and guide her to the bed. She didn't want to startle the old woman awake, unsure of how she would react. So she walked to her bedside and gently placed her hand on Ms. Calhoun's shoulder and lightly shook her awake.

"Ms. Calhoun?" Nicole whispered, trying to keep her head from blocking the light on Ms. Calhoun's face. She wanted to see when the woman opened her eyes. "Ms. Calhoun?" She offered another gentle shake, and then the old woman groaned, and Nicole leaned back.

Ms. Calhoun shifted beneath the covers, and it took a few moments for her to blink away the sleep. Once Ms. Calhoun was awake and noticed Nicole on the bed, and then glanced at Jake by the door, she recoiled to the other side of the bed.

"No, it's okay," Nicole said, holding out a friendly hand. "That's Jake. He's my husband. He's not here to hurt you. We just wanted to ask you some questions."

Ms. Calhoun started to breathe heavy, and sweat broke out on her forehead and upper lip. Nicole imagined that it was difficult for the old woman to comprehend all of this, especially since all of it was out of her normal routine. But Nicole desperately wanted answers, and she believed that Ms. Calhoun wanted those answers too.

"I saw Aubrey," Nicole said.

Ms. Calhoun remained on the other side of the bed, the covers clutched to her chest, still eyeing Jake suspiciously.

Nicole gestured to the picture frame in her hand. "Do you remember Aubrey?"

The second mention of her sister's name pulled Ms. Calhoun's attention back to Nicole, and the fear was replaced by confusion.

"I brought you some pictures," Nicole said, then placed the album in the center of the bed. "Would you like to look at them?"

Ms. Calhoun stared at the album the same way she had just stared at Jake, unsure if the object so close to her would bring joy or pain.

When Ms. Calhoun wouldn't look at the pictures, Nicole reached for the album and opened it to the first page.

"It's your family," Nicole said, then looked back to Jake. "Will you turn on the light?"

Light filled the room, and both Nicole and Ms. Calhoun winced from the brightness. Nicole pointed to one of the pictures on the page. "This was you when you were little, right?" She flipped the album around so Ms. Calhoun could see the pictures.

Ms. Calhoun leaned closer, then touched the bottom left corner of the page with a single finger. It was like she was poking it to make sure that it couldn't hurt her. When she determined that the album was harmless, she inched closer, pulling the album onto her lap, and studied the pages.

Nicole watched carefully, looking for any triggers as Ms. Calhoun turned the album's pages. For a long time, Ms. Calhoun's expression remained blank. But halfway through the album, she pointed to one of the photographs.

"This was when Father took us down to California," Ms. Calhoun said.

Nicole jumped from surprise, and then quickly glanced to Jake to make sure that she hadn't imagined it. When she saw the same expression of surprise on his face, she knew that she wasn't crazy. The woman had actually spoken.

Ms. Calhoun was smiling now, staring down at the pictures, and she grew more animated the longer that she stared into the past. "We were such a close family. Very loving." She giggled at that. "My mother used to tell us that we'd have to find husbands that agreed to buy homes right next to each other so we could still see one another every day."

Nicole watched Ms. Calhoun as she went through the pictures. She was turning into a different person, and it was amazing to watch the cloud of confusion lift from her mind, and for the first time since she arrived at the estate, Nicole believed that she was looking at the real Ms. Calhoun.

"My mother was a wonderful cook," Ms. Calhoun said, pointing to a picture of a pretty, middle-aged woman with red hair pinned up in curls and makeup, wearing a dress and a pearl necklace. "My father always said that she should have opened a restaurant, it was why we had such a big kitchen. She was practicing, and she would hold big dinners for everyone in town." She laughed. "After a few weeks there was a line out the door, and there weren't enough seats in the dining room for everyone that wanted to come, so she had tables set up outside, and if the weather was nice, people would eat dinner outside at sunset and under the stars."

Jake walked over, joining Nicole on the bed, and both of them watched Ms. Calhoun as she continued to look through the pictures and recount her childhood memories. It was nice watching her relive and remember so many positive things about her life.

Ms. Calhoun pointed to a picture and laughed so hard that she only wheezed. She bounced up and down like she was on a pogo stick, rattling the bed. She leaned into a pile of throw pillows, and then her joyous mirth finally echoed to life. She had a good laugh, a contagious one, and Nicole and Jake couldn't help but chuckle themselves.

Finally, Ms. Calhoun turned the album around so they could see what she had pointed at, and Nicole laughed harder too.

"What was she doing?" Jake asked, smiled.

The picture showed Ms. Calhoun's sister with some kind of whipped cream all over her face, with her mother and herself laughing in the background.

"My father had a birthday tradition," Ms. Calhoun said. "At some point during the day, and you never knew when it was coming, he would sneak up behind you and pie you in the face with a big pan of whipped cream." She giggled again, wiping the tears that had collected at the corner of her eyes. "It made birthdays more exciting for the rest of us, and you prayed that Father got you early in the day so you wouldn't be walking around dreading when he was going to do it." She smiled, turning the album around and slowly, the smile disappeared.

Nicole studied her face, wondering why the old woman was so concerned, and worried that she was slipping out of the lucid memories of her past and back into the terrible fog that caused her to stare blankly for hours at a time.

But the smile slowly turned into a frown, and Ms. Calhoun sighed, shaking her head. "My father was a good man. I had always believed that. Was he perfect? No. But no one in this world is ever perfect, and if they tell you otherwise, then they're selling you up the river to the funny farm."

Nicole leaned closer, knowing that this revelation about Ms. Calhoun's father was important. "What did your father do?"

The moment the question left Nicole's lips, she watched Ms. Calhoun's face change again. Disappointment turned to horror, and she pushed the album away from her as if it were diseased and contagious.

"She was so angry," Ms. Calhoun said, her voice trembling. "So violent. She killed everyone." Her eyes watered. "My sister."

Nicole reached for Ms. Calhoun's hand, trying to pull her back, trying to keep her in the moment before she slipped too far back into oblivion. "Who killed everyone? Your sister?"

Ms. Calhoun reciprocated Nicole's squeeze. "So much blood. She hunted all of us down like we were animals. So much rage." She locked eyes with Nicole. "We have to hide before she finds us!"

Nicole leaned closer, holding Ms. Calhoun's terrified gaze. "Who do we have to hide from? Who is hunting us? Is it your sister? You just mentioned her, is she the one who killed your family? Why?"

Ms. Calhoun opened her mouth, and Nicole's hopes were smothered as she watched dementia's fog roll back over Ms. Calhoun's memory, and then she started to scream. She released Nicole's hand, tossing it away, and then quickly crawled out of bed and retreated to the far corner of the room near the windows.

Nicole, knowing that Ms. Calhoun's outburst would catch Melissa's attention, quickly turned to Jake. "Get out of here! Hide!"

"Where?" Jake asked.

But before Nicole could answer, Melissa called from down the hall, her alarmed tone matching Ms. Calhoun's.

"Mrs. Harper, what is going on?" Melissa asked.

"Everything is fine," Nicole answered, shouting back, and then looked to Jake, quieting her voice. "Pick up those albums and hide in the closet, hurry!"

Jake scrambled for the albums, scooping them up in his arms, and then hurried to the closet. It was a walk-in, with plenty of space, and he quickly shut it while Nicole focused on Ms. Calhoun just as Melissa burst into the room.

26

It took an hour before Ms. Calhoun stopped screaming, and Melissa's presence didn't seem to help. But once the old woman calmed down, Nicole managed to get her back into the bed and tucked her in, and she was asleep before Nicole walked to the door and turned off the light.

Nicole followed Melissa out of the room, and the lawyer crossed her arms and set her brow in a straight line.

"What the hell was that?" Melissa asked.

"I'm not sure," Nicole answered. "It must have been one of her episodes."

"And that's the second episode she's had around you since you started this job." Melissa narrowed her eyes, giving Nicole a good look up and down. "What are you up to?"

Nicole knew that Melissa was only fishing to see what Nicole would give up. She took the opportunity to forge her own narrative. "Jake and I are having problems. It started before we got here, but it's spilling over into my work." She lowered her gaze. "I'm sorry."

Nicole hoped that the small nugget of truth in her lie would make it more convincing. And she was right.

"Marriages can be… complicated." Melissa eased up on her tone and uncrossed her arms. "I'm sorry you two are having trouble."

Nicole nodded. "Thank you."

"But you need to make sure that this doesn't affect work," Melissa said. "Send him home if you have to."

"I might do that," Nicole said.

She waited until Melissa was down the stairs before she re-entered Ms. Calhoun's room. She moved toward the closet, making sure she didn't wake her patient, and retrieved Jake and brought him out into the hall.

"That was close," Jake said.

"Do you still have all of the pictures?" Nicole asked, unsure if he was able to hold all of them while he waited.

"I've got them," Jake answered. "So, what now?"

Nicole exhaled, exhausted from the ordeal of getting Ms. Calhoun back into bed. She leaned back against the door and then rubbed her eyes. "I don't know what to make over Ms. Calhoun's episode."

Jake chewed on the end of his thumb. "She's clearly distressed."

Nicole scoffed. "Obviously."

Jake dropped his hand and then rubbed his own eyes. "Something about her sister seemed to trigger the outburst."

"If Aubrey did it, then what is she doing trying to help me?" Nicole asked.

Jake wrapped his arms around himself and then shrugged. "I don't know, but it might explain why Ms. Calhoun has remained quiet for so long. After witnessing such an important person in your life kill the rest of your family, I would think anyone would have a hard time coping with that."

Nicole nodded. The sister might have done it, but neither of them could make much sense out of the ordeal.

"Is there anything you're not telling me?" Jake asked.

Nicole had withheld a lot of information about Kate and Rick, and she wasn't sure how much she should tell him. She found it odd to be on the opposite end of lying. Jake had lied to her about the affair for weeks until she caught him in the act. But she knew that she couldn't keep it a secret forever.

"I think Rick and Kate are after the jewels," Nicole answered.

Jake raised his eyebrows. "The chef and the groundskeeper? What makes you think that?"

"I heard them talking in the kitchen," Nicole answered. "And I followed Rick out into the woods and saw him digging up graves. They thought the jewels were in the coffins."

"Oh my God," Jake said. "We need to report this."

"And tell them what?" Nicole asked. "That I'm snooping around and going places that I shouldn't because I'm being egged on by the ghost of a woman that's been dead for thirty years?"

Jake nodded. "We need to learn more about the family. Real information, not stuff that I found online." He locked eyes with Nicole. "I need to get into Melissa's computer."

"Are you crazy?" Nicole asked. "You're not even supposed to be in the house right now."

"I know I can break into her hard drive," Jake said. "And think of what we could find out about the family with access to their lawyer's personal files?"

"It's risky, Jake," Nicole said.

"Yeah, but I don't have a better option other than going to the police," Jake said. "And it's like you mentioned, we've already broken nearly every major section in our contracts."

Nicole finally agreed to the plan and told Jake to wait upstairs while she checked Melissa's office. Once she was sure the coast was clear, the pair went to work.

"I don't know how much time we have," Nicole said. "She could be back at any moment."

"Watch the door." Jake moved behind the desk and went to work on the computer. "It shouldn't take me long."

Despite the danger, Nicole couldn't deny the rush of staying on the lookout. And this was the first time that she and Jake had done anything but watch TV together and go to therapy. It was a refreshing change of pace.

"Okay, I'm in." Jake rubbed his hands together.

"Check the files on Kate and Rick," Nicole said. "We

JAMES HUNT

might be able to find some dirt on them that we can use as leverage."

"Good idea." Jake typed quickly at the keyboard, but a minute later, he had nothing. "They're clean."

Nicole turned away from her lookout post at the door and walked toward the desk. "What?"

Jake pointed to the screen. "She did a background check on both of them, and neither have any arrest records. A few traffic violations, but nothing major."

Nicole joined Jake on the other side of the desk, confirming the news for herself. "That doesn't make any sense. I heard Rick talking about going back to jail."

"Maybe you misheard?" Jake asked.

Nicole knew she hadn't misheard, but she couldn't ignore the facts staring her in the face. "What else can you find on the computer? Anything about wills for the family? There had to have been a reason why Rick dug up the graves."

Jake searched through the computer and found a file with some of the information regarding the burial of the family after the murders. "This might be something." He clicked on one of the documents, and they scrolled through it.

"It's the burial instructions," Nicole said.

"Looks like the family had requested to be buried together and with some of their most 'precious personal items.'" Jake raised his eyebrows. "Sounds like Rick might have been onto something."

"Keep looking." Nicole looked up toward the door,

afraid that Melissa would return and the pair of them would be whisked away in handcuffs.

"Whoa," Jake said.

Nicole returned her attention to the computer screen. "What did you find?"

"The motherlode," Jake answered. "Read that."

Jake leaned back, giving Nicole a better look at the screen. Her brows creased together as she concentrated.

"Aubrey Calhoun, the eldest daughter of Richard Calhoun, shall hold the key to the vault." Nicole raised her eyebrows. "Wow."

"The jewels might not have been buried with her, but the key to the vault was," Jake said. "Nic, this is huge!"

Nicole leaned back. "Maybe. But we still don't know where the vault is."

"Hey, one step at a time, huh?" Jake smiled. "We make a pretty good team."

Nicole returned the smile. "I guess we do."

Jake drummed his fingers on the desk for a minute, and she could tell that he wanted to say more. "Nic, listen, I know that we're still working on us, and like I said, I'll wait for as long as you need me to, but... how are you feeling now? About us?"

The question caught her off guard. "I'm not sure."

"Oh." Jake lowered his head, defeated.

Nicole shut her eyes. "That came out wrong." She took a breath and started again. "I think I'm learning to trust you again. But I'm not... all the way there."

Jake brightened a little bit. "Hey, it's progress, right?"

"Right," Nicole said, and then she straightened up, wanting to change the subject quickly. "We should probably get out of here."

"Yeah," Jake said, shutting down the computer and erasing his digital footprint. "We have some graves to dig up."

Nicole pressed her finger against Jake's chest, pushing him back a step. "Just so you know that you'll be doing the majority of the digging."

With the night as their cover, Nicole and Jake snuck their way out of the mansion and back toward the shed where Rick kept his tools. It wasn't locked, and with the help of the flashlight on Jake's phone, they located two shovels and then slipped into the darkened woods.

Nicole couldn't remember the exact location of the gravesite, but she knew that she headed due west from the shack, so she did her best to keep herself in a straight line until she found the gravesite or the pair of them got lost in the woods. She wasn't sure which would happen first.

But after a few minutes of moving forward, the forest opened up into a small clearing, which allowed the moonlight to break through the trees, and she saw the same hole that Rick had been digging.

Nicole stopped just short of the hole, and Jake peered over her shoulder to look down inside. "Watch that first step, it's a doozy."

Nicole saw that the grave was still empty. The detective must have gotten his wish to re-examine the body at the morgue. She hoped that he would find something that would point toward more tangible evidence against the person who killed Donald. She didn't like looking down at the empty grave, knowing who it was for. Donald had been kind to her, and from what she could tell, had been kind and dedicated to Ms. Calhoun's family. "He deserved better."

"Who?" Jake asked, catching up to her.

"Donald." Nicole didn't know why she was getting so emotional over this now. She had barely known the man. "Even if it turns out he did kill himself, he deserved better than to die alone in a bathroom all by himself. He spent his whole life caring for a woman after her family was killed, and he genuinely cared about her." A thick ball of grief filled the back of her throat. "You don't see loyalty like that anymore."

Nicole wiped her eyes on the shoulder of her sleeve, and then Jake grabbed her hand. She looked up at him, the moonlight outlining most of the features on his face. But the way that he was looking at her, he hadn't done that in a very long time.

"I'm sorry that I wasn't faithful to you," Jake said.

It was hard to tell in the darkness, but Nicole thought she saw tears glistening in his eyes. It was the first time that he'd shown any kind of emotion like that since their first therapy session when he broke down. At the time, Nicole was ashamed to admit that she had been glad to see him so wrecked. Because he had broken her heart.

But now, watching Jake grieve for the mistakes of his past not because of how it made himself feel, but how it had made her feel, Nicole felt no joy. Only sympathy. She knew how hard he had been working to re-establish their trust.

"And I'm sorry for making you suffer for so long," Nicole said, reaching for his face and wiping away the slick tears on his cheeks. "I know that you made a mistake, and I know how much that mistake drove you away, and I know that I haven't made it any easier on you over the past few months." She took a breath and then nodded. "We both need to be able to move on from the past and not dwell on the mistakes that were made. But I want you to know that… I forgive you."

It was the first time that Nicole had actually spoken the words to him aloud. She had already forgiven him a dozen times in her mind, but she had never said it to him directly.

And judging by the way that Jake teared up, bunching his face as the tears leaked from the corners of his eyes and rolled down his cheeks, she knew that she had waited too long to tell him.

The pair embraced, both of them holding onto one another tightly. They anchored one another, keeping safe in each other's arms. That was what married people were supposed to do, and that's what they would continue to do until they had made it out the other side.

The pair lingered in the embrace for a long time, and it wasn't until Nicole pulled back that Jake did as well. Both of them had been crying, both of them emotionally and physically exhausted. But it felt good to tell Jake that she forgave him. She didn't know why she had been holding on for that long, and it made her wish that she had forgiven him a long time ago.

"Well," Jake said, clearing his throat and sniffling a little bit. "I didn't expect that to happen."

Nicole smiled. "No. Me either."

Jake collected himself and waited until he was a little more composed before he bent down and gently kissed her lips. The motion was so light that Nicole barely felt the touch, but when he pulled away, she felt the absence of his warmth, and in that absence, the desire to feel that warmth again started to grow.

It was the first kiss that they had shared since the affair. It seemed that tonight was a slew of more first times. And while Nicole wanted to act on her desires, she knew that they had come out here to find answers.

Jake smiled, and Nicole smiled, and the pair laughed together like a pair of kids on a playground who had liked each other, but never said anything until now.

"Well," Jake said. "That was nice."

"It was," Nicole said, then took a breath. "We'll build on that later, okay?"

"Who says we have to wait?" Jake asked, his voice sliding into that lower octave the way that most men did whenever they were becoming intimate with a woman.

"The ghost that was communicating to me beyond the grave," Nicole answered.

"Oh," Jake said, clearing his throat. "Right."

"The rest of the family graves are a little farther." Nicole led Jake deeper into the darkness, unsure of the exact location where the graves were marked. "I don't know what Aubrey will have buried with her, but I'm hoping that—" Nicole stopped when her shoe landed in a mound of freshly turned dirt. She lifted her foot, staring at the imprint from the bottom of her sole. "What the hell?"

Jake joined her side and then pointed to the puffy soil that they stood on. "This soil was recently packed down from when Rick had dug up the graves." He pointed to the grave at the head of the fresh soil patch. "Is that one of the Calhoun family gravestones?"

Nicole walked toward it to try and get a better look, but even close up, it was hard to make out the weathered writing on the stones. She squinted, trying to read, and managed to make out the name, which was the largest print on the stone. "Richard Calhoun."

"We need to find Aubrey's grave," Jake said.

The pair fanned out, checking the headstones, and it was Jake who found the headstone in the darkness.

"Nic, over here," Jake said.

Nicole walked over to him and stared at the stone that marked the grave for the woman that Nicole had seen wandering around the house. "It's strange to think that her body is down there after… seeing her so many times."

"Are you all right?" Jake asked.

"I will be." Nicole picked up her shovel and then planted it into the dirt as the pair began to exhume the thirty-year-old grave.

27

A heavy layer of dirt and sweat had collected over both Nicole and Jake as they sank deeper into the earth and closer to Aubrey's coffin. Nicole had to take more breaks than Jake, her shoulders, arms, and lower back burning from fatigue. She couldn't imagine having to do this in the middle of the day. A lifetime of working inside with air conditioning had spoiled her. And judging by the way that Jake was huffing and puffing, she suspected that he felt the same way.

"How deep do they dig these things?" Jake panted between words and heaved another mound of dirt over the side. "I mean we've already had to have gone like what? Five feet?" He paused to take a break, stretching his back. "I don't think I can make it much further."

Nicole dug up more soil and pitched it out of the hole. "I don't know how much deeper it is, but we need to keep going." She also knew that they were low on time. They had already been at this for several hours, and she wasn't sure how much longer they would have until dawn. The last thing she wanted was to still be stuck out here when the sun came up. "We have to be close." Nicole raised her shovel and then speared it into the dirt, but instead of hearing the soft impact of soil, the tip of the shovel struck something solid.

Both Jake and Nicole exchanged a glance, and then both dropped to their knees and started clearing away the dirt to find the edges of the coffin.

Jake looked up from working and smiled. "It's just like Indiana Jones in the Raiders of the Lost Ark. You know that scene where they're digging for the well of the souls?"

"You know that I fall asleep during every movie we watch," Nicole answered, clearing out the top half of the coffin. "I don't remember that part."

Jake nodded. "Yeah. Now that I think about it, you probably wouldn't like what happened to them after the fact."

Once the edges were cleared, they had to dig a little deeper to be able to find the lip of the coffin's hedge so that they could open it. Jake used his shovel as a lever, and when he couldn't do it alone, Nicole added her own shovel to the cause.

Both of them pressed down, the coffin groaning from the pressure that they were putting on it, and then just when Nicole thought that she wouldn't be able to press down any harder than she already was, the resistance ended, and the shovel fell out of her hands as the coffin's lid popped open.

Jake tossed his shovel up and out of the hole and

then gripped the edge of the lid, but Nicole reached for his arm and pulled him back to stop. "Wait."

Frozen in his position, Jake looked up at her with a quizzical expression. "What? We came all the way out here and dug this thing up, don't you want to know what's inside?"

"I do," Nicole answered. "But I don't want to be disrespectful. We look, but we don't rummage through her stuff like it's a yard sale, okay?"

Jake nodded. "Got it."

"Okay." Nicole stepped off the lid and out of the way. "Open it."

Nicole wasn't sure what to expect when they looked inside the coffin. Her exposure with death had been limited to its first moments when the body had yet to start the decomposition process. Of course, most of the bodies she had seen were so close to death that Nicole was convinced that they had already been a part of the decomposition process, but she knew that was only the first phase, because a person who was living and dying looked completely different than a person who had already been dead for thirty years.

Expecting to find nothing but maggots finishing off the flesh of a corpse that had been rotting in the ground for thirty years, her senses blasted with the scent of decomposition, Nicole was surprised to find a face that was still intact, though the skin had become grey and thin over time.

Aubrey Calhoun's hair had thinned, and no longer held the vibrant brown that Nicole had seen when she was visited by her spirit, and the beauty had definitely faded. She was nothing but skin and skeleton now, dressed in a long black gown, with a similar black lace veil that covered her face. She looked peaceful in her final resting position, and Nicole was flooded with guilt at disturbing her, but she remembered that Aubrey had wanted her to do this.

"Do you see anything?" Jake asked, still panting, keeping a step back.

Nicole looked at him and saw the expression of fear on his face as he looked down at the body. She had never seemed him afraid, at least not like this. She had seen him express regret, but not genuine fear. But he wasn't as acclimated to death as Nicole was. She saw it every day. "It's okay to get closer, you know."

Jake shook his head. "I think I'll stay back here if that's all right with you."

Nicole turned away to hide her smirk and then studied Aubrey's body more closely. She gently patted down the corpse, and even though she had been around dead bodies her entire professional career, she was still hesitant before the first touch. The skin was thin, like paper mâché, and Nicole worried that if she pressed too hard, she would poke through the skin and spiders would crawl out and cover her own body.

Nicole took her time as she examined Aubrey, moving down the body slowly to ensure that she didn't overlook anything that would provide her with some positive information. But she didn't find anything.

Defeated, Nicole leaned back from the coffin, sitting in the dirt with her back against the hard soil behind her. "No key." She rubbed her face, smearing some of the dirt that she had collected onto her own face, and then took a deep breath.

"Hey," Jake said, keeping his voice gentle and soft. "It's going to be all right. We're going to figure this out."

Nicole looked at him. She knew that he was right. She was just letting all of this get to her head. She needed to calm down and take a breath. She picked herself up and then returned her attention to the coffin, then glanced down at Aubrey's hands, which were folded over one another on her stomach. Nicole leaned closer for a better look and realized that something was sticking out around the edges of the woman's frail palms. It wasn't noticeable at first because the paper was the same color as the black dress, so it blended in perfectly.

Nicole carefully reached for Aubrey's hand, and while she was gentle on her approach, she still heard the crack of bone as she lifted the palm, and even though she knew that Aubrey was long dead, Nicole winced from the noise.

Beneath the dead woman's palms was a piece of paper that had been flipped upside down, and the image was only black on the back, but when she turned the paper over in her hand, she saw that it was a photograph. A picture of Aubrey and her sister.

Jake stepped closer at the sight of the discovery and crouched by her side. "What is it?"

"It's not a key but... It's a picture of the Calhoun sisters," Nicole answered, studying the photograph, which had aged like the woman who had held it.

Jake frowned, pinching his eyebrows together as he got a closer look. "Looks like they're in a library."

Nicole tilted the picture from side to side, trying to see if there were any other clues to the photograph other than the location. "It's probably the library in the house."

Jake's eyes widened with excitement. "What if that's where the vault is hidden? Behind a bookcase or something?"

Nicole wasn't sure if that was true or not, but it could be possible. "I haven't really been in the library to get a good look around, but you might be right."

Jake nudged Nicole with his elbow, smiling. "Look at that. It's like our next clue!"

Nicole placed the picture back beneath Aubrey's palms, and Jake reached for her wrist to try and stop her.

"What are you doing?" Jake asked. "What if Rick comes back to look and he finds the picture?"

"We don't need it," Nicole answered, removing Jake's hand, and then finished tucking the picture back beneath Aubrey's frail palms. "She wanted to buried with this for a reason. I'm not going to take that away from her just because we think we found a clue."

Jake didn't protest, and then the pair closed the casket and climbed out of the hole. They picked up their shovels and started working to fill the hole that they had dug, and as Nicole dumped shovel after shovel of soil back on the casket, she had a feeling that she wasn't going to see Aubrey anymore. She felt as though the disruption of the grave had severed the tie of whatever connection that Nicole might have shared with the world beyond. She just hoped that she had enough information now to see this through to the end.

Once they were finished filling the hole, both Nicole and Jake had to use the shovels as a cane to help keep themselves upright.

"What do we do now?" Jake asked, smearing more dirt across his face as he tried to rid himself of the sweat that was collecting on his forehead.

"I think we need to take a break," Nicole answered. "We'll wash up, eat dinner, and then go check out the library. It's not going to go anywhere anytime soon."

Jake wanted to protest, but he didn't, and instead only nodded as they left the graveyard and returned to the guest house, dropping their shovels off at the shed along the way.

Dead tired by the time that she reached the guest house, Nicole didn't even stop to look at the dinner that had been dropped off by Kate, which was still covered on the kitchen table, but Jake made a beeline toward the food the moment he trailed in behind her.

"I don't think I can wait to eat," Jake said, lifting the cover of one of the plates, which still billowed steam from the warm contents beneath the dome. "My stomach is starting to eat itself. I need food before I pass out."

Nicole turned back toward the kitchen as she walked down the hallway to the bedroom. "Don't eat everything without me!"

"I'm not making any promises," Jake said.

Nicole staggered toward her room, overwhelmed by waves of exhaustion. She shed her clothes the moment she stepped into her bathroom and turned the hot water on as high as it would go.

She shut the bathroom door and let the room fill with steam before she finally entered the shower and started washing away the grime.

The long day rolled off of her in the form of the dirt and sweat that had collected on her skin, and circled the drain and disappeared. But while the physical effects of the day were gone, she couldn't shake off the fatigue.

Nicole lost track of time as she lingered in the shower, and when she saw that her fingertips had pruned from the steam, she finally turned off the water and then lingered in the sauna she had created.

It had always been hard for Nicole to block out her inner thoughts, and they'd been especially difficult for her to control since the affair, but at that moment, she had been blessed with the serenity of silence. It was a rare treat, and she basked in the warmth. She wondered if this was what it was like to be at peace with herself, to truly be free from the worry of everyday life.

Work contributed to most of her stress. Every day she poured so much of herself into her patients; there was barely anything left for herself. She loved her work, but it was emotionally draining.

Nicole hadn't said any of that in her therapy sessions with Jake, because she had been afraid of what that meant in her own relationship. It would mean that she shared the blame for Jake's infidelity. She knew that she hadn't been able to give him everything that he needed, and because of that, he turned to another person to fulfill what he wasn't getting at home.

Still dripping wet, Nicole reached for a towel as she stepped out of the shower and placed her bare feet on the plush bath mat.

Nicole dressed, putting on shorts and a t-shirt, and forgoing a bra, she walked over to the kitchen, a smile creasing her face as she neared the end of the hallway just before the kitchen entrance. "Jake, I hope you didn't eat everything because I'm starving—"

Nicole only made it two steps as she rounded the corner of the hallway when she saw Jake motionless on the floor, the chair knocked on the side behind him.

"Jake!" Nicole rushed to her husband and quickly felt for a pulse. It was faint, but it was there. She removed her fingers from his neck and then listened for him breathing, and when she saw his face, she knew exactly what happened.

Jake's face had swollen, his lips puffy and blue. He wasn't breathing because his airway had closed up. She looked to the plate that he had uncovered and realized that Kate must have put some shellfish in the food. He needed an epi-pen.

"Hang on, Jake!" Nicole quickly got up and then sprinted toward her bedroom. She always packed an epi-pen for him in case of an emergency.

Feet still slick from the shower, Nicole slipped and smacked hard against the tile when she rounded the corner of the hallway. She grunted, and the force of the impact sent a sharp pain through her leg but concentrated around her right hip.

Nicole struggled to get off the ground, and she limped forward when she finally got to her feet. She moved as fast as she could, but every time she put pressure on her hip, she was greeted with another fresh well of pain that brought tears to her eyes.

Nicole grabbed the epi-pen and then ripped it out of the paper bag as she quickly turned around and headed back toward the kitchen. She tried to keep track of the amount of time that had passed between when she checked Jake's airway, but the spill in the hallway combined with her own panic had blocked her ability to multitask. The only thing that she was concerned about was getting Jake the pen to make sure that he didn't die.

The limp subsided a little by the time that she returned to the kitchen, but flared up again when she promptly dropped to the floor and shoved the needle into Jake's arm, pressing down on the syringe.

Once all of the medicine was released, Nicole then removed the pen and reached for Jake's pulse. It had grown even weaker, and when she checked his airway, she found that he still wasn't breathing.

Nicole adjusted Jake's neck and head to open the airway, and then pinched his nose as she gave him mouth to mouth. His lungs filled with air, and Nicole continued to monitor his pulse. But the longer that Jake went without breathing, she started to panic.

Even if she was able to call for an ambulance, she didn't have the confidence that they would make it all the way out here in time to actually do anything to save him.

"Don't leave me, Jake." Nicole whimpered before she puffed another breath into his motionless body, pressing her red lips against his blue ones. "Please don't leave me. I need you back." She sobbed between breaths, but when he still wouldn't respond, she collapsed onto his chest.

In all the years that Nicole had cared for the sick and dying, she had witnessed more grief than any other person she knew. She had seen what the death of a loved one looked like and how it affected the people who cared for them after they had passed, but even with all of that wealth of knowledge, she never realized how difficult it would be for her to let go of her own family members.

"I'm so sorry," Nicole sobbed into Jake's chest, bunching his shirt beneath her fists. "I love you so much. I love you more than anything in this world—"

Jake drew in a gasp that caused his body to tremble, and Nicole jumped off of him and allowed him to roll to his side where he caught his breath.

"Jake?" Nicole reached for his shoulder. "Oh my God, Jake!"

When Jake finally turned around to look at her, his lips weren't blue anymore, but his face was still slightly puffy from the allergic reaction, which caused his left eye to swell shut. But he was alive.

Nicole wrapped her arms around her husband, and then shut her eyes as she whispered her thanks to whatever god that was listening to her prayers.

Eventually, Nicole let Jake go and helped him over to the couch in the living room. He might have been alive, but he was still in bad shape. She squatted down in front of him as he struggled to keep himself upright on his own steam, his non-swollen eye blinking.

"What happened?" Jake asked, his words still a little slurred from his swollen tongue.

"I think Kate put shellfish in your food," Nicole answered. "I think she was trying to kill you."

Nicole touched his knee, and then he placed one of his swollen hands over hers.

"You saved me," Jake said, his one good eye watering.

Nicole kissed the top of his hand, then took a moment to catch her breath, and she realized that the people who did this to her husband were still nearby. "I'll be right back."

Nicole rushed to the bedroom and retrieved her phone and then tried to search for reception as she walked back to the living room. With no signal found, she returned to Jake, who still had a dazed and confused look in his eyes. "Jake, do you have your phone? Is it on you?"

Jake stared at her for a moment before he finally tried to fumble his swollen fingers into his right pocket. But Nicole stopped him before he could reach inside, and then pulled the phone out herself. She checked the reception on his screen and found his phone roaming too.

"Shit," Nicole said, and then glanced outside through the kitchen windows. It was dark, and she didn't like the idea of going out there on her own, but she knew that she needed to call the police. She turned back to Jake. "I'm going outside to make a call."

"No," Jake mumbled and lurched forward, but because of his fragile condition, she was easily able to push him back into the cushion.

"I'll be fine. I'll stay close." Nicole stood and kissed his forehead. "I'll be right back."

Nicole headed out the door, both phones in her hands, holding both up as high as she could, searching for any hope of a signal while simultaneously keeping her eyes peeled for a potential ambush.

"C'mon, c'mon, c'mon!" Nicole shook both phones in her hands, trying to get better reception, but no matter how far she marched toward the house, she still had nothing.

And just when Nicole thought she might have to venture into the house to try and use a landline, a piercing scream erupted from inside the house, draining the blood from Nicole's cheeks. She was paralyzed until the scream erupted from the house again, and she sprinted toward it, unsure who was being murdered this time.

icole entered through one of the back doors at the mansion, and the blood-curdling scream was even louder once she was inside. Blinded by all of the house lights, she realized that the screams were coming from the first floor, which meant that Ms. Calhoun was still safe upstairs.

The woman screaming was Kate.

Nicole sprinted down the hall toward the kitchen, Kate's screams now dwarfed by the throaty roars of a man and the heavy metal clanging of dishes and pots and pans. She reached the kitchen with no plan of action, armed with two phones that still had zero cell reception.

Nicole skidded to a stop when she entered the kitchen, and she saw that Rick had his hands around Kate's throat, choking the life out of her. Kate's cheeks were so red that Nicole thought that the woman's brains were going to pop out of the top of her head.

Rick had all of his attention on Kate and didn't

notice that Nicole had walked into the kitchen. Knowing that she didn't have much time to spare, Nicole picked up one of the kitchen knives and then sprinted toward Rick.

Leading with the tip of the blade, Nicole was halfway toward Rick when Kate locked eyes with Nicole, which triggered Rick to turn around to see who was behind him. He saw the knife in Nicole's hands and dropped Kate to intercept the blade before it pierced his back.

Nicole screamed as she lunged forward with the blade, and while Rick was able to catch her wrists in time to stop the worst of it, she still managed to slice his love handles before he knocked her to the ground with a backhand and wrenched the knife from her grip.

Nicole hit the ground, stars popping in her eyes, and the pain from her hip had suddenly gone numb as she lay on the cold tile. Her vision cleared in just enough time for her to see a dark figure reach for her from the shadows. And by the time she realized it was Rick, he already had his hands around her neck, choking her the way that he had been choking Kate.

"Dumb bitch!" Rick bore down on his grip, his own face red as he climbed on top of her, using his massive frame to keep her pinned down. He leaned close enough for Nicole to smell his sweat and body odor. "I should have killed you in the woods when I had the chance, buried you out there." The rage subsided from his expression for a moment, and Nicole felt his length along her stomach. "I guess I should have some fun before it's all over. Give you one last thrill?" He chuckled. "A little something to remember me by."

Nicole squirmed and kicked, writhing her body beneath Rick to try and get away, but he was too big, too strong.

Keeping one hand on her neck, Rick reached for Nicole's pants, yanking them down around her thighs, revealing her underwear.

Exposed, Nicole kicked and bucked even harder, the steady pressure rising in her head from Rick choking her, and she grew more frantic as she saw him reach for his own pant buckle. She glanced around the floor, her peripheral vision blurred from the pressure in her head, as she looked around for anything that she could grab and use to defend herself. She couldn't find the knife that she had used to attack Rick after it had been dropped to the floor. But that didn't mean that she was completely helpless in fighting back.

With only her nails to defend herself, Nicole used both hands to dig into Rick's forearm, clamping down with all of her strength, and then raked downward with her fingers like claws, drawing blood on his arm.

Rick released Nicole's throat, and he screamed from the pain. "Damn you!"

Knowing that she didn't have much time, Nicole kneed Rick's groin, which triggered an even bigger scream from the piece of scum hovering over her, and he collapsed to his side next to Nicole on the tile.

Nicole tried to scramble away, catching her breath with every raspy inhale as she was resigned to crawling along the tile. She didn't have a destination in mind other than to get away from Rick, but she didn't make it very far when she realized that Rick had collapsed onto her leg.

Nicole yanked her leg free, Rick still wallowing on his side, both hands on his groin as he moaned in pain. Her own mind was swirling, and she knew that she had bought herself a little time, not much, but enough to try and turn the tables in her favor.

Blinking away her own pain and the blurry images of the kitchen, Nicole did her best to keep her wits. She needed to think quickly. Call for help? She still hadn't gotten a signal on either cell phone when she entered the kitchen. She could scream, hoping that Ms. Calhoun or Jake would be able to hear her, but her voice was so raspy she couldn't even muster a whisper. The only option was to find another weapon and put Rick down for good. And while killing him would put an end to discovering what he was doing, she didn't see any other way in how she was going to get out of this scenario. She needed to move, and she needed to do it quickly before she ran out of time.

But while Nicole was processing her next moves, struggling on all fours as she slowly crawled across the kitchen tile, Rick had been collecting himself, regaining his strength, and while he was still wounded, he was still strong and powerful enough to make Nicole regret what she had done to him.

"No!" With one long arm, Rick snatched Nicole's ankle, and with one powerful tug, she was flattened against the tile again. "You're not going anywhere!"

Nicole kicked back as she lay on her stomach, but

she was helpless as he pulled her back toward him and then flipped her around to her back. She was still disoriented from the altercation, but she was lucid enough to see the pair of angry eyes that had once been full of lust filled with nothing but blind rage.

Rick used both hands to constrict Nicole's throat, and her eyes bulged as the pressure returned to her head. She couldn't think straight. She couldn't do anything but watch as her vision slowly darkened.

Nicole struggled against him, but she knew that this was it. The last image that Nicole would see in this world would be the evil face staring down at her. She couldn't believe that after everything that had happened, she would die here.

But just before Nicole's vision went completely black, she saw something smack against the side of Rick's head, the force of the blow powerful enough to knock him off of her as he rolled to the side.

Nicole coughed and gagged, her body and mind numbed from the lack of oxygen, but she was aware of another pair of hands on her, dragging her backward, away from Rick and the kitchen.

She managed to make it to a wall and was then propped up against it, and with her vision returning to normal, she saw Jake kneeling in front of her. She reached up and touched his cheek, making sure that he wasn't some kind of apparition. But it was him. He was real.

Face swollen, Jake did a quick scan of Nicole's body, his speech slightly slurred. "Are you all right?"

Nicole tried to answer. Only raspy gasps came from

her throat, and when she realized that she couldn't speak, she nodded.

"The phones," Jake said. "Where are the phones?"

Nicole heard the question, but she was distracted by the lumbering figure that had risen from the floor behind Jake. Her vision was still blurred, and at first, she thought she imagined it, but her eyes widened in terror as Rick sprinted toward Jake. She opened her mouth to warn him, but only raspy breaths escaped.

Jake turned around just in time to be greeted by Rick's fist, the powerful blow cracking him across the jaw and then knocking him sideways.

Blood dripped from Rick's scalp, the top part of his head matted with blood from where Jake had cracked him over the head. He staggered a step, breathing heavy, his black beady eyes staring down at Jake with an animal rage. He wasn't a man anymore, he had crossed over into a different plane, and he saw nothing but red. He was a bull in the center of the pit, ready to charge and kill anything that got in his way. And right now Jake was in that path.

Rick turned his blood-red gaze to Nicole. "I'll kill him first. Make you watch. Then you're next." He walked toward Jake, who was struggling to get up from the ground, and then punched him again, this time landing a swift cross on the other side of his cheek, and then knocked him to the floor once more.

Helpless, Nicole tried to stand up, but the strength in her legs had vanished, and she fell right back down on her bottom. She could only watch as Jake struggled to defend himself against the larger and stronger man.

Nicole's heart cracked as she watched him take blow after blow, doing everything that he could to keep Rick away from her. But she knew that he couldn't keep up for much longer. He was reaching the end of his rope, and when the pair locked eyes as he went down for the final time, she saw him mouth 'I love you.'

Nicole mouthed the words back, and Rick stepped over Jake, lording over him and prepared to deliver the final blow. But Rick staggered for a moment. He was tired, exhausted from the beatings that he had doled out, but also wounded from the crack to the head. If she could just reach him, try and hurt him with one last-ditch effort, she thought that she might be able to turn the tide. But she was fading as well, and her one hope was that she wouldn't be conscious when Rick killed her or did whatever he fantasized of doing to her.

But just before Nicole blacked out, she saw a blurred image sprint toward Rick, something big and grey in its hand. The blurred figured clashed against Rick, collapsing the big man to the floor next to Jake.

For a moment she thought that it might have been Ms. Calhoun, that somehow the old woman had gotten out of bed and made it down the stairs to save all of them. Then she thought that it could have been the ghost of Aubrey Calhoun, coming to rescue them at the last moment. She also considered that it was nothing more than the final wishes of her dying mind.

$\mathcal{I}$t was the light that brought Nicole out of her daze. She was numb but was aware of hands touching her, of bodies around her. Her first instinct was to fight back, thinking that it was Rick trying to have his way with her. She quickly swung her arms around, smacking her hands into the pair of bodies that were on either side of her, but instead of resistance, both of them backed off, and she heard not the angered roar of Rick's voice, but the level-headed concern of someone else.

"Mrs. Harper?" The blurred figure stared at her. "It's Detective Salvor."

Nicole blinked a few times. Her mouth was dry, and her heart was hammering in her chest. But when her vision finally cleared, she calmed down a little bit, because she did see Detective Salvor hunched down, looking at her, and she saw the paramedic next to him, who had been shining the light in her eyes.

Detective Salvor raised his eyebrows. He looked

tired, the bags under his eyes pulling the rest of his face down. "Can you hear me?"

Nicole swallowed, and it hurt. She winced, then nodded. "Yes." The answer came out in a raspy whisper, but she was glad to know that while her voice was raw, it had returned. She took a moment to gather her strength, sorting through the million questions that raced through her mind until she came upon the only one that mattered. "Is Jake alive?"

"Yes," Detective Salvor answered. "He's been beaten up pretty bad, but he's going to be okay."

Nicole tried to stand. "I need to see him."

Both the detective and the paramedic immediately put their hands on her shoulders and set her down.

"You need to let the paramedic finish examining you," Detective Salvor said. "Once he clears you, I'll take you out to the ambulance to see your husband."

When the detective got up to leave, Nicole reached for his arm, stopping him. "Don't let Jake go before I see him."

The detective smiled sadly and then patted Nicole's hand. "I won't."

Nicole let him go and then relaxed a little bit as the paramedic went about checking her vitals. Her blood pressure was still slightly elevated, and there was some bruising around her neck from where Rick had grabbed her. Aside from those larger injuries, the only thing else wrong with her was a few scrapes and bruises.

Nicole was still in the kitchen, and from her position on the floor, she saw police officers snapping pictures, looking around the crime scene. She glanced over to where she had seen Jake on the floor, Rick towering over him, ready to deliver that kill shot, and then she remembered the blur that had come in at the last moment and crumpled the big man to the ground.

"Kate," Nicole said, whispering to herself.

The paramedic had the stethoscope in his ears, checking her heart rate and breathing. "What was that?"

Nicole shook her head. "Nothing." But the question lingered on the tip of her tongue. Had it been Kate that had come running to save her and Jake? Had she been wrong about Rick and Kate working together? Or was it an argument between partners who couldn't agree on how to get rid of the troublesome married couple that was slowly exposing their plans?

"All right, Mrs. Harper, you are good to go." The paramedic stood and then helped Nicole do the same. She took a moment to steady her legs, the floor uneven at first, but once she was up for a few minutes, the world corrected itself. And once she felt better about standing on her own two feet, she walked out of the kitchen in search of her husband, and for answers.

The scene outside of the estate was something that Nicole had never seen at the mansion since she arrived. Crowded.

Police and emergency vehicles clogged the driveway, their red and blue lights painting the ground and the house itself the same color. She saw Jake propped up in a gurney in the back of an ambulance, another paramedic tending to the injuries that he sustained during his fight with Rick.

Nicole broke out into a run when she saw him, and her heart leaped from her chest when she realized that he was awake. But while the swelling from the shellfish had gone down, they had been replaced with the welts that Rick had left behind. Still, it was a miracle he was alive.

When she moved closer, she saw the bandages around his head, and the splint on his leg, which kept it straight and immobile, along with his right arm in a sling. Despite all of his injuries, he smiled when Nicole reached the ambulance.

Crying, Nicole climbed up into the ambulance and wrapped her arms around Jake's neck, squeezing so tight that she heard him groan.

"Sorry." Nicole pulled back, wincing as if she had hurt herself too. She wiped away the tears and then got a better look at him. "Oh no, just look at you." She was afraid to touch him, unsure of just how severe his injuries had become.

"I'll be all right," Jake said, then gestured to the arm. "It's just a shoulder sprain, and the leg brace is only a precaution until I can get an X-ray."

Nicole couldn't believe his condition, and the longer that he stared down at his broken body, the more she realized how much punishment he had taken for her. "You saved me. He would have killed me if you hadn't shown up."

Jake gently grazed Nicole's cheek with his good arm. "So long as you're safe, it was worth it."

Nicole leaned into his touch. It was good, familiar, and warm. She wanted to kiss him hard at that moment, but unsure if she could stop herself from causing it to escalate, she settled for a peck on the cheek instead.

The paramedic removed his stethoscope and looked at Nicole. "We're going to take him down to the hospital. You can ride along with us if you want."

"Actually, I need to speak to her." Detective Salvor appeared at the open doors, speaking to the paramedic before looking at Nicole. "I can take you there once I'm done."

"No," Jake said. "I want you to stay here. Get some rest. I'll probably just pass out by the time that you get there, and sleeping in a hospital is never comfortable."

Nicole grabbed his hand. "I'm coming."

Jake smirked. "All right."

Nicole kissed his hand and then climbed out of the ambulance. The doors swung shut, and she stood in the driveway watching it leave until she no longer saw the red and blue lights.

"Mrs. Harper?" Detective Salvor touched her elbow, pulling her attention back to the matter at hand. "I need for you to go through step by step of what happened."

Nicole nodded, and she didn't leave anything out, not now, except for the premonitions. But she told him everything else. The threat made by Rick when she was alone in the woods after she followed him out there, the argument between him and Kate that she heard in the kitchen, and the fact that Ms. Calhoun did speak when Nicole showed her the family albums. "I know it sounds hard to believe, but when you speak to Jake, he'll be able to confirm everything I just told you."

Detective Salvor raised his eyes. "Jake heard what Ms. Calhoun said?"

"Yes," Nicole answered, and then she remembered that Ms. Calhoun was in the house during the entire ordeal, and her thoughts turned to the old woman. "Is she all right?"

Detective Salvor nodded. "She's fine. In fact, she was asleep when the authorities arrived. She was a little spooked until Melissa showed up, and then she calmed down."

Melissa, Nicole thought. She couldn't imagine what the lawyer would have to say when the pair spoke. Nicole imagined that she would be fired on the spot, maybe even dragged through the legal process, but now that it was over, she was ready to face the consequences. She had practically broken every house rule, but in the end, it helped save an old woman from whatever Kate and Rick had planned.

"Where's the chef?" Nicole asked, glancing around the yard.

"We took her to the station." Detective Salvor was consulting his notes. "She claimed that Rick attacked her."

"Did she also tell you that she was sleeping with him?" Nicole asked.

Salvor nodded. "She did. She said that she thought Rick was planning something and was getting nervous about what he might do, so she tried talking to him about it and there was a big fight."

Nicole figured that might have been the argument that she overheard. "She tried to kill my husband."

Surprise flashed over the detective's face. "Do you have proof of this?"

Nicole gestured to the guest house behind the mansion. "The food that she cooked for our dinner had shellfish in it. Jake is extremely allergic. We disclosed that to her, and she did it anyway."

"I'll be sure to bring that up," Salvor said.

"Detective." Melissa appeared in Nicole's peripheral vision. Even with the late hour, she was immaculately put together. Hair and makeup done, she looked like she might have been ready to go out on a date, but that would mean the robot of law would require human interaction, and Nicole never sensed that Melissa had wanted that sort of thing.

"Did you have the file for me?" Salvor asked.

"Yes." Melissa handed over a vomit green folder, the same kind that Nicole had seen in her office when they first arrived. It was what she had used to store all of the employee information on the folks who worked for the estate. "I think you'll find everything that you need."

"Thank you." Detective Salvor nodded and then turned to Nicole. "Mrs. Harper, if I have any more questions about tonight's events, I'll be sure to reach out, but it looks like we'll have everything handled from here on out. I wish you and your husband nothing but the best."

And just like that, the detective that had doubted

everything that Nicole had to say up until the very end shook her hand and then disappeared.

But there were still pieces missing, things that Nicole needed to understand, and the only person that could answer them was the least likely person that would talk: the lawyer.

"What did you give him?" Nicole asked.

Melissa pursed her lips, and for a moment, Nicole didn't think the woman would talk, but she finally released the words like water spurting from a leak in a dam. "Turns out Rick Dunst isn't who he said he was. It was a fake name. His real name was Kevin Horner. He is a convicted felon from Oregon. He managed to get some convincing papers, though, because my people believed the documents he provided were authentic. It wasn't until I arrived here and took a closer look at his paperwork that I realized the documents were forged. And then the detective was able to identify him through fingerprints because he was already in the system."

Nicole frowned. "What about Kate?"

"Her background was clean, and from what I've heard the detective say about her, she was just someone who got caught up with a bad love affair. Something I'm sure we've all done."

Part of it made sense, especially the fact of Rick's true identity. Nicole knew that he was a violent man, and now this proved it.

"So he was after the jewels?" Nicole asked.

"Yes," Melissa answered. "Apparently he believed that they might have been buried with the family members themselves, but when that didn't pan out, he started to become more violent and angry."

"And Donald?" Nicole asked. "Did Rick, I mean Kevin, kill him?"

"I don't know," Melissa answered. "He hasn't pleaded guilty to anything, but it's possible. I know that Detective Salvor will be questioning him about all the events that have transpired at the mansion over the past two days."

Nicole watched Melissa, who she found was surprisingly calm, maybe even a little nervous. It was a far cry from the confident woman who had greeted them upon their arrival to the estate. But even with the lawyer's shift in demeanor, Nicole knew that there was something else coming, something that Melissa wanted to say.

"I know that I can be difficult sometimes," Melissa said. "But I think it's important for you to understand that the Calhoun family and my own have been inter-twined for a long time. My father was the lawyer for Mr. Calhoun, and after he passed last year, I took on the family business and was charged with taking care of the estate." She lowered her eyes, almost as if she were afraid to look at her directly. "I create strict rules because I know how fragile Ms. Calhoun is. And she is also one of my family firm's wealthiest clients, so it's also out of self-preservation that I get so defensive." She rubbed her forehead, grimacing. "I can't believe I didn't catch the notes about the groundskeeper. It was stupid. A stupid mistake."

Nicole wasn't sure if the lawyer was trying to get

her to feel empathy for her or not, but Nicole still wasn't sure if she was buying it.

Melissa took a breath and composed herself, returning to the curt woman that Nicole had grown to know. "I tell you all of this because what you have done for Ms. Calhoun went above and beyond the call of duty. If you hadn't come in when you did, then Rick planned on kidnapping Ms. Calhoun and holding her for ransom. You saved her from that. And I am forever in your debt."

It wasn't the scolding that Nicole had anticipated.

Melissa cleared her throat and then twisted the tips of her fingers on her left hand. "And I hope that we can come to an arrangement outside of the courts to handle any... compensation that you might require in order not to press any charges about the... difficult working environment."

And there it was, Nicole thought. The reason why Melissa had been trying to butter her up. She was worried that Nicole and Jake would sue her, instead of the other way around. "I'm sure we could work something out."

Melissa smiled. "Good." She extended her hand. "Well, you can stay here as long as you like, but I'm sure you'll be wanting to move on to another assignment."

Nicole nodded. "I'll wait until my husband is well enough to travel." She glanced to the second-floor room, again seeing the outline of a woman in the window staring down at her, but this was someone who Nicole knew was real. "Until then, I'd like to continue to care for Ms. Calhoun. If that's all right?"

"Of course. I'm sure she would love to have you." Melissa wiped her palms on the front of her jacket and then offered a small bow. "Thank you again, Mrs. Harper. I know I speak for Ms. Calhoun when I tell you that she is forever in your debt."

Nicole lingered out on the lawn for a moment after Melissa had gone, watching all of the lights bathe the world in the blues and reds. She was awake now, but she knew that it was only from the lingering drops of adrenaline that had flooded through her system from the fight and the fact that she had made it out of all of this alive.

She had wanted to go to the hospital, but she didn't think she would be awake by the time she arrived. She thought that maybe Jake was right, and she should just stay here. Plus, she needed to make sure that Ms. Calhoun got back to bed.

30

*M*ost of the police and emergency workers had left by the time Nicole reached the second floor. She didn't bother going back to the kitchen, which she knew was a mess that would still need to be cleaned up.

When she arrived at Ms. Calhoun's room, Nicole expected to find the old woman still at the window, staring out into the night and watching the strangers that had come to her home. But to her surprise, Ms. Calhoun was already lying in bed, the covers pulled up to her chin, though she was still awake.

"Are you all right?" Nicole asked, lingering in the doorway. She wasn't sure if the old woman would answer or not, but she thought she'd give it a try.

Ms. Calhoun only stared back at her, looking more like a frightened child than an elderly woman. She didn't speak, but she shook her head.

Nicole smiled and then entered the room and sat on the edge of Ms. Calhoun's bed. "I know you've been through a lot, but you don't have to worry. The bad people are gone."

Ms. Calhoun slowly lowered the covers from her chin and then studied Nicole for a moment. When she was finished, she removed her arm from beneath the covers and then grabbed Nicole's hand. "Will you stay?"

Nicole's heart softened, and she nodded. "Of course."

Ms. Calhoun smiled and then reclaimed her hand, placing it back beneath the covers, and closed her eyes and got a little more comfortable as she fell asleep.

There was so much more that Nicole had wanted to tell Ms. Calhoun. She wanted to tell her how sorry she was about her family, and for thinking that the old woman had anything to do with the murders thirty years ago. Because while she still hadn't proved who killed the Calhoun family, Nicole no longer believed Margaret Calhoun had anything to do with it.

Nicole lingered there on Ms. Calhoun's bed, watching her sleep. She hoped that the old woman found some kind of peace now that all of this was over, but there was still something troubling in the back of Nicole's mind that she just couldn't figure out.

What did Aubrey really do the night of the murders? Was she the killer? And if she was, then why did she help Nicole find out the truth about Rick and Kate?

With her adrenaline fading, Nicole's eyelids drooped. She needed sleep.

Nicole found one of the spare bedrooms, not

wanting to walk out to the guest house where she would be alone.

Nicole shut the door behind her, blocking out the light in the hallway, and crawled beneath the covers. The sheets were cool as she laid her head down on the pillow. When she closed her eyes, she drifted off to sleep immediately.

_N_icole wasn't sure how long she was asleep when she was awoken by the frigid cold, but the room was still pitch black, and she couldn't stop shivering. Nicole blinked, wiping away the sleep in her eyes. Her mind was glazed with the exhaustion of coming out of a deep sleep.

She knew that she should get out of bed to see if Jake had called, and to check the time, but the cold made her linger beneath the covers. But she stayed awake and stared out the window, and the longer she stared, the more she realized that something was falling outside.

Nicole sat up, not hearing the pitter of rain on the roof or against the window, and squinted in the darkness. She removed the covers, exposing herself to the cold room, and gingerly walked to the glass and realized that it wasn't rain that was falling.

It was snow.

Nicole's heart hammered, and with her back turned

toward the door, she felt that familiar pinprick at the base of her skull, and she turned around to find Aubrey Calhoun standing in the room.

The woman said nothing, but there was something different about her. She was no longer translucent. She looked more solid. More real.

Nicole walked toward her, frowning. "Where am I?"

Aubrey said nothing. She only smiled and then turned for the door.

Light flooded into the room when Aubrey stepped into the hallway, leaving Nicole alone in the bedroom, shivering with her questions.

Nicole followed, but when she stepped out into the hallway, Aubrey was gone. Instead, she found holly and figs running along the banisters, and wreathes adorned all the doors in the hall. They were Christmas decorations. Boisterous laughter drifted up the stairway, and Nicole headed downstairs to investigate.

The laughter grew louder on Nicole's descent, different voices blurring together in the way that busy conversation tended to when you were listening from far away.

When she reached the first floor, Nicole followed the voices to the dining room and found it filled with a family enjoying a very large and sumptuous Christmas feast. It was the Calhoun's last Christmas together. Nicole wasn't sure how she was here, but she knew that she was meant to witness what happened all those nights ago. Aubrey had pulled her from her sleep and transported her back to the night of the murders.

Mr. and Mrs. Calhoun sat on either end of the table,

and Aubrey and a much younger Ms. Calhoun sat on the sides across from one another. Everyone was all smiles and laughs.

Nicole stood by the door, watching them interact with one another, and she saw how happy everyone looked. And then she realized that if she was here, then maybe they could hear her.

"Hey." Nicole waved her arms, walking right up to the table to try and get their attention. "Hey!" But none of them would look at her. She wasn't brought here to save them, she was brought here to watch them die.

Nicole walked over to Margaret Calhoun, listening to her chat away about her day at work. She had gotten a position at her father's company, and she was enjoying the work. She was so pretty, much prettier than the pictures revealed.

"Richard." A voice pulled everyone's attention to the entrance of the dining room. A woman held a pistol in one hand, her large jacket damp from snow, wearing large snow boots.

Everyone in the room stared at the woman with a mixture of shock and confusion. No one spoke at first, no one even moved. But then Mr. Calhoun slowly stood from his chair.

"Maggie," Richard said, his tone very cautious. "What are you doing here?"

Nicole had heard that name before. It took a moment for her to place the name and the face, but then she remembered the photograph that Jake had shown her. That was Maggie Farr. Melissa's mother.

"What?" Maggie asked. "You don't want me here?"

Ms. Calhoun turned from her seat, and she rose as well. "Maggie, I don't know what this is about but—"

"Shut up!" Maggie shouted and turned the pistol on Ms. Calhoun. "Of course you don't know what this is about! None of you know what this is about. And that's because he's done such a good job of hiding it." She looked at Richard. "But it's time to confess, Richard. It's time to finally come clean."

Mr. Calhoun's face reddened, but Nicole couldn't tell if it was from fear or from anger. "Maggie, this is enough. Put that gun down and leave this house at once—"

Maggie raised the pistol to the ceiling and fired one shot, sending some dust and plaster down over her head, making all the women scream, then she lowered the weapon and pointed it back at Richard. "You don't get to tell me what to do!"

Everyone froze, the gunshot cracking the air like shattering ice. Nicole studied everyone's reaction carefully and found that the only person that wasn't surprised by this violent visitor was Mr. Calhoun.

Richard raised his right hand to calm his girls. "It's all right." He stood slowly. "Maggie. I understand that you're upset—"

"You understand nothing." Maggie twisted her face in an expression that was half-anger, half-grief. Madness overrode her reason, and she pointed the gun at Mrs. Calhoun. "Tell her, Richard."

Mrs. Calhoun frowned, looking from Maggie to her husband with a puzzled look. "Tell me what?"

"Dad?" Aubrey asked. "What's going on?"

Richard stepped from around the table, maintaining a smooth, slow, and methodical pace toward Maggie. "If you're upset with me, then that's fine. But my wife and my daughters don't have anything to do with this."

Maggie had the gun trained on Mr. Calhoun now. Tears filled her eyes, and the snow that had collected on her shoes, jacket, and hair were melting. "I think your wife and daughters have everything to do with this."

Mrs. Calhoun was becoming restless. "Richard, you need to tell me—"

"Quiet, Bethany!" Richard barked the words harshly but kept his attention on Maggie. It was almost as if his gaze on her kept the woman from pulling the trigger. "Aubrey, Margaret, you two take your mother into the next room. Now."

"No, everyone stays, Richard," Maggie said. "You tell them the truth or I kill them." She aimed the gun at Margaret. "I'll count to three."

Margaret hyperventilated, looking to her father. "Daddy?"

"One," Maggie said.

Richard's calm demeanor shattered. "Dammit, Maggie, enough!"

"Two," Maggie said.

Margaret started to cry, and Aubrey reached for her sister's hand across the table.

Nicole could do nothing as she watched the scene unfold, but she was certain that Maggie would pull the trigger. She had a wild look in her eye that was reserved for only those that had reached the end of their rope. She had nothing left to lose.

"Three—"

"I had an affair," Richard said.

The fear on Mrs. Calhoun's face shifted from terror to the incredulous disbelief that accompanied such a heart-wrenching betrayal.

"Richard..." Mrs. Calhoun's mouth hung open, lingering there as she struggled to find the words.

A thin smile creased Maggie's lips, and she drew in a deep, satisfying breath, the kind that released a weight that had been pressing her chest down for a very long time.

"That's good, Richard," Maggie said, keeping the weapon trained on Margaret. "Now, tell them the rest."

Nicole empathized with Mrs. Calhoun. She recognized that expression she wore, that one that hollowed you out, turning you into a glass shell that was slowly cracking with every second that you had to linger with the shame and embarrassment that accompanied the infidelity.

"What else, Richard?" Ms. Calhoun's voice trembled.

Mr. Calhoun had lost all of his confidence, leaving him exposed and vulnerable.

Ms. Calhoun slammed her fist on the table, rattling the dishes and glassware. "What else!"

Maggie aimed the pistol back on Richard and then crossed the room, placing the barrel of the gun a mere three inches from his forehead. "Say it. Tell them about her. Tell them the truth."

The three Calhoun women looked at one another nervously, the daughters still holding onto one another by their hands across the table.

Tears were rolling down Maggie's cheeks, and she struggled to keep the weapon steady in her hand. "Tell them, Richard. I want to hear you say it out loud. I want to hear you acknowledge the truth. For once, I want to hear you say it out loud because you know that I'm right. You've always known."

Mr. Calhoun straightened his back and stiffened his jaw, a little bit of that confidence returning.

The room was held hostage by both Maggie and Richard's hidden secret. But the longer that Nicole studied Mr. Calhoun's face, the more she realized that he wasn't going to speak. Whatever truth that Maggie wanted him to reveal would be buried with him.

And Maggie must have sensed that as well because she pressed the barrel of the weapon against his forehead and Nicole was convinced that she was going to pull the trigger.

But that couldn't be right. Because Nicole remembered that the family was butchered with a knife.

And almost as if Nicole's thought transferred to Mr. Calhoun through some psychic connection, the man reached for Maggie's wrist, moving it to the side, and wrestled the weapon out of her hand.

"No!" Maggie screamed and tried to fight back, but the moment that the weapon was out of her hands, she lost her power, and she was tossed to the floor.

The three Calhoun women all stood from their seats, both sisters with their hands covering their mouths. But Mrs. Calhoun looked at her husband, who was now unloading the bullets from the pistol.

"Bethany, take the girls out of the room and call the police," Richard said.

Nicole saw that Mrs. Calhoun wanted to say more, but another harsh glare from Richard caused the wife to lead her daughters out of the room, both of whom followed with hasty, jerking movements.

Maggie lay on her stomach on the floor, sobbing, hands balled into fists. She kept her head hung low, slowly swinging it back and forth in the cadence of a person who was wallowing in the defeat of the end.

"You shouldn't have come here, Maggie," Mr. Calhoun said. "I told you that it was over."

Maggie kept her back to Mr. Calhoun as she pushed herself to all fours and crawled toward the table. "You're a bastard." She reached one hand up to the table and used it to help pull herself up.

From where Nicole stood on the other side of the table, she had a front-row seat to the expression on Maggie's face. Tears and snot were glued to the woman's cheeks and upper lip. She was a ragged mess, defeated in her mission for revenge.

But Nicole knew that Maggie wasn't finished. Because if this was the night that the Calhoun family died, then the bloodshed was just beginning.

And because Nicole knew how Maggie was going to murder the family, her eyes found the carving knife next to the turkey that was within arm's reach of Maggie.

"She's your daughter," Maggie said, her eyes on the

knife and her back to Mr. Calhoun. "She is yours, and you know it."

Richard sighed, slowly walking toward Maggie, the gun now empty and held limply in his left hand. "Maggie, you don't know what you're talking about. We had our fun, but Melissa is not mine."

Nicole gasped, her reaction unnoticed by the people in the room.

"She is your daughter," Maggie said, her voice thick with phlegm, still eyeing that knife. "I loved you. I just wanted us to be a family. A real family."

"I already have a family, Maggie," Richard said. "And so do you. Go home to Devon."

Maggie straightened up, her pain and grief suddenly replaced with the serenity of someone who was no longer in control of their actions. "No."

When Maggie reached for the knife, Richard was already in striking distance, and because he thought that the confrontation was over, he was too slow to react when she spun around and plunged the knife into his gut.

Mr. Calhoun's face went pale, and his cheeks wiggled from the shock of pain that gripped his body.

"Melissa is your daughter." Maggie removed the knife and then plunged it into his stomach again. "She has always been your daughter." Another plunge. "And now I'm going to rid you of the family that you wouldn't leave for me."

Mr. Calhoun helplessly groped at Maggie's arms and shoulders as he collapsed to the floor.

Maggie stood over him, bloody knife in hand,

staring down at the man who she believed had ruined her life, a man whom she loved and was betrayed by.

"Richard, I called the police and—" Bethany Calhoun turned into the dining room and saw her bloodied husband on the floor, and almost instantly all of the anger and hate that she had felt for him just moments ago vanished in the blink of an eye. "Richard!"

Without concern for her own life, rushed toward her husband, only to be met with the same blade to the gut that killed her husband.

Bethany froze when the knife entered her belly, and a small bit of blood formed in the corner of her mouth, the color running from her face as quickly as the blood that poured from the wound in her gut.

Maggie removed the blade, and then Bethany crawled on her stomach toward her husband, who now lay lifeless and bloodied on the floor. Nicole could do nothing but watch as the woman reached out a shaking hand to hold her husband's hand as her last gesture in this world, because even after learning about his infidelity, she still loved him.

Bethany eventually touched Mr. Calhoun's lifeless hand, her own life draining from her, and then rested her face against the floor, the last bits of life draining from her as well.

Nicole looked to Maggie, who still held the knife, staring down at the people that she had just killed. Her eyes contained a wild, maddening expression that she had only seen the eyes of the most advanced dementia and Alzheimer's patients.

Maggie raised the knife high and then plunged it down into Bethany's back, shoving the blade all the way into the body until it disappeared and nothing was showing but the hilt and her hand. Her knuckles had blanched white from the tight grip, and she bared her teeth, pushing foam from the corners of her mouth. She was a mad dog off the leash.

Maggie knifed Bethany's body a dozen more times, and then turned her frenzied rage onto Richard's stomach, carving up his body like he had done to the half-eaten bird on the table.

Blood splashed over the floor and coated Maggie in thick globs that covered her arms, torso, legs, and face. She resembled a gory Jackson Pollock, all confusion and rage and pain. She stabbed the bodies until her arm grew tired, and she sat on her knees, panting, leaning back, laughing as she turned her face up toward the ceiling.

It was hard for Nicole to look away. It was like watching a train wreck in slow motion. She was so close to the murders that she could smell the heat and stink of the bodies. She tasted the metallic texture of the blood in the air. The heavy metal tasted bitter on her tongue.

Nicole was meant to see all of this because she was meant to understand what happened tonight. And the night still wasn't over.

Maggie stopped laughing and then lowered her gaze from the ceiling and stared at the bodies on the floor. The skin around her eyes twitched, and the same madness pulled the corners of her mouth up into jittery smiles. "The girls." She spoke the words with a hint of joy in her voice. "I still need to kill the girls." She stood, blood dripping from her body like Carrie from Stephen King's classic horror novel. She kept the knife in her right hand then slowly turned toward the hallway in search of her next victims.

Nicole remained in the dining room for a few seconds after Maggie had walked out. She found that she was unable to move, lost in the wake of the bloodshed that had been left behind. She didn't know these people other than from the stories and rumors that had been spread about them. And while Mr. Calhoun was wrong for his adultery, the punishment didn't fit the crime.

Nicole might have been familiar with death, but she was new to murder, and it was a cold and unforgiving act. She felt her own soul darken from witnessing it.

A pair of screams snapped Nicole from her stupor, and she sprinted from the dining room, skidding into the hall. A second scream pulled her attention toward the staircase, and she watched as Aubrey led Margaret down the staircase, the maddening shouts of Maggie echoing from somewhere on the second floor.

Nicole stood in the hallway and watched as the girls sprinted down the hallway, and then quickly veered into one of the rooms off to the right. She sprinted after them, knowing that it was important for her to see what happened next, knowing that this was what Aubrey had wanted her to see.

Nicole hurried into the room and saw Aubrey pulling at different books from the shelves on the wall.

Margaret stood behind her, looking directly at Nicole, but only seeing through her.

"Hurry, Aubrey, hurry!" Margaret bounced with a nervous energy that made her look like a little girl.

"Where are you, girls?" Maggie's crazed voice was coming down the stairs, and this prompted Margaret to retreat to her sister, who was still working on pulling books, but as to why, Nicole had no idea.

Margaret tugged on her sister's sleeve, clawing at her with the kind of panic that was reserved for life-or-death moments like the one the sisters currently found themselves in as the young Ms. Calhoun dropped her voice to a whisper. "Aubrey, she's coming."

Aubrey reached for one last book on a nearby shelf, and with that final pull, the bookcase that covered the wall on the far end of the library opened a single column, exposing a vault that was no more than six feet high and two feet wide.

When the safe opened, Nicole saw the walls and shelves were lined with jewels.

"Get inside." Aubrey manhandled her younger sister and shoved her inside. When she started to close the vault door, Margaret planted her palm on the door, stopping it from closing.

"What are you doing?"

"There isn't enough room," Aubrey said.

"Oh girrrrrlllsss!" Maggie's voice was closer now, and Nicole turned to see the bloodied woman step off the bottom staircase and head toward the library, and Nicole quickly ducked inside, thinking that she might be the one to give away the girl's position.

It was a foolish thought, but seeing the events of the night that changed Ms. Calhoun's life forever play out provided a texture that made it real.

"Go," Aubrey said, giving her sister another shove inside.

Margaret resisted, but only a little bit. She resisted in the way that a tired child tried to fight their parents about going to bed. They didn't want to do it, but sleep had already blanketed the child's mind with the prospect of rest.

The only difference here was that Margaret's emotion was fear, and it had overridden the rational mind that wanted to save her sister. Because at that moment, the young Ms. Calhoun only wanted to save herself.

Before Margaret could protest any further, and with Maggie's eerie and terrifying calls growing closer and closer to the library, Aubrey shut the vault, swung the book column back in place, and spun around just before Maggie entered the room.

"Aubrey," Maggie said, smiling wide as she saw her next victim. The blood that covered her face and body helped brighten her teeth. "Where's your sister?"

Aubrey was a deer caught in headlights. All of the courage and bravery that she had displayed to protect her younger sister from the crazed woman that had walked into their home and murdered their parents melted away when she saw her parents' blood on Maggie's clothes and skin.

"Y-y-you need to leave." Aubrey swallowed and

nervously shifted her feet from side to side. "I already called the police, and th-they're on their way here."

Aubrey's frightening words rolled off of Maggie like oil on water. "The police won't save you. No one can save you. You're going to die, you little bitch. I only wish that your father was here to see me kill you!"

Maggie sprinted toward Aubrey, who screamed as she tried to run away. The pair sprinted around the library, Aubrey throwing every piece of furniture that she could in front of Maggie to try and get her to stop, but Maggie refused to let up, continue to reach toward the back of Aubrey's shirt or snatch a snippet of her hair.

Watching the chase would have almost been comical had it not been for the stink of fear that filled the room. It was also hard to ignore the jolts and screams that pierced the eerie silence of the room, the frantic cries of Aubrey as she screamed for someone to help her. The help which Nicole knew would not make it in time.

And slowly, inch by inch, Maggie gained on Aubrey, until the eldest Calhoun daughter twisted her ankle as she rounded a love sofa to try and escape the room. The moment she hit the floor, the chase was over.

Maggie pounced on the Calhoun daughter, Aubrey still fighting back to the bitter end, but her efforts were futile. One quick slice of the blade across Aubrey's skin, and the pain from the sting of the steel sucked the fight right out of her.

After that, Nicole screamed as she watched Maggie drive the knife into Aubrey's body again and again.

Nicole knew that it had been Aubrey who had suffered the worst fate of the family, but what the police had told reporters about the harrowing incident didn't do it justice in the least.

By the time that Maggie was finished, Aubrey's torso was nothing but a bloody stump. The blood that covered her body was so thick that you couldn't even tell she was wearing clothes.

And even after all of that carnage and death that she had just drummed up, Maggie still wore an expression of revenge. She wanted to find the last Calhoun daughter.

But young Ms. Calhoun was locked away in the family vault, and Maggie wouldn't get the chance as the faint wail of sirens echoed from beyond the estate walls.

It was the sound of those sirens that seemed to finally snap Maggie out of her bloodlust, and Nicole watched as she blinked away some of the blood droplets that had fallen into her eyes.

Maggie stared down at herself for a moment, then at Aubrey, who still had the knife plunged into her heart. Her mouth formed an oval of sorts, and a soft moan crawled out of it, but she quickly stopped as if the sound of her voice horrified her to no end.

Maggie pulled the knife from Aubrey's chest and then stood. She stared down at the butchered body as she slowly retreated from the library, the sirens growing louder as Maggie sprinted down the hallway and back out into the snow, where the heavy snowfall would cover her tracks.

Nicole walked over to Aubrey, staring down at the slain girl's body. She gave the ultimate sacrifice to protect her younger sister.

The book column behind Nicole opened, followed by the vault, revealing a frightened Margaret, her face as white as the ghost of her sister.

The young Ms. Calhoun glanced around the library for a moment, unable to see her sister's body on the floor, which was hidden behind the sofa that she had fallen behind. But as she carefully stepped forward, probably worried that Maggie was still lurking about, she finally saw the outstretched hand that was hidden behind the couch, bloodied and lifeless.

"Aubrey!" Margaret shrieked and sprinted toward her sister, but the moment she turned the corner and saw the bloodied mess, she stopped dead cold. She covered her mouth, her body dissolving into a pile of shivers that she couldn't control. She finally lowered her hand, and then slowly, carefully as if she would wake the dead, walked to her sister's side.

Nicole watched Margaret kneel, looking only at Aubrey's face, and then Margaret picked up Aubrey's bloodied hand and held it close to her chest.

Margaret said nothing, her eyes wide, as she slowly rocked back and forth, holding Aubrey's hand, looking at her sister's lifeless, bloodied face.

Nicole moved closer and then knelt right next to Margaret. This was the moment that broke Ms. Calhoun, the one that fried that speech circuit in her brain. It wasn't just the murder of her family by the hands of a woman who had lost her mind, it was the sacrifice of her sister, the guilt of knowing that she was the only survivor.

And then, unexpectedly, the young Ms. Calhoun turned her attention directly on Nicole, as if she could see her right there in the dream, and Nicole froze on the spot, the way that she had when Aubrey had spoken to her in the basement.

"She's still in the house," Ms. Calhoun said.

And when she finished speaking, Nicole was thrust awake from the dream.

*N*icole gasped when she woke, bolting upright in her bed, dripping sweat, and cold from the dream. Or was it a premonition? Had she really gone back in time? Was she still there?

Nicole ripped off the covers and walked to the window, but she saw no snow. She pressed her palm against the glass and felt that it was cool, but not the frigid cold of winter.

Nicole removed her hand, leaving behind a print on the window, and then turned around. She was still breathing heavy, and she slowed her breathing down by drawing some deep breaths to help.

When Nicole was confident that she had calmed down, she tried to remember everything that happened in the dream, afraid that the memories would float away like the smoke from a fire that had been doused with water.

But she remembered everything, even the smells,

and taste in the air, both of which she could have done to forget.

"Melissa," Nicole said, thinking out loud. "Melissa is the love child of Richard Calhoun and Maggie Farr."

The Calhoun family murders had been ones of passion. It was also the same reason why Maggie Farr had killed herself shortly after the murders. She wasn't losing her mind, she had already lost it, and she was wracked with the guilt of what she had done.

But had Melissa's father never told her about the truth? Surely he would have known what happened that night when Maggie came home covered in blood. According to the articles, he had been called to the scene himself after the police had assessed the situation.

"He helped cover it up," Nicole said, pacing the bedroom, gaining momentum with her line of thinking. "He was protecting his wife, his daughter, his own legacy. He needed Calhoun's business, the name, and if their name were brought down in scandal, if it were uncovered what Maggie had done, then he would have been ruined."

It all made sense, the pieces slowly being put together. Nicole glanced at the clock. It was late, but not too late. She could still get to the station in time. She headed for the door, remembering something else from the dream, right before she woke up.

Ms. Calhoun had tried to tell her something. Nicole opened the door, remembering the phrase 'she's still in the house' when a heavy force hit the back of her head and knocked her unconscious.

33

The pain was nothing but a dull throb for a while, but when it started to break through to Nicole's subconscious mind, it sharpened to a surgeon's knife, and she awoke bound and gagged in the Calhoun library.

Nicole's head swam in a sea of confusion. She blinked a few more times, trying to clear her vision, and when it finally did clear, she saw that Melissa was still working on the bookshelves, the same bookshelves that she had seen Aubrey open during the vision that she had seen during her dream.

"You're his daughter," Nicole said, wincing as she spoke. It was hard even trying to stay awake.

Melissa turned at the sound of Nicole's voice and smiled when she saw her. "You're up. I was afraid that I'd hit you too hard." She returned to trying the different combinations on the shelves. "I apologize for that."

Nicole remembered that the vault was behind the

library wall. "You're going after the Calhoun family jewels?"

Melissa spun around, her movements fast and jerky. "I'm going after what is rightfully mine!" Her cheeks had reddened with anger. "Do you think that old woman knows the kind of wealth that she has? She can barely remember her own name now! Today, I take back what should have been mine for my entire life!" But the anger slowly vanished, and she frowned. "How did you know they were here?" She crossed the room, leaving the books on the shelves and hovered over Nicole. "I had to pry it out of Donald, threatening to kill Ms. Calhoun if he didn't tell me, but how did you know?"

Nicole looked up at Melissa, the well-mannered lawyer who always crossed all of her T's and dotted all of her I's. "You're the one who killed Donald?"

Melissa smiled, but it held the same kind of madness that Nicole had seen Maggie display on the night of the murders thirty years ago. "No. You killed Donald." She laughed. "At least that's what the police will think when they find the murder weapon in your guesthouse after you've stabbed Ms. Calhoun and yourself to death." Melissa turned her gaze to a table nearby where a knife rested on top.

Nicole recognized the knife. It was the same kind of knife that she had just seen used to butcher the Calhoun family the night of those brutal murders thirty years ago. And she was betting that was also the real knife that had been used to cut Donald's wrists, the knife that Detective Salvor had been looking for.

"I needed someone that I could pin the blame on," Melissa said, picking the knife up and handling it with a practiced apathy. "You see, Rick and Kate were just the distraction for the police. It was a way for me to lure them in with a false narrative." She pointed the tip of the blade at Nicole. "But when they learn what you were really after... what you wanted to find in the house, and to take advantage of a poor old lady, well, that's going to throw them for a loop."

"What are you talking about?" Nicole asked. "Detective Salvor practically thanked me when he left."

"That's because he hasn't searched your room," Melissa said. "But when he does, he'll find this blade. The same blade that you used to cut up your Donald, and then kill your employer, Ms. Calhoun."

Nicole studied Melissa's expression. There was something different in her eyes, something maddening that hadn't been there before. It was like something, or someone else, had taken control of her body and mind. "You never told Kate about the shellfish, did you?"

Melissa smiled. "No. At least not officially. I put it in the paperwork of course, but I never relayed that information to Kate."

Nicole shut her eyes, her mind swirling with questions. She shook her head. "Why would you do all of this? Why hire Rick if you knew he was a criminal?"

Melissa smiled, twirling the blade around in her hands. "Because right now what's happening is both Kate and Rick are squealing on one another about how it was the other person's idea to go after the jewels, but this will re-open the investigation into Donald's murder, and the police will find some damning new evidence when they get the search warrant to look in your guest house." She lifted the blade in her hands. "This was what I used on Donald after I gave him the sleeping pills that knocked him out. It was difficult getting him into the tub, but I managed."

It was almost too impossible to believe. But then Nicole remembered how Melissa's mother butchered three people in this very home. The madness was in her blood.

"You don't think I didn't do my homework?" Melissa asked. "If my father taught me one thing, it was to always be prepared for any possible outcome. You think that I would have agreed for a nurse to bring her husband if I hadn't known that you two have been having marital issues?"

The creases along Nicole's face deepened. "How would you have known that?"

"You're not the only one who is resourceful," Melissa said, still holding the carving knife in her hands. "But I was disappointed that you two didn't argue more. It would have painted a more convincing picture for your descent into madness. A lover's quarrel always make for popular headlines. And it's because of your difficult marriage and the betrayal that you felt that drove you mad while you were working here."

Slowly, Nicole was starting to catch on. "That's why you didn't want the police to search our rooms. You wanted to plant the seeds of suspicion."

With her mind still fatigued, Nicole struggled to

figure a way out of her predicament. She knew that she couldn't work through the restraints. They were too tight, and she was too weak to break them. But she also knew that she couldn't just sit there and do nothing while she waited for Melissa to kill her. And then she remembered that Jake was at the hospital. If she could just keep her talking, then Nicole might stay alive long enough for him to come home, and he might bring the police with him. She just needed to keep her talking, keep her engaged and distracted.

"How long have you been planning this?" Nicole asked. "Or did you send the woman that broke my marriage into Jake's arms?"

Melissa smiled, shaking her head. "No, I didn't plan that far ahead. But I did do a background check on you before I even contacted your firm. It wasn't hard to locate hospice nurses on the West Coast with a track record and qualifications that I was looking for. But it was difficult finding one in a currently troubled situation. To be honest, I didn't even really know what I might have been looking for, but when I called into your employer to find out more about you, I knew that I found the right mark. The perfect nurse to take care of poor old Ms. Calhoun was the same nurse I would frame for the murder of the very patient that she was charged with taking care of, and I don't think it could have worked out any better than it did." She smiled. "Because everything that I needed to happen to achieve my success has unfolded, and now the time has finally come for me to inherit what I had lost all of those years ago. To have what was rightfully mine."

"Why did you kill Donald?" Nicole finally asked, this more out of honest curiosity than trying to bide her time until help arrived, help that she wasn't even sure was coming. "He was a good man."

"And a man who was incredibly loyal to Ms. Calhoun," Melissa said. "I wasn't about to let a butler come between me and the life and money that has always been rightfully mine. I have come too far."

Hearing Melissa talk now was like listening to another person. She was a far cry from the composed and serious woman that had greeted Nicole and Jake when they first arrived at the mansion. She had grown wild and untamed. She had become dangerous in a way that she had never seen before. And Nicole wasn't sure how much time she had left before everything fell to pieces.

"So you killed him for the money?" Nicole asked.

"I killed him because he would have stopped me from having what has always been mine!" Melissa hunched forward, arching her upper back as she screamed into Nicole's face. She was losing her mind, and there was nothing that Nicole could say that was going to bring her back from the edge. "He was the last connection to the old woman's past. With him out of the way, all that was left was to take care of Ms. Calhoun herself."

Nicole leaned away from the rage, but because of her restraints, she couldn't move directly out of the path of the creature that was tormenting her, so she was forced to sit there and take it.

But when Melissa was done with her outburst, she

248

twisted her face up in disgust. "Don't sit there and look at me like that. You don't have any right. None! You're nothing but a weak woman who couldn't even hold onto her own husband. So don't blame me for taking your situation and using it to my advantage." She spat the words with such hate and vitriol that Nicole was forced to turn away lest she was covered in spittle.

Nicole wiped her cheek on her shoulder, removing some of Melissa's spit, and then looked the woman in the eyes. When she had first arrived at this house, she had been so intimidated by the woman that stood in front of her now. There was nothing that she couldn't imagine Melissa doing to her, but now, seeing the veil of civility and calm that had made her so intimidating disintegrate, Nicole found that she was no longer afraid.

Because she had been running for too long, running from the truth about her marriage, running from confronting the husband that had wronged her, running from the truth that she had learned in therapy that she had refused to believe.

"Life isn't about getting what you think you deserve," Nicole said. "It's about how you play the hand that you're dealt."

Melissa smirked. "You're a fool if you really believe that." She leaned away. "If you have enough money, you can buy however many cards you want and however many decks are needed. That's what I will continue to do until I have all the cards I need to do whatever the hell I want." But then Melissa frowned when she moved closer to Nicole, and that familiar lawyer's gaze returned to her. "How did you know?"

"Know what?" Nicole asked.

Melissa straightened up, looking down at Nicole with casual indifference. The woman's mood shifted, like a cold breeze coming off of a lake on a spring day. She smiled and then slowly turned toward the table in the middle of the library. "How did you know that I was the daughter of Richard Calhoun?" She paused when she reached the table, but Nicole saw that she picked something up.

Nicole broke out in a sweat. She knew that she had said too much. "I-I-I don't know."

Melissa kept her back to Nicole, hiding the object that was in her hand. "How much did Kate and Rick tell you?"

Nicole shook her head, unsure of where the conversation was going. "They didn't tell me anything." That wasn't exactly true, but Nicole wasn't about to start telling the truth to a woman who was clearly losing her mind. "I thought that they were after the jewels, that's all."

Melissa narrowed her eyes. She tightened her grip around the handle of the blade and started a slow, methodical walk toward Nicole. "Tell me."

Nicole wasn't going to tell the woman anything. The fact that she had learned the truth about the murders by the grace of the house might be her one trump card in this situation. And she was going to keep Melissa guessing. "I'm not ready to show my hand yet."

Melissa laughed, and that familiar sound of

madness returned, made more ominous by the blade that she still held in her hand. The laughter died slowly, and Melissa shook her head, wagging the knife like she would a finger to scold a child. "You're smarter than you let on. I'll give you that." She finally turned to face the bookcase again, and she set the knife on the table as she walked toward it. "When I get what I want, I'll deal with you."

Nicole watched as Melissa reached for the last few books on the shelves, pulling them in the same order that she had seen Aubrey do it in the dream that she saw just moments ago.

The books acted like the combination number on a safe, adding another layer of protection that was in plain sight.

Melissa pulled on the last book, and the old bookcase swung open, the dust popping at the cracks and hinges. It had been closed for a long time, and Nicole suspected that it probably hadn't been opened since the last time that Aubrey had hidden Ms. Calhoun in the vault the night of the murder thirty years ago.

When the door finally opened all the way, revealing the massive vault inside, Melissa pumped her fists in the air and screamed as if she had just won the lottery.

"I've been so patient," Melissa said, hands clasped together at her chest. "It was my father that told me the truth on his death bed." She turned around to look at Nicole. Some of the madness had left her face, and a child-like wonder had taken its place. "I didn't believe him at first, but he was so sincere. Being the person I was, I couldn't just sit and wonder if it was real or not.

I had to make sure that my father was telling the truth. After he died, I looked into the case from thirty years ago more closely, and the closer I looked, the more I realized that it all fits with what my father had said." She swallowed, her face darkening with a more serious expression. "I can't imagine what it was like for my father all of those years ago, finding that not only was his wife having an affair, but that I wasn't his blood daughter." A tear fell from her eyes, and she took a breath to catch herself. "But he never treated me like anything less than his real daughter. He still loved me, still trusted me with his business after he was too old to run it himself. He was so much stronger than anyone that I had ever known, but there were some things that he just couldn't handle. And that was letting the truth come out. My father helped cover up what my mother did out of love." Melissa wiped at her eye and then took a breath, better composing herself. "But it will be for vengeance that I burn this place to the ground. And I'll make sure that you burn down with it."

Nicole struggled against the restraints, hoping that she would be able to set herself free, but there was nothing that she could do, and she helplessly watched as Melissa reached for the handle and pulled open the vault.

It was empty.

"No," Melissa said, her voice nothing but a panicked whisper. "No, that can't be." And then she broke through her paralysis and lunged for the empty space, as if reaching inside would suddenly make the jewels appear out of thin air. "NO!"

Melissa spun around, the rage returning and her face reddening so hot that it had turned a shade of purple. She slammed the bookshelf closed again, screaming until her voice was raw. The sounds that came out of her were raw and primal. She raked her fingers through her hair and breathed so quick and heavy that she looked like she was about to pass out.

Nicole could do nothing but sit and wait for Melissa to figure out what she was going to do next, but she figured that it would involve driving that carving knife into Nicole's heart.

When Melissa finally set her eyes on Nicole, the air was sucked from the room.

"Where are they?" Melissa asked.

Nicole played dumb. "I don't know what you're talking about—"

"Liar!" Melissa sprinted toward Nicole, grabbing the blade off the table along the way, and then pressed the edge of the blade up against Nicole's throat. "You're a fucking liar! You've known about the jewels. I heard you and Kate talking about them. And I know all of the research that your husband did on his laptop about the murders thirty years ago. So don't cut me that bullshit!"

Nicole tried to lean away from the blade so it wouldn't slice her throat, but she was limited in her range of motion from the ropes around her ankles and wrists.

But an idea struck Nicole, something that she might be able to use to her advantage. "I did find them." She swallowed, trying to gather the spit in her mouth. "I found them and then I hid them. I thought that I could get them after all of this was over, especially since Kate and Rick were out of the way. But I didn't think that you were still looking for them. I didn't think you were involved."

Nicole waited for Melissa's reaction. She wasn't sure how convincing she sounded, but she hoped that the woman would buy it. Because Nicole had learned that people could convince themselves that anything was true, so long as they wanted it bad enough.

Melissa finally removed the edge of the blade from Nicole's throat, but she kept that intense gaze focused on her until there was nothing left for her to do. "You found the jewels and hid them. Why?"

Nicole didn't break away from Melissa's gaze. She was afraid that if she did, it would be the end of her. "I needed a getaway plan. You know that my marriage hasn't been great. It's on the verge of collapse, and there isn't anything that I can do to save it. I thought the jewels were my way out. I thought that I could help myself by taking from someone who already had so much."

Again Nicole waited, hoping that she was being convincing. Because if she wasn't, then her life was going to end right then and there.

Melissa refused to let her expression betray her thoughts, but with the blade still so close to Nicole's flesh, she wasn't sure if the woman was going to make good on her promise to kill her or let her go.

But when Melissa finally cracked a smile and relaxed her posture, Nicole was certain that her deception had worked.

"You're a clever girl," Melissa said, chuckling. "You think that if you can convince me that you have the jewels hidden away somewhere that I won't kill you for it."

Nicole swallowed, hoping she didn't look as nervous as she felt.

"It's a smart play," Melissa said. "But I think that you forgot one pivotal piece of information."

"What's that?" Nicole asked.

Melissa leaned closer, her nose only an inch away from Nicole's face. "You care about people. But I don't." She smiled. "So you know what I'm going to do? I'm going to go and grab that old bitch and pull her out of bed, and bring her down here and sit her down in front of you." She held up the knife. "And then I'm going to place the edge of this knife to her throat, and then we'll see how much longer you'll keep quiet about where you stashed the jewels, or if you were even telling the truth about the jewels in the first place!"

The lights in the house shut off after Melissa was finished screaming, casting them in darkness. The sudden contrast from the brightness to the darkness made it difficult to see, and Nicole panicked for a moment from the blindness. She was afraid that Melissa would start slashing the blade through the air in a blind rage, and it would get caught in her throat and send her flying to the floor to bleed out in the darkness, alone.

But Melissa remained frozen as well. Neither woman said anything as they waited for the lights to turn back on, but after a few seconds passed and nothing happened, it was Melissa who stomped around the room.

"It's that old fucking bat!" Melissa screamed. "She's playing with the lights again."

But Nicole didn't think that this was something that Ms. Calhoun had done, because, like all the times since she arrived at the house when something like this happened, she again felt that cold sensation run down her spine, flowing to the base of her skull, freezing her in place. And while she still couldn't see, Nicole swore that when she exhaled a breath, she thought that she could see the cloud of vapors that had collected because it was so cold.

"Fine," Melissa said, and then she grabbed hold of Nicole, dragging her across the floor. "I'll deal with the bitch, and then I'll deal with you after I find her."

Nicole didn't struggle when Melissa dragged her across the floor. She knew that trying to fight back now was pointless, but the scrapes and pains that she received across the floor made it difficult to take the trip without wiggling.

Melissa finally manhandled Nicole into the safe. "You'll stay here where I know you won't cause any trouble, and then I'll deal with you when I come back!"

The vault door slammed shut, and then Nicole listened to the clank of the lock engaging.

34

*O*nce the door to the vault was closed, Nicole was sealed in darkness. She was blind and deaf to the outside world. Space was cramped, with barely enough room for her to fit. But what was worse than the cramped space was the lack of mobility due to her restraints. And the longer that Nicole was forced to sit in that vault, the more the walls seemed to close in around her.

Nicole wanted out. She wanted this to be over. Her nerves were frayed, and she was exhausted, and she wanted to go home. But she now found herself locked in a vault by a woman that had hired her for a job, only to frame her for murder.

All of the frustration and pain reached a crescendo, and she screamed. Her voice bounced around the steel walls, reverberating right back at her. But no matter how loud she screamed, she knew that no one would hear her cry for help.

Nicole rested the back of her head against the cold

steel wall behind her, unable to tell the difference between the darkness of the vault and when she closed her eyes.

For all of it to end this way after Jake and her had come so far was soul-crushing. She bowed her head in defeat. Suddenly, that familiar prick returned at the base of her skull, and her spine was flushed with ice.

Nicole perked up, her skin breaking out in goose-bumps, and she thought that she felt the restraints loosen. Just a little.

With what little space that she had, Nicole wiggled her arms and legs to try and get a hand free, and after working her hands in a seesaw motion, moving them repeatedly back and forth, she finally managed to work for her hands loose.

Hands no longer bound, Nicole was able to remove the restraints around her ankles. She couldn't stand, but she could now maneuver more efficiently in the dark and cramped space.

Nicole reached for what she thought was the flat surface toward the door, and then she pushed as hard as she could to try and open it, but it wouldn't budge. Before she was too overwhelmed again by the fear of being trapped, Nicole stopped and then fell backward into the vault.

It wasn't long enough for her to straighten her legs, but it was the most comfortable position that she could find. She knew that there had to be a way to get out of here somehow. She refused to believe that her life would end locked away in the vault of a family who had haunted her since—

Nicole paused, perking up in the darkness. She had already seen that it was possible to get out of this vault. She had watched Ms. Calhoun make the great escape when Aubrey had locked her in the vault to protect her from Maggie.

After Aubrey had died, Ms. Calhoun walked out of the vault on her own steam. There must be some kind of hidden key or access panel nestled into the walls of the vault.

Nicole pushed herself to a crouched position, running her palms against every inch of the surface of the vault. She struggled to check the surfaces thoroughly, wanting to speed through the process so she could escape the coffin that she had been buried in, but the longer that she went without actually feeling anything, the more worried she became that she wasn't going to find her means of escape.

Heart pumping harder, Nicole gritted her teeth and forced herself to calm down before she had a panic attack. She didn't need to have an episode here in the darkness. But she felt the cold bullets of sweat collecting all along her body, and once again, she felt those storm clouds circling overhead. The ones that had plagued her since the affair. And that little voice returned to tell her that she was doomed. She was helpless. She would die.

"No," Nicole spoke aloud, her voice reverberating off the walls that encased her, and the strength in her voice surprised her, despite it coming out of her own mouth. She clenched her hands into fists, squeezing so tight that she thought her joints were going to crack.

She had fought for too long and too hard to regain control of her life. She refused to quit.

Reinvigorated, Nicole started again on the wall behind her, pressing her palms in a smoother, calmer fashion. She worked the walls in a grid, moving carefully to make sure that she didn't miss anything that might have given away a crease or a handle or a divot, anything that might grant her an escape.

When she made it to the third wall, still having found nothing, Nicole felt that voice of doubt yell from the back corner of her mind where she had put it. She tried to drown it out, but it was getting louder.

Nicole neared the front door of the vault. She was still moving her palms slowly across the surface of the walls, and when she neared the bottom of the wall she was searching, she felt the lightest divot appear in the metal.

Nicole froze, quickly moving her hands back over the divot so that she could find it again before she lost it forever. But then she remembered to slow down again, and when she did that, she was able to relocate the groove that she had felt before.

Nicole ran her index finger over it to try and see if there was anything else around it, and when she circled her finger outward of the divot an inch, she was able to find another crease.

Slowly, methodically, Nicole worked her finger around the creases until she had traced the outline of a panel.

Using both hands now, Nicole placed her fingers on either end of the panel and then tried to lift it up, taking great care to make sure that she didn't break anything. But time and rust made it difficult to lift, and the first attempt broke both of Nicole's nails down to the cuticle.

"Ouch!" She quickly retracted both hands, the pain at the end of her finger screaming and making a slow trail down her hands and into her forearms. She placed both fingers in her mouth, hoping to ease the burning pain, and after a few minutes, it finally subsided.

Hands trembling when she returned them to the panel, Nicole forced her fingers back into the divots. The flesh was exposed and raw from where the nail had broken off, but she knew that this was her only shot at escape.

Pushing through the pain, Nicole applied pressure, pulling on the cover with all of her strength, fighting back the urge to quit. She dug her fingers into the side of the panel so hard that blood pricked from her skin, and the liquid made her fingers slip, and she lost her grip.

But when she pulled her hands back the second time, there was no scream of pain. Nicole simply stared at her bloodied, shaking hands, still unable to see them, but she could feel them. She had never been backed up against a wall like this before. She had always had a safety valve that she could reach for, something or someone that she could call for help, but there was no one to call on. It was up to her to dig deep enough to find the courage to break through the pain and her own self-doubt.

Blood still dripping from her fingertips, Nicole

reached for the plate once more. She closed her eyes, knowing that the moment those bloody prints touched the metal, she would be greeted with a fresh dose of pain.

It was masochistic. It was brutal. But it was the only way that she would get out of this alive.

Gingerly, Nicole placed her fingertips back onto the board and, realizing it was the slow progression that made the pain worse, she bore down on the plate quickly with the remainder of her strength.

The tips of the metal dug deeper into her flesh, but it worked to her advantage as it gave her a better grip on the plate. She wasn't sure if she would be able to get it open again before the flesh across her fingertips ripped and she wouldn't be able to hold it at all because her bone would be exposed. Nicole pulled back with everything she had, tears streaming down her reddened, sweat-stained cheeks from the pain and the heat and pressure of the moment.

And then, just when Nicole thought that her fingers were going to give out and she would have to start this whole process over again, she was flung backward with the panel in her bloodied hands.

Nicole dropped the piece of metal and then fumbled her bloodied fingers over the open space. The pain had numbed her fingertips, and it had become difficult to tell what she was touching.

Nicole reverted to the use of her pinky, and she managed to locate a small bar inside the panel. She was able to hook her pinky finger around it and then added as many fingers that would fit. She pulled and then heard the heavy groan of the bookshelf beyond the door.

Another second after that, she heard the pop of a lock, and she pressed against the vault's door. Instead of finding resistance, it opened.

Muscles cramped from the tight fit, Nicole struggled to get out of the vault and then collapsed on her hands and knees when she finally managed to squeeze herself out.

Arms and legs trembling, Nicole heard Melissa screaming from somewhere in the house. She was looking for Ms. Calhoun. And Nicole knew that she would have to find Ms. Calhoun before Melissa, or they wouldn't survive the night.

---

35

*B*efore Nicole left the library, she immediately looked for a phone, realizing that Melissa had taken both cell phones away. But when she reached the phone in the kitchen, she found it was dead. She was on her own.

Nicole knew that she couldn't confront Melissa without her own weapon. She wasn't sure what else the lawyer might have, but Nicole grabbed her own knife from the block in the kitchen. It was the biggest, sturdiest one she could find.

It was odd holding a weapon in this way, one that Nicole realized that she might actually have to use to kill someone. Gripping the blade, she thought of Maggie when she butchered the Calhouns.

Did Maggie believe that there was no other way? Did she convince herself that it was necessary to kill every member? What would happen if Nicole had to plunge the knife into Melissa's body? Would she be able to do it? Would it change her? Push her over the edge until all she was able to feel was the rush of killing someone?

Nicole pushed the thoughts out of her head, knowing that they would be answered in due time. However horrible it would be.

Muscles still cramped and swollen from her confined quarters, Nicole limped up the staircase, listening to Melissa upstairs.

"Ms. Calhoun," Melissa said, her voice echoing with a sweet cadence that made her sound more sinister than before. "Ms. Calhoun, where are you?"

Melissa's voice drifted through the air like smoke, and Nicole was having a hard time trying to figure out where it was coming from.

Nicole followed the sound of Melissa's voice as she approached the second story. She tilted her head to the right and to the left, trying to pinpoint exactly where the voice was coming from. Because just when she thought she had figured out where the woman was, it sounded like she was coming from somewhere else.

Nicole was about to ascend to the third floor when she heard the high-pitched scream of fear. It was coming from a room down the hall on the second floor. She kept the knife up and raised on her sprint down the hallway, following the horrific screams from the room as she moved closer, turning the corner sharply. She saw Ms. Calhoun on the floor with Melissa lording over her.

Nicole froze in the doorway, staring as Melissa held a clump of Ms. Calhoun's hair in one hand and the knife in the other. Ms. Calhoun lay on her side on the ground, cowering with her hands in the air to try and protect herself, but the old woman wouldn't survive the death blows that Melissa planned to deliver.

When Melissa saw Nicole in the doorway, she pulled Ms. Calhoun closer and used her as a human shield as she pressed the edge of the blade to her throat.

"Don't come any closer!" Melissa barked with aggressive panic. "How... How did you get out?"

Nicole realized that she had caught Melissa off guard and that she had missed her one big element of surprise, and she kicked herself for not taking advantage of it.

"How did you get out!" Melissa screamed again, this time louder, and Ms. Calhoun shivered in fear.

"Let her go, Melissa." Nicole locked eyes with Ms. Calhoun for just a moment, hoping that the old woman was all right. In her age and her condition, the shock of the moment could put her in cardiac arrest. Or worse. When she flicked her gaze back to Melissa, she took another step, closing the gap between the two of them. "You're not getting the jewels, Melissa. You'll be lucky to get out of this house with your life. Now, let Ms. Calhoun go."

Melissa chuckled, the laughter rolling off of her tongue in heavy waves. She shook her head. "You're unbelievable, do you know that? But you have confidence, I'll give you that. I suspect that you were forced to rebuild it after what your husband did to you." She cocked her head to the side. "Do you think he's flirting with any of the nurses at the hospital right now?"

Nicole knew that Melissa was just trying to get into her head. But it wouldn't work. "My husband isn't your concern."

"Are you sure about that?" Melissa asked. "Did he tell you that he called me after our meeting?" She raised her eyebrows in a childish attempt to make her accusation more provocative, and Nicole hated that it worked on her just a little bit. "He said he wanted to ask a few follow-up questions, and said he preferred that we speak in private." She smiled, which only accentuated her features. She was an attractive woman.

"I know that you don't believe me," Melissa said, her voice still in that annoyingly high-pitched tone. "But I also know that a part of you still wants to ask him about it. A part of you still wants to pick at that little scab until it bleeds because you want to know what's beneath the surface." She took another step toward Nicole. "Because breaking a trust like that was so evil, so vile, that I know that you couldn't imagine it ever healing again. Because even if it does heal, even if it's all put back together, you can still see the cracks. Scars always remind us of the past."

Nicole wanted to cut the smirk right off of Melissa's face, but she knew that an attack on Melissa now would put Ms. Calhoun's life in danger.

Nicole needed for the pair to separate, and she hoped that what she did next would be the trick to finally do it.

"I'm going to count to three," Nicole said. "And if you don't let Ms. Calhoun go, I'm going to throw that chair at you." She gestured to the chair at the vanity in the corner of the room.

Melissa laughed. "You try and move another muscle, and I'll slit her throat. I have to kill you both anyway, so who says that I have to wait to find out the truth?"

Nicole shook her head. "I won't have to move a muscle. One."

The smile faded from Melissa's face, and she snarled. "You're a liar. This isn't some game, Nicole. I will kill her, and then you, and then I'll still get away scot-free after I pin the blame on you. Do you understand me?"

"Two," Nicole said.

Melissa grew even more frantic, her movements fidgety and nervous. She kept looking between the chair and Nicole. "Enough games, Nicole! I'm serious!"

"So am I," Nicole said. "Three."

Both women looked at the chair, but it didn't move.

Melissa relaxed. "So, what happens now? Are you going to count to six? Ten?" She laughed. "It doesn't matter how—"

The chair moved three inches away from the vanity, pulling everyone's attention to it. And while a smile graced Nicole's lips, Melissa's grin faded.

"What the hell was that?" Melissa moved back a few steps, giving up the ground that she had gained. "What the hell did you do!"

"I didn't do anything," Nicole said, keeping her voice eerily calm. "I'm not the only person that's seen what you've been doing, Melissa."

Melissa kept her eyes glued to the chair. "That's impossible. I've been so careful. No one knows what I'm doing. No one knows what's really going on!" But it was the hesitation in her voice that gave away the fear and uncertainty. She didn't really believe what she was saying. She didn't believe it, because she had just seen something unbelievable. "I don't care about your little parlor tricks!"

Nicole shook her head. "It's not a trick."

The lights flickered on and off, strobing with that ominous glow that Nicole had seen when she was down in the basement collecting the cleaning supplies. It was Ms. Calhoun's sister. She was close. She was trying to help, but Nicole knew that she could only do so much. If they were going to save Ms. Calhoun from whatever terrible fate that Melissa had planned, then she just needed the right distraction.

The flights finally flickered dark again, the bulbs in the room still humming from the intermittent flow of electricity that had flooded the circuits.

With the light show over, Melissa turned her attention back to Nicole, who had gotten closer while Melissa had backed herself into the wall. She didn't have anywhere else to go.

"It's over, Melissa," Nicole said. "I won't let you leave. And the house won't let you leave."

Melissa kept the blade close to Ms. Calhoun's neck.

Nicole took another step. She needed to get rid of the knife in Melissa's hand before she made any sudden moves. Because one wrong slip and it could be game over for Ms. Calhoun. One nick of the wrong artery was all it would take to kill the old woman and have her bleed out on the floor.

"Where are the jewels!" Melissa barked the question. "Tell me where they are right now, or I will cut her throat. I swear on my mother's grave that I will."

"You don't have to do this," Nicole said. "You don't have to make yourself into the bad guy. You're better than this. You're better than your mother. You don't have to be doomed to repeat the same mistakes."

"It's not about repeating mistakes," Melissa said, her voice filled with grief. "This is about fixing what happened all of those years ago. Do you have any idea what it was like growing up with a mother who killed herself? Do you have any idea what I would have given to have a normal family? A normal life?"

Nicole stopped herself, not daring to move any closer than her current position. She was close enough to make a move if the opportunity presented itself, but she wasn't going to make that move until she was certain that Ms. Calhoun wouldn't be in any danger. She needed to make sure that the old woman was protected at all costs.

"It was all Richard Calhoun's fault," Melissa said, unable to hold back the tears any longer as she rattled Ms. Calhoun in her arms. "If he had just left his family for my mother, then my life would have been different. I wouldn't have to do this. But he couldn't do it, and I want to know why!" She screamed, her cheeks growing red, and there was a frantic nature in her voice, a pleading kind of scream that Nicole recognized. She had done it herself when she had found out about Jake's affair.

"I know what it's like to lose a part of yourself, to lose something that should have never been taken in the first place," Nicole said, hoping that trying to relate to Melissa and her situation would help pull her out of the emotional tailspin that could lead to some very deadly consequences. "You know about my husband's affair. You know what happened between the two of us. But I can tell you after going through that experience that I would have saved myself a lot of heartache and time if I just accepted the fact that he made a mistake." She shrugged. "That's all it was. Because that's what people do. They make mistakes, and sometimes those mistakes affect the people that are closest to them."

Melissa's eyes watered and her mouth trembled, the fight slowly running out of her. "My mother was supposed to be the one to protect me, to make sure that I didn't get into trouble." She sniffled and then wiped her eyes. "She was the one who was supposed to make sure that I was okay. She was the one that was supposed to take care of me!" She pointed to herself, and Nicole watched the knife that was still near Ms. Calhoun's throat closely.

"I understand how you feel," Nicole said, trying to sympathize with the woman. "But you have to deal with what happened to you healthily. And this isn't healthy."

Melissa couldn't hold back the tears anymore.

Nicole knew that the woman was on the verge of breaking. She just had to push a little bit harder.

"I know that you want to make them pay," Nicole said. "I know you think that taking their jewels and all of their money will make you feel better. But it will only destroy an old woman who can't even remember her own name." She shook her head. "That's not what you want, is it?"

Melissa struggled to keep a straight face. She was losing a part of herself, losing a piece of her that she wasn't sure that she could get back. But Nicole couldn't tell if she was going to cross the line. "What I want?" She swallowed and then took a breath and exhaled it slowly as she closed her eyes. "What I want can't be bought. It's not about the money. It's about getting back what I lost."

"But you won't get it back," Nicole said. "It's all gone, Melissa. You need to accept that fact and move on. It's the only way that you'll find any peace. Trust me."

Nicole waited, watching Melissa's expression, trying to look for any sign that the woman understood what was at stake, but she gave no such signal as to what she might do.

"You're right," Melissa said, her voice soft, but still trembling. "I can't get it back. I won't find peace." Keeping hold of Ms. Calhoun, she straightened up and then drew in a breath. "But it's not the peace that I'm after anymore." She tightened her grip on the handle of the blade and then curled her upper lip into a snarl as her face darkened. "It's about revenge. And I think killing the legitimate daughter of my real father would make him turn over in his grave!"

"Melissa, no!" Nicole lunged, but she was thrown off balance by the rumble of the house.

The floor itself shook, sending all three women to the floor, but Melissa made sure to keep a tight hold on Ms. Calhoun.

When the quake stopped, it was Melissa who was the first to rise, pulling Ms. Calhoun back to her feet as well, forcing the old woman to stand on her trembling legs. "What the hell was that!" She looked to Nicole. "What are you doing?"

Nicole finally stood, straightening herself up and shook her head. "It's not what I'm doing. It's what you're doing." She gestured to Ms. Calhoun. "You have the daughter of the man who built this house. And I don't think he's taking very kindly to your treatment of her."

Melissa looked around the room as if she expected to find Mr. Calhoun standing somewhere in the darkness, but there was nothing but the darkened room and the slight feeling of vertigo that lingered after the small quake that they had just experienced.

"You need to let her go," Nicole said. "It's the only way that this is going to end with everyone alive. You have to understand that."

But when Melissa readjusted her grip on the handle of the blade, Nicole knew that she wasn't going to stop. She was too far down the rabbit hole, and there wasn't a lifeline that Nicole could throw to her that would reach her now.

"This," Melissa said, taking a breath, "is the only way to make it right. My mother meant to kill all of the Calhouns thirty years ago. It's my job to finish it. For her."

Nicole saw the look in Melissa's eye, she saw the way that the woman was going to slice Ms. Calhoun's throat, and at that moment she lunged forward. She knew that she wasn't close enough to make a difference, the movement was more out of instinct. The instinct to protect innocent life. The instinct to make sure that a woman wasn't killed out of circumstances that were no fault of her own.

But before Nicole could reach it, something came flying from the corner of the room. It was nothing but a silver blur at first, but when Nicole got a better look at it, she saw the face of Aubrey Calhoun materialize at the head of the ghost.

It was an apparition, just like the one that Nicole had seen in the basement. But this had movement to it, and enough force that it trailed a wake of wind behind it. And when Melissa caught sight of the ghost figure that was barreling toward her she let go of Ms. Calhoun to defend herself.

Nicole, already in midstride in her rescue of Ms. Calhoun, managed to grab hold of the old lady's frail wrist and pull her out of the way as Melissa slashed at the ghost of a woman who had already been torn to pieces.

Still holding Ms. Calhoun's hand, Nicole led the woman out of the room and hurried down the hall.

"C'mon, Ms. Calhoun," Nicole said, holding up as

much of the old woman's weight as she could without collapsing.

"Stop!" Melissa stepped out of the room, knife still in her hand, and sprinted after her prey.

Nicole struggled to keep Ms. Calhoun upright. She saw the stairs up ahead, and she knew that there wouldn't be enough time to get the old woman down to the first floor to keep her safe. They just weren't moving fast enough. So Nicole quickly changed direction, heading toward the nearest door, and then shoved Ms. Calhoun inside. "Lock it and stay hidden!"

Nicole slammed the door shut and turned around just in time to miss the broad slash of Melissa's blade. The knife scraped against the door as Nicole backtracked, still holding her own blade in her hand, and Melissa quickly lunged for the door handle, giving it a twist, but the lock held up.

With her access to Ms. Calhoun denied, Melissa turned her focus and rage on Nicole. "You won't be able to stop me!" She thrust the blade forward again, but Nicole was well out of range. "I'm going to kill you, then kill her, then burn this whole wretched place to the ground! Wherever those jewels are, they'll be destroyed with the rest of the house!"

Nicole continued to keep as much distance between herself and Nicole as she possibly could, but it was difficult with her constant backpedaling. She needed to stop Melissa, but she didn't know how to do that without hurting her. But then a thought hit her.

The basement.

It only had one exit and entrance, and if Nicole

trapped Melissa down there, then she could bar the door and that would give her enough time to get Ms. Calhoun to safety and call the cops.

Nicole reached the stairs and then hurried down, moving as quickly as she could without taking a tumble down the steps herself. She didn't dare look behind her to see how close Melissa was, because she knew the moment that she turned, she would lose the advantage of not knowing how close to death she truly was.

Nicole beelined it to the kitchen, feeling that Melissa was getting closer. The shadows of fingers were clawing at her neck, and she knew that if she couldn't get out of this place, she was going to lose her mind and her life.

Nicole skidded to the basement door and then opened it, looking back behind her, only to find nothing.

Melissa didn't follow her. Nicole was alone in the kitchen. She frowned, her heart beating with the quick rhythm of a drumline in her chest. She slowly rose from her crouched position, keeping the long counter between herself and the door in case Melissa tried to hurt her in the process.

After another minute of silence, Nicole finally worked up the courage to move back toward the entryway. She held the knife tight, her arm slightly raised and poised to strike at anything that jumped out at her. She struggled to keep herself calm, knowing that any misstep could be her last.

When Nicole neared the front entryway, she knew

that she would have to make a move. So instead of going through the doorway slowly, she lunged forward, swinging her arm around wildly, slashing the blade through the air.

Nicole looked up and down the hallway, searching for any signs of Melissa, but found nothing. And then she looked back to the staircase, thinking that maybe she had gone back up to the second floor to go after Ms. Calhoun.

Her mind already blocked by the fact that she was about to go into this alone, she didn't think that she had much time to try and figure out what to do next, so she hurried down the hall, her eyes locked on the stairwell, hoping that the old woman was still alive.

But her distracted mind didn't see that Melissa had ducked back into the library and she rushed out, slashing the knife across Nicole's arm and sending her to the floor.

The impact with the ground knocked the blade loose from Nicole's hand, and she clutched her now-wounded arm, her palm warm from the blood that was oozing out of the wound.

"You fucking bitch," Melissa said, lording over Nicole with the knife still in her hand, blood dripping from the tip. Nicole's blood. "You really thought that you had a chance at beating me, didn't you?"

Nicole crawled backward on her feet and elbows, the motion causing more blood to pour from the wound on her arm.

Melissa laughed as she followed. "You're weak. It's why I wanted you to come here in the first place. You were too weak to save your marriage, and you're too weak and stupid to stop me." She stared down at the knife in her hands. "I think I know what my mother was trying to do all of those years ago. I think I finally understand what she had planned." She turned her murderous gaze to Nicole. "She wanted to end the pain." She gripped the knife with both hands and prepared to drive it down into Nicole's flesh. "Time to say goodbye, Nicole."

Melissa screamed as she drove down with all of her weight, aiming the tip of the blade into Nicole's chest, but Nicole thrust her arms out, griping Melissa by the forearms, and she managed to stop the blade just before the tip reached her upper abdomen.

Pain flooded Nicole's arm as she struggled to keep Melissa's weight from bearing down on her. The woman was tall, but she was lighter than Nicole expected, and that worked to her advantage.

Confidence growing, Nicole managed to roll Melissa to the right, the pair latched onto one another with the knife between them, and when they flipped to the side, Nicole managed to twist the blade flat so the end wasn't pointed into her stomach.

Surprise flashed over Melissa's face at the turn of events, but the expression passed quickly, and she gritted her teeth. She added pressure to the blade, and it started to turn toward Nicole again. "You can't win."

Nicole felt her grip on the blade slipping. She knew that she wouldn't be able to hold on for much longer. Throwing caution to the wind, Nicole slammed her forehead into Melissa's face, and a bright white light of pain blinded her vision for a moment before the dull ache of the headbutt finally set in.

But the surprise attack rendered Melissa without protection, and Nicole quickly snatched the blade out of her hands and then stood up, hovering over the lawyer in the same manner that she had done only moments before.

Nicole kept her left eye squinted and was panting heavily, the pain still roaring in her head. "It's over, Melissa."

Melissa covered her nose with both hands, blood seeping between the fingers, staring up at Nicole with the same rage in her face that she had worn all night. "No." She lowered her hands, her nose busted and bloodied, a red smear across her upper lip and more blood dripping off of her chin. "You'll have to kill me."

Nicole kept both hands on the blade, keeping it tight in her hands. "I'm not killing you."

"You want to stop me?" Melissa slowly backtracked and tried to give herself some room to stand, but Nicole closed the gap, keeping the woman on the floor. "Then you have to kill me. Because you're a fool if you don't think that I can't get out of this. I'm a lawyer, remember? You don't think I wouldn't have a backup plan?"

Nicole knew that Melissa was just grasping at straws, but the clouds of doubt started to return. "You don't have anything."

Melissa smiled. "Are you sure about that? Is it something that you'd be willing to bet your life on?" She tilted her head to the side. "Your husband's life?"

"Stop it." A part of Nicole knew that she was right. But she couldn't let Melissa's words betray her own confidence now.

"You can't beat me—"

Nicole kicked her heel into Melissa's face as hard as she could, and the force of the blow flung Melissa's head back, and it cracked against the floor, where she was knocked out cold.

Shocked by her sudden act of violence, Nicole lingered in the hallway for a moment, staring down at the motionless lawyer. She checked her pulse and made sure that Melissa was breathing, and once both were confirmed, she retrieved the rope that was used to tie her up, and she bound Melissa's wrists and ankles in the same fashion that she did to Nicole.

Once Nicole was certain that Melissa couldn't move, she turned to leave the library but found Ms. Calhoun standing in the doorway. She looked at Nicole, then to Melissa on the floor, and then she slowly approached.

The old woman could barely do more than a shuffle, but when she reached Melissa, she bent down and gently brushed Melissa's bangs out of her face. It was done with such a gentle and natural caress that it surprised Nicole.

When Ms. Calhoun finally stood, she turned back around to Nicole and wrapped her in a big hug. The old woman clung to Nicole for a while, and when she finally let go, she was smiling and pinched Nicole's cheeks.

"Thank you."

Nicole frowned, and then looked past Ms. Calhoun and saw Aubrey standing next to Melissa's unconscious body.

Aubrey smiled. "Hello, Margaret."

Ms. Calhoun took a few steps toward her sister, but then stopped herself from getting to close, almost as if she were afraid that she would send her sister away if she got too close.

"Aubrey?" Ms. Calhoun asked, her voice barely above a whisper.

"Yes, sister, it's me." Aubrey wiped a silver tear from her cheek and smiled again. "I've wanted to speak to you for so long, but I don't have much time." She walked close enough to Ms. Calhoun so that the pair could almost hold hands, but they never touched. "I know how much guilt you've held over yourself of the past thirty years about what happened. About why you survived, but no one else did. And while I've had a lot of time to think about it, the only answer that I could come up with was... because I wanted to save you. It was my choice to put you in that vault. My choice to sacrifice myself so I could protect my little sister." She took one step closer, eliminating almost every inch of open space between the two of them. "Let go of the guilt. Let go of the pain that you've held onto for so long. It wasn't your fault what happened all those nights ago. It was our father. He made a mistake, and we all paid the price for it."

Nicole knew that Aubrey was talking to her sister, but she couldn't help but feel those words also applied to her. She needed to let go of her own pain. It was no way to live.

Ms. Calhoun nodded and then cleared her throat, stuttering a bit before she was able to spit out her response. "I will. I promise."

"Good." Aubrey looked past her sister and to Nicole. "And thank you for helping her. I only had so much ability to interfere, but you did a wonderful job of saving the rest of them. I couldn't have done it without your help. Thank you."

A light opened up at the end of the hallway, so bright that Nicole and Ms. Calhoun had to turn away as Aubrey walked toward it.

"Margaret," Aubrey said, stopping to turn just before she passed through the barrier. "I'll tell Mother and Father that you said hello. I know they've been worried about you." She smiled one last time and then disappeared to the other side.

Once Aubrey was gone and the white light disappeared, the power came back on in the house, and Ms. Calhoun turned to Nicole with tears in her eyes.

"She's really gone," Ms. Calhoun said.

"Yes," Nicole replied. "She's finally at rest."

36

*I*t was nearly morning by the time that the police arrived, Detective Salvor leading the group of officers that flooded into the house to collect evidence and Melissa, who was still tied up inside.

Once Nicole caught Salvor up to speed, he shook her hand.

"I suppose I should offer you a job on the force," Salvor said, a hint of teasing in his voice. "So far you've caught more bad guys than the other detectives have all year."

Nicole smiled but shook her head. "I don't think I want to worry about any more police work for a while, Detective. But I appreciate the offer."

"Thank you again, Nicole. Stay safe." Detective Salvor smiled and then walked over to a group of forensic techs to follow up on the evidence that would put Melissa away for good.

Exhausted from the long night, Nicole walked

around the side of the house toward the guest house, hoping that she could catch some sleep.

But along the way, something was troubling her, something that she couldn't get out of her mind no matter how hard she tried.

Where were the jewels?

There had been three people after them, and the one place where they should have been, in the vault, was completely empty.

"It's just so weird," Nicole said, talking to herself as she staggered a little bit from side to side.

For so much wealth and value to just disappear into thin air seemed odd. And then Nicole stopped, remembering something that Donald had said the first day that Nicole arrived at the house. It was about the pictures that she and Jake had found in the room with the blue door.

"They were her greatest treasures," Nicole said.

She looked to the house, wondering if what she thought could be true, and then headed inside. She walked past the forensic officers taking evidence, no one saying anything to her as she quickly moved through the house, and she saw that the blue door was open.

Nicole stepped inside and opened one of the first boxes that she could get her hands on. She lifted one of the pictures in the frame and then flipped it over. She undid the four small latches, and then carefully opened the backside of the frame, her eyes widening in surprise.

"Oh my God," Nicole said.

Taped to the back of the picture were several small diamonds. Nicole glanced back behind her to make sure that she was alone, and then she set that frame aside and picked up another one.

The back of the next frame held a ruby. Another frame held two emeralds. The next three had more diamonds and one sapphire.

Nicole stopped and looked at all of the boxes that filled the room. If every picture frame had jewels on the back of them, then there had to be millions stashed away in here.

When Nicole turned to the door, she froze when she saw Ms. Calhoun standing in the doorway. The old woman was expressionless, looking at Nicole instead of the open frames and her family jewels.

Nicole smiled. "Don't worry. I wasn't going to say anything. I was just curious to know where you put them."

Ms. Calhoun smiled as she shuffled inside and then picked up one of the open frames. "It was Donald's idea. He told me that the safest place to keep them would be in a place that only I cared about." She flipped the photograph around so she could see the picture. "This was a trip down to the shore one summer."

It was the memories that Ms. Calhoun cherished the most, not the jewels. And for a woman slowly losing her mind, Nicole suspected that these pictures were worth even more now.

"You know, now that all of this is done, you could probably put the photographs back up," Nicole said.

Ms. Calhoun nodded. "Yes, I suppose I could do that. Though it will make me miss them more."

Nicole placed her arm around the old woman's shoulders and pulled her close. "You should embrace that while you can."

Ms. Calhoun nodded. "I think you're right." She then flipped the picture around and peeled off the jewels that were taped to the back.

"What are you doing?" Nicole asked.

Once Ms. Calhoun collected the jewels in her palm, she reached for Nicole's hand and tranferred them into her palm, and then closed her fingers over them. She looked up at Nicole and winked. "I'll leave these with you, and step outside for a moment to watch the door." She walked away, leaving Nicole stunned at what she was suggesting.

"Ms. Calhoun, I can't—"

"You can." She stopped at the door and turned around. "You're the only one that can." She winked again and then smiled as she stepped outside.

*N*icole pulled into the driveway and shut the engine off. She smiled at the front porch swing, knowing that she and Jake would be sitting on it when the sun went down to enjoy the evening. They had picked a place right on the coast, a nice bluff over-looking the ocean.

It had been out of their price range before the visit up north and Ms. Calhoun's generous bonus, but that all changed the moment that they came back from their trip four years ago.

Nicole stepped out of the car and walked through the front door without any fear or hesitation about what might be on the other side because she already knew without a doubt what was waiting for her, and she couldn't have been happier about it.

The smell of dinner graced her nostrils when she entered, and she smiled when she saw three-year-old Annie running toward her with outstretched arms.

"Mommy!"

"Oh, my lovely dear," Nicole said, and scooped her daughter up in her arms, planting a big kiss on her cheek. "It's so good to see you."

"Babe, are you home?" Jake called from the kitchen and then popped his head out. "Hey, how was work?"

"It was great." Ever since the Calhoun home, Nicole had decided to focus only on patients suffering from dementia. It was a way to give back, help them remember who they were, and it was also a way for her to remember what was most important to her. "And how was your day, little one?"

"It was fun!" Annie raised her arms above her head, splaying out her little fingers. "I made a picture, do you want to see?"

"I would love to see it." Nicole smiled and then set her daughter down, and she ran into her room.

Jake finally emerged from the kitchen, removing his apron, and planted a big kiss on her lips. "Dinner will be ready in ten minutes. Just needs a little more time in the oven." He smiled and then Annie came running back from her room, holding the picture in her hands.

"Look, Mommy!"

Nicole grabbed the picture from Annie's little mitts and then smiled. "It's beautiful, sweetheart."

"It has you, and me, and Daddy on the swing in the front of the house to watch the sunset!"

An unexpected tear formed in Nicole's eyes, and she quickly wiped it away. After waiting so long for life to improve, she was so thankful for where she was now. She had everything she ever wanted.

"Are you okay, Mommy?" Annie asked, her tone concerned.

"Yes, baby, I'm fine." Nicole smiled again, looking to her husband and daughter, pulling them closer. "Everything is wonderful."

Made in the USA
Coppell, TX
11 June 2024